"Thanks, Judd..." Adrienne murmured.

"For what?" he asked her, surprised.

"For listening. And understanding."

"Adrienne, you're an idealist. By any stretch of the imagination, the world can use more like you."

"What a nice thing to say."

"Well, you'd better treasure it," he told her. "I try never to say more than one nice thing a month."

Maybe she wouldn't be so tough to work with after all, Judd thought. As long as he stayed on his toes, kept his thoughts away from that night he'd spent with her and didn't spend a lot of time remembering the kiss they'd just shared, he'd be okay.

After all, they'd be in public ninety-nine percent of the time. It wasn't as if they had to *live* together to get the job done.

Yeah, handling a few days would be okay.

He hoped.

Dear Reader,

Many of you love the miniseries that we do in Intimate Moments, and this month we've got three of them for you. First up is *Duncan's Lady,* by Emilie Richards. Duncan is the first of "The Men of Midnight," and his story will leave you hungering to meet the other two. Another first is *A Man Without Love,* one of the "Wounded Warriors" created by Beverly Bird. Beverly was one of the line's debut authors, and we're thrilled to have her back. Then there's a goodbye, because in *A Man Like Smith,* bestselling author Marilyn Pappano has come to the end of her "Southern Knights" trilogy. But what a fantastic farewell—and, of course, Marilyn herself will be back soon!

You won't want to miss the month's other offerings, either. In *His Best Friend's Wife,* Catherine Palmer has created a level of emotion and tension that will have you turning pages as fast as you can. In *Dillon's Reckoning,* award-winner Dee Holmes sends her hero and heroine on the trail of a missing baby, while Cathryn Clare's *Gunslinger's Child* features one of romance's most popular storylines, the "secret baby" plot.

Enjoy them all—and come back next month for more top-notch romantic reading...only from Silhouette Intimate Moments.

Yours,
Leslie Wainger
Senior Editor and Editorial Coordinator

Please address questions and book requests to:
Silhouette Reader Service
U.S.: 3010 Walden Ave., P.O. Box 1325, Buffalo, NY 14269
Canadian: P.O. Box 609, Fort Erie, Ont. L2A 5X3

DILLON'S RECKONING

DEE HOLMES

Silhouette® INTIMATE™ MOMENTS®

Published by Silhouette Books

America's Publisher of Contemporary Romance

SILHOUETTE BOOKS

ISBN 0-373-07628-2

DILLON'S RECKONING

DEE HOLMES

would love to tell her readers about exciting trips to Europe or that she has mastered a dozen languages. But the truth is that traveling isn't her thing, and she flunked French twice. Perhaps because of a military background where she got uprooted so much, she married a permanent civilian.

Dee is an obsessive reader who started writing casually, only to discover that "Writing is hard! Writing a publishable book is even harder." She has since become involved in her local RWA chapter and says that she loves to write about "relationships between two people who are about to fall in love, but don't know how exciting it is going to be for them."

Chapter 1

Judd Dillon had no trouble spotting Adrienne Trudell, despite the chaotic noise and scrambling hospital staff. Knowing she would be here should have prepared him, but he braced himself, anyway. He didn't want to even consider the thought of working with her.

Seeing her every day.

Concentrating on managing his unwanted and unwelcome feelings.

And the worst of it all: remembering too vividly how he'd used her.

Dammit, he thought, he hadn't even gotten close enough to speak to her and already his gut was twisting. What he needed were those steely nerves and the cool distance he'd perfected over the past few years.

Judd stepped around a deserted cart of lunch trays. He made his way down the wide corridor of the maternity floor to where Adrienne was talking softly to a sobbing young woman who looked barely out of her teens.

The sound of tears interspersed with wailing grew louder as he got closer.

Adrienne turned and saw him, her eyes catching his for a fleeting second before she resumed patting and reassuring the weeping woman. She urged the younger woman back into her room and then walked toward him.

Despite his preference not to, he noted her curly auburn hair, and the misty blue eyes that made him think that innocence had a color all its own. He took in the flush of her cheeks, and the fitted navy suit that defined her slenderness without looking provocative.

In fact, had he not known her credentials, he would have immediately concluded that she was too young and inexperienced for the job she held.

"Ms. Trudell," Judd said in a low voice, trying to ignore the lilac freshness of her scent filtering through the antiseptic hospital odor.

"Detective Dillon."

The automatic formality should have pleased him. On one level it did, but he was still too conscious of the effort it cost to deny and ignore the bitter edges of his past with her. This, in turn, made him aware of just how careful he had to be around Adrienne Trudell. Dealing with suppressed tension was always a dangerous proposition.

Judd nodded toward the room where the woman had gone. "I presume she's the mother."

"Yes. Tanya Whitewell."

He knew the first investigating officers had already been there and would be filing preliminary reports. Right now, Judd also knew, questions were being asked in other parts of the hospital, at the admittance and visitor's desk, as well as outside, with outer security. Although the sight of a woman leaving a hospital with a baby wasn't unusual, babies often did cause many a fond second look. With any luck, someone might have noticed a significant detail. From what Judd had learned so far, the extent of the description was that the "snatcher" in question had been a woman. Closer questioning of the mother was why he was here.

"Where's the father?" he asked abruptly.

"Not here yet. He's a carpenter and is working on a project in Massachusetts. He's been notified to come to the hospital immediately."

Judd nodded and made a mental note to make sure the father was questioned. "Have you learned anything from Mrs. Whitewell?"

"Only that she has no idea who the woman was or why she would take her baby."

"I have a better question," he said with sharp irritation. "How in hell did the woman get close enough to the baby to take him in the first place?"

She caught her breath and Judd immediately realized how fierce and angry he sounded.

"That wasn't directed at you personally," he said gruffly, wondering why he felt any need to apologize for being outraged at what had happened.

"I'm as angry as you are."

"You're just better at keeping it in check."

She stared at him. "Should I take that as a compliment or your recognition of a flaw?"

He gave her a measuring look, wondering if her question was some kind of attempt to make him more pliable about working with her. Deciding against it, he looked away from her. His cynicism was in top form, he decided grimly.

Deciding to take a different tack, he said, "Let's just call it an observation. Maybe I've been at this job too long, but I'm short on patience and sympathy for carelessness and stupidity by people who should know better."

"You mean the hospital."

"For starters."

"They've already started internal inquiries. As you can see by just looking at the nurses and the other staff, everyone is very upset."

Judd pulled a notebook from his pocket along with a pen and reminded himself that he wasn't a judge, but a cop assigned to get the facts and find the infant who'd been kidnapped from the hospital. Maybe it was the feeling of sheer helplessness of the situation or the deeper fear of failure that was riding him. He didn't know what it was but he had to work quickly. Statistically, the longer the infant was missing the less likely the possibility of a favorable outcome.

To Adrienne he said, "Give me the name of the person who's coordinating the internal inquiries."

"Ralph Fairfax, the hospital administrator. His office is in the annex."

Judd jotted down a few notes and then said, "So fill me in on the mother."

"From what Tanya told me, she'd just finished feeding her son. By the way, his name is Caleb. The suspect came into her room saying she'd come to get the infant and return him to the nursery."

"So the baby wasn't staying in the room with Mrs. Whitewell?" Judd tightened his fingers on the pen, recalling when his wife had given birth to their son. Diana had wanted the baby with her. Diana and Travis ... God, it had been three years since he'd allowed himself to think of them this way. Three hellish years since they'd been killed by that drunk driver. He'd gotten on with the business of living, but his personal life, by his own choice, was a barren stretch of emptiness.

"No, Tanya had a difficult delivery and her doctor felt she needed the rest, so the baby stayed in the nursery."

Judd nodded, busily taking notes and refusing any more self-indulgent forays into the past.

Adrienne continued, "Tanya said the woman made some comments about how much she loved babies, and when she took Caleb, she looked at him so adoringly and was so nice that Tanya wanted to cry."

"A *nice* woman?" Judd rolled his eyes. "One who just happened to steal a kid from a hospital?"

"The fact she stole Caleb doesn't mean she's devoid of feelings," Adrienne said.

"You're defending her?"

"Of course not, but I don't think this woman, whoever she is, is a total monster, either. In fact, her positive reaction to the baby may be a plus. Just because *you* have no heart, Detective Dillon, is no reason to assume that every emotion shown by a criminal is just part of some con job."

"Yeah, well, given that we have a missing infant, I'd say my instincts are dead-on. As far as a con job goes, to take an infant from a large hospital without arousing any suspicion requires a hell of a lot of deceit—including those cuddly smiles the suspect tossed around." Placing the notebook and pen back into his pocket, he'd already started to move around her and toward Tanya Whitewell's room, when she touched his arm.

He glanced down at her fingers. Her nails were polished a pale pink and in a clear flash he recalled the way she'd tunneled them through his hair, lightly scraped them along his belly, down to his—oh, hell, he thought in self-disgust. The vivid images spiraled through his conscience with maximum damage before he forced the memory away.

"Please be gentle with Tanya," Adrienne said softly, and for a few seconds he could swear that those same words had been uttered in an entirely different context.

"You'll be gentle with me, Judd, I know you will."

Judd took a deep breath. Her trust, her faith in him, the giving of herself—he'd had them all and had hurled them back at her. He'd made it clear with his predawn departure from her apartment a year ago that he wanted nothing to do with Adrienne or any of her feelings. It had been too late for him then. He'd given himself wholly and totally to Diana and when he'd lost her and their son, he'd lost himself, as well.

Damn the memories. Damn them—

"Judd? Did you hear what I said?"

Judd could have sworn that her nails had penetrated through his jacket and his shirt. "I heard you. Look, I've been a cop for more years than I want to think about. Dealing gently with distraught victims isn't exactly a new concept. But I have to get some answers and that means questions."

"I understand that, but she's so young and so confused." Then after a pause, she asked, "Would you object if I stayed while you talk to her?"

He peered at her, a little surprised she would ask permission. She worked at the Seapoint police headquarters in a new department that dealt exclusively with children's issues. The mayor had okayed the innovative idea six months ago at the request of Child-Aid, a publicly funded program that specialized in missing children and that often worked closely with the police. Moving a branch into the police station had saved taxpayers money and provided in-house timeliness in dealing with the growing number of missing children's cases.

Judd knew Adrienne had worked in various capacities for Child-Aid since graduating from college. She preferred to do the legwork of dealing directly with the parents and children rather than the office paperwork. When Judd had learned that she'd turned down the job as director, and along with that, a significant pay raise, he'd been astonished. That decision of hers highlighted one of his major problems with Adrienne—she deserved a lot more than she ever took and for reasons that he himself didn't understand, this infuriated him no end. She always saw things from a higher, more idealistic perspective than others.

His taste for idealism had crumbled early on in his law enforcement career, but it had disappeared when Diana and Travis had been killed by that drunk driver. The bastard responsible had done two years on a plea bargain and the last Judd had heard, the man had moved north. Some had expected Judd to go after him—and he'd come damn close to doing just that, but instead he'd done something, in his opinion, far more damaging.

He'd used Adrienne; to forget what a cold bastard he'd become, to block out Diana and Travis, to make himself feel . . . God, he didn't know what he'd wanted to feel.

Alive? Aware? Warm? Not so damn alone?

Shaking off the emotions, he reminded himself once again just how complicated working with her would be.

"You're asking me permission to be in the room? You know I don't have jurisdiction over the Child-Aid department."

"But you are going to handle this case, aren't you? I assumed that's why you're here."

"That's why I'm here." He studied her, his eyes narrowing. "I suppose it's too much to hope that you were just called in on a temporary basis."

She shook her head slowly as if she didn't want to give him the unsettling news.

"That's what I was afraid of," he grumbled. "Yeah, come on in with me. Your being there will probably help."

"Why, Judd Dillon, is that an acknowledgment that I might know how to do my job?" she asked breezily.

He wondered if she was trying to ease the tension. Too bad it wasn't that simple. "I've never questioned your ability to do your job, I just don't like your doing it with me."

"In other words, the farther away from me you are the better you like it."

"Look, it's not because—"

"You'd be working with a woman?" she interjected quickly. Judd scowled, feeling a new tension develop. They'd been together all of five minutes and already he was in trouble.

Shrugging, he finally said, "I admit it's not my first choice."

She gave him a cool detached perusal. "I'm so glad it's just your sexist attitude. I was beginning to think it might be because we made love once and you're afraid I might not be able to separate the personal from the professional."

The bald comment or perhaps just the casual way she used it brought him up short. Not once since that night had they discussed it or even referred to what had happened between them. For her to throw it out now like some barb or gauntlet rattled him, although he had no intention of showing her any reaction.

Besides, he guessed he was ten times more worried about being with her than she was disturbed about being with him. He had no doubt any positive feelings she might have had for him had been shredded and forgotten long ago.

Adrienne smiled one of those winning smiles notable for an obvious victory. Damn her, anyway.

Just outside Tanya Whitewell's room, he folded his fingers around her wrist. He could feel her pulse pound and he knew his own was none too steady.

Scowling, he said in a low voice, "Don't play cute with me, Adrienne."

She pulled away and he let her go. Not looking at him, she said firmly, "All I was going to say is that I'm quite aware of your disinterest and dislike of me and I wouldn't dream of trying to change that. In fact, the feeling is mutual."

"Good," he said flatly. "Finally we understand each other."

For some strained seconds, neither spoke.

Then Adrienne added, "You know, now I can appreciate what makes you such a good cop. Nothing fazes you, does it?"

"Damn little. Now, can we get on with why we're here?"

She drew herself up, her back arrow stiff, and walked ahead of him into the hospital room. Sighing, he followed her. God, he didn't need this kind of hassle. A tiny core inside of him hoped for a miracle. Maybe the woman who'd taken the infant would find her conscience, realize what she'd done and return the baby by tonight.

But his more cynical side knew that was as likely as getting Adrienne Trudell off the case.

Adrienne walked across the room to where Tanya sat in a chair, staring out the window. Wearing a ruffly yellow robe and fuzzy slippers, she looked barely more than a child herself. Vases of congratulatory flowers sat near the bed. Cards stood open on the dresser.

She sobbed intermittently and Adrienne had to apply all her professional objectivity not to cry herself. Getting emotionally involved was not only nonproductive from the standpoint of those she dealt with, it was also intensely, personally, draining.

She glanced back at Judd, and wished she had his ability to distance himself. Sighing inwardly, she admitted the main problem here. For an entire year, Adrienne had managed to avoid any sustained contact with Judd, with the same doggedness that he had avoided her. Oh, they'd nodded to each other occasionally, exchanged polite chatter, wherever they ran into each other during a workday, but that was all.

Now suddenly, a kidnapped infant had flung them together and the unspoken rule of maintaining distance and coolness had disappeared. Wary and resolute, each was determined that neither would breach the shell of the other.

"Tanya?" Adrienne said softly. "This is Detective Judd Dillon. He's a police officer and he wants to ask you some questions about what happened here."

For a moment, Tanya looked surprised. "I already talked to the police." Then she glanced toward the door, her eyes darting and scared. "Where's Ronnie? They said they called him. Why isn't he here? He was so proud to have a son. He took this job to give us some extra money for the baby. Now my baby is gone. Stolen..." Tears flowed down her cheeks.

Trying to reassure the woman, Adrienne squeezed the young mother's balled-up fists. "Yes, your husband has been called. I'm sure he will be here shortly. But Detective Dillon needs you to answer some questions so he can find Caleb quickly."

Tanya sniffled, her eyes red and her cheeks salty with dried tears. "All right, but I don't know anything that will help."

Judd pulled a chair over and sat down. Adrienne moved to the side.

He took out his notebook and pen from his inner jacket pocket, then in a friendly, but professionally objective voice, Judd asked, "How old are you, Tanya?"

"Twenty."

"And Caleb is your first baby?"

"Uh-huh. Ronnie and I want two boys and two girls. We planned it all before we got married."

"That sounds very organized."

"Ronnie and I are careful," she said fiercely, as if she expected to be accused of carelessness given how she'd allowed the stranger to take Caleb. "We didn't want me to get pregnant before we were married. We wanted to do things right for our baby." Her lower lip began to tremble and new tears fell. "It's not fair. We did things right and proper and look what happened. Oh, my poor Caleb. Why did this happen to him and to us? Why?" She buried her face in her hands and Adrienne started forward. Judd grabbed her wrist to stop her, shaking his head.

Adrienne frowned, but he didn't release her wrist.

"Tanya," he said in a low voice.

More sobs.

"Tanya, I want you to stop crying and look at me."

Adrienne tried to free her wrist, but Judd held it firmly.

What are you doing? she mouthed.

My job, he mouthed back.

But Adrienne heard something else underlying his two words. *Don't interfere.* She guessed this was but a tiny example of why he had a reputation for thoroughness and cool professionalism. She also concluded it was the reason he didn't want to work with a woman.

She drew back and he released her. Reluctantly, she admitted to herself that she was interfering. Finding Caleb as quickly as possible was more important than indulging Tanya's tears.

In a soothing tone that was nonetheless firm, Judd said, "Tanya, I want you to tell me what the woman who took Caleb looked like."

She shook her head back and forth. "I don't know. I don't remember."

"Someone in the corridor said they saw a woman who was large, with red hair tied back with a scarf."

Adrienne frowned. As far as she knew, no one had seen anyone they would have described in such a way. Unless Judd was throwing out a description to get Tanya's attention?

When Tanya shook her head, Adrienne knew that was exactly what Judd had done. Very impressive, she thought with admiration. His reputation as a skilled investigator wasn't exaggerated.

"The woman who took Caleb was skinny," Tanya said. "Her hair was dark."

"How old?" Judd asked.

"Jeez, she was old. At least thirty-five."

Adrienne suddenly felt ancient. She knew Judd was close to thirty-seven and she herself was thirty-three.

"Any scars, marks, broken teeth, did she wear makeup? If so, how did it strike you? Carelessly or carefully applied? Anything that stood out that you might remember?"

Tanya bit her bottom lip thoughtfully. "She had a friendly smile...oh, and a yellow ribbon in her hair. She even had a blue rattle that she said the hospital gave to the baby boys. Pink to the girls, I guess."

Judd made notes and Adrienne frowned, but before she could decide what bothered her about Tanya's blue rattle comment, Judd asked, "How did she hold Caleb, Tanya?" At the woman's puzzled look, Judd explained, "Up over her shoulder as if to burp him? Or did she cradle him in her arms?"

"I'm not sure." Suddenly, she looked stricken.

"Let's see if we can help you remember." He turned. "Adrienne, would you get the pillow? We'll see if we can reconstruct what Tanya saw."

Adrienne did what she was told and Judd drew her close. He arranged the pillow in a cradling position in Adrienne's arms, then placed her arms and hands as if she were holding and rocking an infant. She watched the quickness of his hands and wondered how many times he'd placed his own son in Diana's arms. Her heart wrenched anew at the thought of the devastation their deaths had brought to him.

Judd said, "Tanya, does this look familiar?"

~ The young mother stared for just a minute. Then, biting her lip, she shook her head.

"All right, let's try the shoulder."

Adrienne held the pillow against her shoulder and placed her hand toward the top, as if supporting an infant's head.

"Yes!" Tanya exclaimed, suddenly excited and sitting up straight. "Yes, that's the way she held him. Adrienne has a ring on and I remembered the woman wore a ring. I was afraid it might twist and scratch Caleb's head."

Judd already had his notebook open to a fresh page. "Tell me about the ring."

Adrienne put the pillow back on the bed and sat down to listen.

Tanya frowned. "It was sparkly. You know, one of those rings that's so big it can't be real. The stone had silver, uh, those things that hold the stone."

"Prongs?" Adrienne suggested.

"Yes, that's it. Prongs."

"What color was the stone?"

"Red. I remember it was red because it made me think of blood."

Chapter 2

"Blood, for God's sake," Judd said a few minutes later. He shook his head in astonishment.

They had left Tanya's room after Leo, a police sketch artist, arrived. He'd promised Judd a composite in the next few hours. In the meantime, Judd had decided to talk to Ralph Fairfax. Adrienne went along to save Judd's having to repeat to her later what he'd learned from Fairfax.

Judd scowled, as if unable to let go of what Tanya had said. "Why would a woman Tanya's age think of blood when she saw something red?"

Adrienne shuddered. "Chilling, isn't it?"

"Why not red roses or valentines or even passion?"

"Probably because she's seen more spilled blood than most women do in a lifetime. The inner-city life of young girls today means ducking bullets more than it does looking for white knights to the rescue."

He didn't answer and Adrienne knew it wasn't because she'd given him any new insight, but more than likely that he was mulling over what she'd so quickly deduced were Tanya's thought processes. She knew Judd well enough to understand how focused he was about his work; anyone careless or incompetent would quickly be dismissed by him as unqualified.

Adrienne sighed. Despite her credentials, she guessed she'd have to constantly show him and reaffirm that she did, indeed, know how to do her job. Given his admission already that he didn't like working with women, and considering their past relationship, Adrienne didn't have to be brilliant to conclude that Judd didn't mean *all* women, just her.

Her attempt to soothe Tanya when Judd was questioning the young mother had annoyed him. Grimly, she realized she had played right into a male assumption that tears required soothing words, embraces and probably an apology for asking painful questions. Judd had been extremely patient with Tanya, and in retrospect Adrienne had to admit that he'd gotten an incredible amount of information from the woman, despite her sobbing.

She stole a glance at him. Saddle-brown hair, the sharp jaw, the stubborn set of his face, granite flesh—if such a thing could exist. Lines fanned from his smoky green eyes even when he didn't smile. His lean body, muscled and hard, made her aware of how he had felt pressed against her once. An awareness she instantly put aside. Judd wasn't handsome, certainly not boyish and rarely charming. Most times, his demeanor gave the message—stay away, it's too late for me, too late for anyone to care.

Adrienne had seen cynicism in adults and even in children. However, Judd's attitude seemed more entrenched and calcified. Then again, she knew nothing about Judd that was simple or easily explained. Losing Diana and Travis had fundamentally drained and emptied him so that any attempt to break the seal he'd created around his life—and most of all his heart—was greeted with cold detachment and immediate suspicion.

She'd learned that fact in a too-painful and too-mortifying way.

Since they would be working together, she had to do her job in the most exemplary way, and she wouldn't allow old and long-buried feelings for Judd to interfere with her responsibility or deter her from her duty.

Once she'd loved him, despite knowing he felt none of those feelings for her.

Once she'd wanted him and given in to that want.

Once she'd trusted him and he'd betrayed her heart by walking away without a backward look.

Well, not again. A fool she wasn't. Perhaps not much older than she'd been that night, but definitely wiser, and she fully intended to prove to him and to herself that keeping cool and emotionally aloof would be the basis of any relationship they had.

Now they turned down another corridor and at the end took the elevator to the main floor. Ralph Fairfax's office was located in a separate building, connected by a glass-enclosed walkway.

As they stepped into the sun-drenched area, Adrienne noted that Judd scowled. She got suddenly tense, but quelled her immediate reaction to ask what was wrong. He would just scowl harder and refuse to answer. She wondered if he had a dislike of closed places, but that theory seemed remote. In the kind of job he had, she doubted any phobia would be long tolerated.

Personally, she loved glass enclosures, whether they were paths from one building to another, the glass-bottomed boat she'd gone on in Florida when she was a child or her very favorite—a greenhouse. She had a miniature one attached to a window in her apartment and working with the plants always brightened her mood after work. Someday, she wanted to have a house with a full-size greenhouse that she could walk in. Someday, maybe.

The view outside the walkway offered gardens profuse with late-summer flowers, two marblelike birdbaths on pedestals that attracted cardinals and hummingbirds. Stone benches were scattered about. Soft music played from strategically placed speakers, giving an ambience of peace and tranquillity.

"Good God, who dreamed up this glass cage?" Judd grumbled.

"From what I heard, the purpose was to give the hospital staff a respite from all the grim things it has to deal with."

Ignoring her explanation, he said, "When we leave, let's use the other exit."

Adrienne nodded, but she wondered what had shaken him. Maybe it *was* that caged feeling, but to her the glass gave a sense of openness and light. As they entered the annex, she saw him visibly unwind and within a few seconds the tightness had disappeared.

"So what do you know of Tanya's background?" Judd asked, picking up on their earlier conversation.

"Her mother never married, but she had a lot of kids who had different fathers. Tanya doesn't know where hers is. She's managed quite well, given such a difficult background. She's spunky, and determined that she and Ronnie beat the stereotypes so often attached to the poor. She resents it if anyone calls her irresponsible."

"Yeah, I got that impression. This kidnapping must make her wonder about her own instincts."

"What do you mean?"

"I mean that growing up under the circumstances you described makes someone pretty sharp about being fooled."

"You sound like you know from experience. But you had an above-average upbringing, with parents who loved you."

"Yeah, I was lucky. But I've also dealt with a lot of kids who don't trust the sun to come up tomorrow. Plus my kid brother—" He cut himself off as if he'd said too much.

Adrienne frowned. "You have a younger brother? I know you have an older one, but..." She'd met the Dillons a number of times and she was positive there'd never been mention of a third son.

"Let's get back to Tanya," he said abruptly and there was no doubt he wished he hadn't strayed off the subject. "As I was saying, I'm surprised some inner warning about this woman didn't kick in."

"Maybe the setting. A hospital is a pretty secure place. Maybe Tanya just assumed, as anyone would, that this woman was only doing her job."

"And now Tanya's blaming herself, when the real blame lies with the hospital."

Adrienne stopped outside Fairfax's office. She would never have guessed that he would truly look at Tanya's emotions as a result of this. Maybe he did have some feelings, after all—at least, when it came to his job.

Judd stopped, too. "What's wrong?"

"Nothing. I'm just pleased that you're seeing Tanya as more than just a woman for a file report."

"Contrary to popular opinion at headquarters, I'm human at least ten minutes every year," he said dryly.

She grinned at his sarcasm and said lightly, "I'm so glad you picked your ten minutes for Tanya. If you'd just fired questions at her, she would have dissolved. And by the way, the pillow demonstration was brilliant."

Judd narrowed his eyes, looking at her so directly, she felt pinned in place. In an even voice, he asked, "What about the way I held the notebook and poised my pen? Was that brilliant, too? Did I lean forward enough? Did I pick the right clothes? Guess it's a good thing I didn't wear old jeans, a black shirt and saunter in with a shoulder holster on. The jacket and slacks were just the right touch."

Adrienne sighed. So much for trying to get along. "Can't you just accept a compliment that's well deserved?"

"I don't do my job for praise and compliments, deserved or otherwise."

"Well, forgive me for trying to extend one. Since we're going to be working together, I thought it *might* be appropriate if we spent at least five minutes not sparring with each other."

"Professionals do their job," he snapped. "I do mine and I don't need some social worker to make me feel good about it."

"Dammit, Judd, I'm not a social worker. I'm a specialist in missing children. You are well aware that Child-Aid is a new concept that takes a personal approach to the problem rather than a governmental one."

"Fine. You do your job and I'll do mine and just maybe we can get this kid back home safe."

Judd opened the outer office door and she walked in ahead of him. After they learned from his secretary that Fairfax was at a TV interview and would return in ten minutes, Judd dropped into a leather chair and sank back in a relaxed position. He took his notebook and pen from his inner jacket pocket and began to flip through it, making notations here and there.

Adrienne sat on the couch and picked up a magazine. She flipped through the pages without paying attention to their contents. Although she stayed silent, she was seething inside. Why did he have to be such a bastard about everything she said and did? She'd never known a man like him, and given that she'd known him for many years, his uniqueness should have provided some clues by now. Then again, he'd shown little need or desire to reveal much about himself.

Admittedly, during most of the years she'd known him he had been her best friend's husband, but since he'd lost Diana and Travis, Adrienne figured he must also have lost a part of himself. Perhaps at some level, she was conscious of that, but it didn't seem to stop the futility of hope—her continually trying to be something he didn't want—someone he acknowledged who cared about him.

But perhaps she was using "caring" to cover up her own duplicitous heart. For still—despite the three years that had passed since Judd had become a widower—Adrienne carried a mammoth load of guilt for the way she'd truly felt about Judd. For having deep feelings for a man that was married to her best friend.

She and Diana had been roommates in college and good friends until Diana's death. Adrienne had been Diana's maid of honor and had often baby-sat their son, Travis. She'd spent holidays with them and remembered clearly one special Christmas. The Christmas when she'd been particularly upset, the awful year her mother, Rhoda, had taken up with some oily gambler and gone to Las Vegas with him. Adrienne was accustomed to her mother's having boyfriends, their number was as prolific as bees on a summer day. But getting used to them didn't mean liking them—the gambler had been particularly odious.

The frustration of watching Rhoda's pride fall and her mother's bitterness increase over the years had left Adrienne leery of her own feelings about love and commitment. Even now, she fervently wished that "love" was as straightforward as it was in the movies—meet, get to know each other, share likes and dislikes, fall in love and marry.

Betrayal wasn't part of the perfect picture and yet Adrienne's mother had once given her heart. Rhoda Trudell had been so cruelly betrayed by Adrienne's father, that Rhoda had actually told her daughter that trust was a four-letter word. Her mother's experience had made Adrienne more careful of risking any feelings for a man. That Christmas, she'd been hurting for her mother's vain search for love, even though, in some tiny place in her heart, she had wanted, and still did desperately want love to be wonderful and fulfilling instead of painful and heartbreaking. She just needed to make sure none of those expectations were connected with Judd Dillon.

Fairfax entered and Adrienne glanced up as Judd rose to his feet.

The hospital administrator was groomed and pressed as if he were about to model for a pipe-and-fireplace scene in a magazine layout. His hair was styled and parted so carefully, not one strand dared to rebel. On the hand he extended to Judd was a college ring; Adrienne recalled he'd graduated from Yale. She'd read a bio on him when he'd first taken the position five years ago.

"Detective Dillon, I understand you want to talk to me," Fairfax said. "I told one of the other officers and, of course, the local television news reporters exactly what our procedure here is as to security. I don't know how repeating it to you will be of any help."

"Perhaps you can indulge me," Judd said, and although the quip seemed to have gone right past Fairfax, Adrienne didn't miss it. Judd didn't like waiting while Fairfax did TV interviews.

Judd turned to Adrienne. "This is Ms. Trudell. She knows Tanya and her husband and will be working on the kidnapping aspect of the case."

Fairfax grinned a little too engagingly. "Well, you certainly don't look like you should be doing such unpleasant things, Ms. Trudell. No, sir." His eyes slid over her and lingered on her legs. The sheer blatancy of the look made her certain she was expected to take his perusal as a compliment.

"Looks can be deceiving, Mr. Fairfax," she said sweetly.

He placed a finger against his lips in a thoughtful manner. "Have you ever danced? Professionally, I mean. You remind me of a young woman I met in Providence last year."

Judd narrowed his eyes, his voice rough with warning. "She's never been to the Bubbles and Brew Club, Fairfax. And I'd suggest you be careful with your comments. Ms. Trudell is very good with her knee." His gaze lowered to Fairfax's impeccably fitted suit pants, especially the zippered area.

Adrienne hid a smile as Fairfax flushed and then hurriedly turned toward his office. Judd had been a little extreme, but his comment had effectively shut down any further eye-stripping looks at her.

"I'm good with my knee?" she asked in a whisper only Judd could hear as they followed Fairfax into his office.

"Aren't you?"

"I don't know. I've never had to do that."

"That's not what I heard."

Gaping at him, she grabbed his arm. She'd always been supremely conscious of not sending out anything that could be construed as a sexual message around the men she encountered at work. Not only was it unprofessional, it smacked of the kind of bimbo mentality that relied on sexual moves rather than intelligence. "What you heard? About me? There has to be a mistake."

"Why? Are you afraid to have a tough-broad reputation? Don't be. It can save you from a helluva lot of hassle."

How strange, she thought, suddenly at a loss as to what to say next. Even though she and Judd worked in the same police department, they were on separate floors and rarely had contact. She didn't even know many of the officers by name on the other floors, and to have them not only know who she was, but learn that she had magically acquired a reputation for toughness boggled her mind.

Fairfax indicated seats and they both sat down, their personal conversation ended. Not as far as Adrienne was concerned, however. She intended to find out from Judd just where her "tough-broad reputation" had come from. *And* Judd knew about it. She didn't think Judd had ever given two seconds of time to think about her, let alone allow himself to listen to others' opinion of her.

Fairfax had already begun speaking tonelessly about the hospital's approach to what he called the "Whitewell baby situation." After giving what sounded like a PR briefing, he added sternly, "This was not a lapse in security, but simply an unfortunate occurrence."

"That's not much comfort to the mother," Judd said.

"But it's necessary that the hospital not show panic. Of course, we're concerned and you can be assured this won't happen again."

"Look, Fairfax, the next time isn't now." While Judd talked, he made additional notes. "Caleb Whitewell has been taken from the maternity floor with the slickness of grease. A lot of people weren't paying attention, if a stranger could walk through the halls, ride the elevators, pass two nurse's stations and then repeat that entire process again, this time carrying a baby."

"Obviously, the woman looked like a professional."

"Ah, and how would she know how to look professional?"

"I don't know. How would I know the answer to that?"

"How about if she might have worked here and knew the routine?"

"Worked here? In my hospital? That's impossible."

"Are you acquainted with everyone who's worked here since..." Judd tapped his pen on his knee. "I believe the hospital opened in the late sixties."

"Certainly I don't know everyone. I've only been here myself for five years."

"Then I suggest you have a somewhat limited knowledge of the former staff."

Clearly rattled, he finally nodded. "All right. I concede your point, but that still doesn't prove this woman was employed here."

"But it's a logical place to start. Since the kidnapper didn't conveniently drop a business card or leave a number where we could reach her, we're stuck with you."

"You don't need to be sarcastic."

"Then get serious. We're talking about a baby, not a missing bedpan. What I want is a list of former employees who were fired or quit. Tanya said the woman looked to be in her mid-thirties so fifteen years back should be enough."

Adrienne leaned forward.

"Mr. Fairfax, what about the women who have given birth here?" she asked. "I know it sounds remote and it's probably a huge number of people to consider, but this woman might be a mother who for some reason wants another newborn."

Fairfax started to refuse when Adrienne added, "Birth records are public. You can save us a lot of time and show the public that Seapoint Hospital is determined to cooperate and get Tanya Whitewell's baby back safely."

"We can get them from City Hall, if you refuse to help us," Judd commented.

"That's a lot of information," Fairfax conceded with reluctance. "It will take some time."

Judd stood. "Didn't the hospital install a state-of-the-art computerized system about a year ago?" he asked, with an edge to his curiosity. "I recall my father's construction company, along with a number of businesses and private donors, gave substantial donations for its purchase."

Fairfax scowled, obviously realizing Judd wasn't just some rookie. "Well, yes, we are computerized."

"Then I'll expect those two lists by eight tomorrow morning. An officer will come by and pick them up." He braced both hands on the shiny mahogany desk and leaned forward. "In the meantime, I suggest you put all your credentials to work and find a better security system. One that keeps the babies in the hospital until their mothers take them home."

Moments later, they wound their way down a carpeted hall toward the exit that avoided the glass-enclosed walkway.

"I'm going back to the station," Judd said. "Leo should have that sketch done by now and I want to check on any new developments."

"I don't suppose you know if anyone saw the woman outside Seapoint," Adrienne commented as she hurried to stay apace with his long legs. "Passersby, perhaps?"

"The ones we could find have been questioned and I've already requested bus and cab checks. Sometimes we get lucky at the routine level."

"What can I do? I feel like I'm just following you around."

"You did great with Tanya. And suggesting we get a list of births might be the key we need. You were telling me earlier about Tanya's mother... What about a family connection to taking the baby? Jealousy or revenge of some sort."

"Offhand, I don't know of any problems, but I can do some checking."

"Good."

They'd followed the walk around to the front of the hospital. The face of the building was of imposing stone softened by ivy that crawled up the sides. Bushes thrived in weed-free mulch. Adrienne was about to say she'd talk to him later, when her attention was drawn to the edge of the mulch. She walked a few steps closer.

"Judd, look."

He frowned and moved to where she had knelt by a baby rattle.

"Remember Tanya mentioned the woman had a blue rattle?" she said.

For a few seconds, he frowned, as if mentally scrolling back through the interview with the young mother. "Yeah, she did, didn't she?" Judd said thoughtfully. But as Adrienne reached down to pick it up, Judd grabbed her wrist to stop her. "Don't touch it."

"Fingerprints?" she asked, excitement filling her voice.

"Yeah, we might get a bonus we didn't expect." He glanced back at the path, then stood to measure the distance. "If this was the rattle that Tanya saw and the woman dropped it—for it to be so far from the walk, she either zigzagged close to the bushes and lost it or she dropped it and it was kicked aside by someone.''

Adrienne stared at the rattle, again sensing something familiar. It was plastic, shaped like a tiny barbell with thin bands of yellow. Puzzling over the familiarity, her mouth fell open in surprise.

My God, she thought. Of course! She'd seen a blue rattle among Diana's things that she'd packed away at Judd's house after the funeral. If her recollection was correct, that rattle was a replica of this one.

"You wouldn't have something in your purse we could wrap this in, would you?'' When she didn't answer, he touched her shoulder. "Adrienne?''

"Oh, I'm sorry.''

He repeated the question and she took out a plastic pack of tissues. After using his pen to slide the rattle from the mulch, Judd carefully folded the tissues around it.

"I know where I saw it,'' she said carefully, hating the fact she had to bring up his wife and son.

"Saw it? The rattle? Where?''

In that moment, when she looked at him fully, she wanted to forget what she knew. Or at the very least, she wished she hadn't said anything, not until she could check with the hospital to be absolutely sure. But she was sure. She knew it as well as she knew her name. But telling Judd...

In as even a voice as she could muster, she said, "When I came over to pack up Diana's and Travis's things, there was a box of stuff that Diana had saved from when Travis was born. In the box was a blue rattle just like this one.''

Judd was silent, staring down at the small object as if someone had just presented him with a time bomb.

Adrienne got to her feet and wished she had the right to put her arms around him and soothe him, but she didn't. She knew he would only stiffen and draw away.

Finally, as if unable to escape the painful yet potentially valuable source of information, he said, "Travis was born in this hospital. It would be eight years ago this November... I remember that Diana had a lot of stuff when she came home. Formula samples, disposable diapers—that sort of thing."

"Yes, most hospitals routinely give out newborn packets. The rattle might have been included."

He nodded and looked away, physically gathering his professionalism into place. "Okay, then Tanya should have recognized it. In other words, she would have had one."

"Maybe they changed the packets. Why don't you let me check on it."

"Yeah, why don't you do that," he said in a gruff voice. He slipped the rattle into his pocket. "In the meantime, I'll drop this at the lab and then—" He took her arm and led her back to the path. "Never mind."

But she guessed what he had been about to say. He was going to go to the house and look for Travis's rattle.

Adrienne swallowed. Looking through that box meant handling his son's things, dealing with suppressed memories, walking through the rooms of the empty house, the house he hadn't been in for three years.

He raised an eyebrow and she knew he had read her thoughts. "You're too damn smart, you know that?"

"It was a logical conclusion. You want to get that baby back safely and if that means searching through your son's things for a rattle, then you're going to do it."

"Stop crediting me with some inner strength I don't have," he said harshly.

Good grief, was every reaction she had the wrong one?

"I'll go with you," she said firmly. At his dark look, she quickly added. "You don't know where I put everything, Judd. My being there will save us some time."

"Afraid I can't handle it?"

Adrienne recalled with far too much clarity the broken man gripped with a black fury she'd met when she'd gone to the house a few days after the funeral to see if there was anything she could do.

He'd looked at her that day with a raw pain and had growled a response that had torn at her heart. "Yeah, give me a good reason to keep on living."

Now she hoped her expression didn't reveal that memory. "Of course I know you can handle it."

"Bull."

She lifted her chin. "If I were your partner, this wouldn't even be an issue."

"But you're not, Adrienne. And that is definitely the issue."

"Because I was Diana's best friend?"

"No, because I took you to bed a year ago and used sex to try and forget my dead wife and son."

Chapter 3

At his desk at the Seapoint police station, Judd gripped the phone. Laid out in front of him was the information on the Whitewell case and there were still too many missing pieces.

He kept looking at the clock and wondering about the baby; he knew from too many police reports that the woman's motive for taking the infant would be a huge factor in how safe the infant remained. Time was of the essence. The longer Caleb Whitewell was missing the greater the possibility of not getting him back safely.

Mike Shelby, one of the officers on the case, took Judd's call. "What have you got at your end?" Mike asked.

"So far, damn little," Judd said in disgust. "No cab picked her up and the bus driver doesn't remember a woman with a baby."

"That's what Carmichael reported. He also talked to Ronnie Whitewell. Kid is really shook up and nothing we have indicates he might be involved. Carmichael said he doubts either of the parents knew anything about this."

"Yeah, for some reason, though, that seems too simple and obvious. Leo has the sketch done and we're getting it out. Have Carmichael show it to the bus driver and see if it jogs anything."

"Gotcha."

"In the meantime, we have to figure the suspect either had a car or she walked," Judd said.

"Vehicle ID or plate number would be nice."

"So would having her stop a cop and turn the baby over." Judd took a sip of his cooled coffee and grimaced.

Mike chuckled. "How is it we always hope for the easy break?"

"Probably from wishing this was a TV drama instead of real life."

"Yeah, probably. You mentioned earlier the rattle you and Adrienne found. Any prints that are usable?"

"Don't know yet."

"Judd, what's your gut sense on this one?"

"Uneasiness. This woman's just boldly going into the hospital and walking out with a baby tells me she's either very smart or not smart enough to know how risky that was."

"So we either have a brilliant kidnapper or a very stupid one."

"Or we have a psycho," Judd said.

Moments of silence followed. "I'll get back to you after Carmichael shows the sketch to the bus driver," Mike said.

"Don't forget to pick up those lists from Fairfax over at the hospital. He's expecting you about eight in the morning," Judd said. "I've got to follow up on something, so if I'm not here, leave a message."

"Sure."

Judd hung up and once again glanced at the clock. Five hours since the reported kidnapping. Five hours, he knew could put a lot of distance between Seapoint and where the baby was right now. Before the phone call, Judd had met with others in the department to hash over past cases involving infants. Sifting through the details often showed similar patterns.

Thankfully, those involving babies were the exception rather than the rule, but what deeply concerned Judd was that the cases—and their related findings—in the past few years were so far-flung and bizarre: a black market for babies had been uncovered, along with some psycho cases where the kidnapper had believed it a mission to save babies from some perceived danger.

Judd had worked on one where a woman had kidnapped two babies for the purpose of saving them from inner-city air pollution. Through some lucky tips, the infants had finally been found, crying but safe, in an old abandoned bomb shelter from the fifties. The woman had left them to go and get another child.

Judd recalled going home and telling Diana that he thought he'd seen everything. Diana had shown much more sympathy than Judd thought the kidnapper deserved—not empathy for what the woman had done, but sympathy for what a horrible life the woman must have had to resort to kidnapping and not know how wrong it was.

Oddly, Diana's determination to see more than just the surface circumstances reminded him too much of Adrienne. Maybe because the two women had been friends since college and tended to share the same willingness to understand the emotions and motives that drove people to do things. Adrienne's work in Child-Aid certainly bore out that fact.

Resigning himself to working with Adrienne on this case without making any attempt to change the assignment puzzled Judd. He had enough clout in the department that if he'd submitted a request to his superiors, they would likely have granted it. Judd's detective work had been flawless in the past, and if anything, he'd worked too hard and was too generous with his skills and expertise.

If ever there was a situation that begged for him to ask for special consideration, his past relationship with Adrienne would certainly qualify. But to use a personal issue meant he'd have to reveal the "why" of his hesitation, and that he wouldn't do.

First, it was no one's business and second, it could hurt Adrienne professionally as well as endanger the Child-Aid project within the department. Their assistant director doing a one-night stand with the cold and aloof Judd Dillon would feed the interdepartment gossip grapevine for months.

Putting aside the personal reason, he had no legitimate or professional excuse for refusing to work with her; she was eminently qualified. She'd proven that this afternoon. Her knowledge of the Whitewell family, especially Tanya, her heads-up thinking on getting the birth records and, of course, the blue rattle.

A fluke or the wind of fate, but with all the endless range of possible clues, Judd would never have thought his dead son and this missing infant would have had a connection.

One small blue rattle and Adrienne's recognition of it had churned his insides into painful knots. The cop part of him rejoiced at what could be a vital link to identifying the kidnapper.

Yet the other side of him resisted going back to the house and looking through boxes for Travis's rattle.

Hell, he didn't even recall the blue rattle, but he did recall too many other things. The old pain as well as the good memories were locked in those rooms. A week after the funeral, he'd simply walked out of the house he'd shared with Diana and Travis and had never returned.

Adrienne had volunteered to pack away all of Diana's and Travis's things in the hope that the house would be easier for Judd to deal with.

But it wasn't the house, it was the reminders and the smells and the noise that lived in the walls. Travis's pride over his drawings on the refrigerator and his determination to ride his two-wheel bike without training wheels. Diana humming the classical music that she loved and the woolly scent of yarn in the needlepoint she created. The third stair that squeaked so that when Judd came in late, he'd automatically skip it, not wanting to wake anyone. The holidays with their rushed meals and mistletoe everywhere; the summer days of pools and picnics and tiny vases of pansies in every room. And finally, the empty, hollow loneliness of grief after his wife and son were dead.

He scrubbed his hands down his face, cursing himself for allowing the memories to slide back into the light of the present. Sighing, he decided he might as well get this over with. He might even find that the three years had done what time was supposed to do—give him some sense that he'd gotten beyond the tragedy, that his life was streaming along and that Diana and Travis were a finality, a horror that he'd put firmly into his yesterdays.

Judd took a breath and stood. He reached for his jacket and had just shrugged into it, when Adrienne wove through the desks and stopped at his. Immediately, he thought of sunshine on a dismal day.

"You afraid I was going to duck out without you?" he asked, suddenly wishing he had. Perhaps going to the house by himself would be best. Then, if he fell apart, no would see him but the ghosts.

"I just thought I'd save you a trip upstairs."

"Always the sweet, considerate lady, aren't you?"

Obviously aware of his sarcasm, she asked pleasantly, "Would you rather I be a snarling bitch?"

"It would be a helluva lot easier to ignore you."

She tipped her head to the side, determined not to be cowed by insults. "You know what your problem is?"

"I'm stuck with the one woman I don't want to be stuck with?"

She fiddled with putting his pencils and pens into the cracked coffee mug holder. With a resolve that frankly surprised him, she said, "You're making too much out of a single night."

For too many drawn-out seconds, he stared at her. She was exactly right, but what was even worse was that he was using that "single night," as she called it, as a reason to remind her he didn't like working with her. He wondered if he was being sexist or just a lousy bastard.

Probably both, he mused grimly. Yet, she'd brought it up and maybe she was right. One single night was hardly a big deal, and obviously she'd put it behind her. If he really wanted to do the same, why did he keep thinking about it as if it had some long-lasting meaning?

"Let's get out of here." He came around his desk and steered her into the corridor, down the stairs and outside to the parking lot where his car was parked. He unlocked the passenger door for her, walked around to the other side and then slid behind the wheel. Starting the car and driving out of the lot, he said, "I owe you an apology."

"Yes, you do."

He chuckled. "At least we agree on that. It's about a year too late, but my behavior that night was outrageous."

She was quiet for a moment and he got the strangest feeling he'd apologized for the wrong thing. Then she said, "That sounds as if you forced me."

"Forced seduction."

"Judd, there's no such thing as forced seduction."

"Dammit, Adrienne, don't pretty it up. Sure, I was fighting some demons and yes, I was damn lonely and feeling sorry for myself, but that doesn't excuse what happened. Suddenly, there you were. I wanted you and I set out to get you into bed. Maybe because you were Diana's best friend and sex with you made me feel as if she weren't dead. Maybe because too much Scotch in a bar seated beside a sweet-smelling woman made me too damn horny. Maybe because back then I was more of a bastard than I was anything else."

Judd caught a glance of her widened eyes from the corner of his own and told himself he should have done this a long time ago. Why in hell, he wondered, was it always so tough for him to apologize on a personal level? In his work, when he made a mistake, he acknowledged it and learned from it. But that night with Adrienne hadn't been just a mistake, it had been an impropriety that he wished fervently had never happened.

But she refused to agree with him. "What happened between us happened because I was just as willing as you were."

"Uh-huh," he said skeptically. "You came there to meet a boyfriend for dinner. When he called and said he would have to cancel, you just shifted gears and decided to go to bed with me?"

"No, of course not."

"Obviously, at some point that evening, you made that decision. We went to your apartment and we had sex."

"Yes, but—"

"Is that your usual routine when one date falls through? Just pick up another one?"

She turned fully in the seat and glared at him. "Maybe I wanted you. Maybe *I* was lonely and feeling sorry for myself. Maybe *I* was madly in love with you. Maybe *I* used *you*. Did you ever think of any of those reasons?"

"No."

"Why? Because you don't want to think a woman would do something like that? Because Diana never would? Well, I'm not Diana. Maybe that's why we were such good friends. We were exact opposites. I watched men use my mother and watched her get suckered into lousy relationships. She told me all about totally trusting a man and then finding out he neither wanted you or your trust. My father did that to my mother and she never recovered from it. It's not going to happen to me." She turned away and stared out the windshield. "I knew you and I wanted to sleep with you. I don't see why I have to explain that any more than you do."

Judd was speechless, but mostly he wondered how he could possibly have missed this facet of her that night. He hadn't had that much Scotch. In fact, he vaguely recalled a fear, at one point, that she would take the night too seriously. *Had* she felt that way or had he just drawn an egotistical male conclusion? "Look, maybe I don't know you as well as I thought."

"No, you don't."

Pushing her for a deeper explanation, he said, "But you can't deny that you didn't come across as some woman just looking for a good time."

"Why? Because I didn't drape myself all over you? Because I didn't talk dirty? Some of us aren't that obvious," she said stiffly.

Judd drove past the city limits, hardly aware of where he was going. He kept casting sideways glances at Adrienne, his mind suddenly swirling with new questions about her and about what had happened that night.

Had he been that blind to her responses?

Was his own hang-up about sleeping with his wife's best friend so front and center in his mind that he'd made himself believe his hormones had clouded his good sense?

Scowling, he faced the sexist side of the issue. "Look, if I've offended you, I'm sorry. You have a perfect right to your own reasons for doing what you did. I just thought we should lay the cards on the table rather than tiptoe around what could be an uncomfortable subject."

"I'm not uncomfortable with it, *you* are."

He shrugged. "Guess I don't have any more reason to be, do I? Hell, if you can view that night as nothing to complicate our working together, I can, too."

But could he? Some gut instinct told him that day-by-day contact with Adrienne Trudell was going to be hellishly complicated.

Liar. Liar. Liar.

The word repeated itself in her head like some wagging finger of accusation. And yet, given the alternative choices...

Accept the apology, when she'd known that "forced seduction" was a thousand light-years from the truth? Or perhaps she should have refused to accept his obvious distress over what had happened and admitted the truth? Her heart nearly stopped at the thought.

She had been in love with Judd. Foolishly, crazily and guiltily. She wished she could acknowledge that the emotion had come upon her after Diana's death, but truthfully, she'd been secretly in love with Judd for more than two years before Diana had been killed. She sincerely doubted Diana had ever guessed, but the fear that she might had prompted Adrienne to quit visiting at the house when Judd was home. She had been terrified that she would give herself away. Oh, not by any overt action or flirtatious silliness, but because she knew her feelings showed in her eyes to anyone who cared to look. And because she didn't trust her ability to hide those emotions, she had stayed away.

Once, when she'd run into Judd in town and he'd asked why she was such a stranger, she'd mumbled some lame excuse about work and a new boyfriend, but her heart had been pumping and she'd been petrified he'd see through the lie. Yet he'd just nodded and commented on how lucky her boyfriend was, before climbing into his car and driving away.

A year ago, the night they'd unexpectedly met, she had encountered a side of Judd she'd never seen—dark and sexually intense. She'd gone from astonished to fascinated, and from there to an eager willingness to go to the ends of earth with him if he'd asked.

He'd dropped an arm around her as if they were old and intimate friends. They'd danced when the song was a smoky ballad about kissing and making out and making the night last till the morning light. He'd held her against him as if that was where she belonged and he'd whispered the forbidden words of all her fantasies.

The practical side of her had known his behavior was the result of a combination of liquor, darkness and loneliness and maybe a need to release pent-up tension with someone he felt safe with. Yet Adrienne hadn't felt cautious. She'd been reckless and a little wanton and had reveled in finally being able to express what she felt for him in ways she'd never dreamed possible.

In the hours that followed at her apartment, she'd thought it a dream, an impossibly wonderful night that might be the beginning for them. Instead, the perfect lovemaking began and ended in those hours, leaving her bereft, confused and finally furious with her own vulnerability. Never again would she allow her heart to be so open, her emotions so defenseless. Never again would she place herself in a situation where her very being was susceptible to so much pain.

But that was a long time ago and meaningless now, she told herself firmly as Judd turned into the circular driveway in front of the sprawling two-story colonial house.

Glancing around, Adrienne had expected the landscape to be overgrown and the house to look deserted. On the contrary, it looked lived in and cared for. An empty house and deserted grounds had been as carefully tended as it had been when Diana and Travis were alive.

"I keep telling myself I should sell it," he commented as if reading her mind. "But every time I start to call a realtor, I can't bring myself to do it."

"Everything and everyone you loved was here. It's understandable why selling to some stranger would be difficult."

He didn't agree or disagree, but said, "On the other hand, I don't want the place to look neglected and run-down, in case I do decide to sell." He pushed open the car door. "Come on, let's get this over with."

Side by side, they walked up the gravel walk to a small porch, where Adrienne recalled standing nervously the day she'd come to pack up Diana's and Travis's things. She'd known that Judd was home. But she hadn't known whether she should just take charge or seek him out and ask what exactly he wanted done with the things once they were in boxes.

In the end, she'd packed and sealed the boxes and moved them all to the guest bedroom, where she'd slept on the few occasions when she'd stayed overnight.

Now Judd unlocked the front door, then turned slightly to her, obviously remembering that day years ago when he'd dragged the door open and gestured that she come in, without even asking why.

With his eyes searching her face, he asked, "How did you know I needed you that day?"

Adrienne blinked at the way he'd phrased the question and then shook off the wave of feeling. Ancient reactions, she reminded herself. Long ago, she'd stopped wanting what he was never going to give her.

"After the funeral, I wanted to do something," she said softly. For you, she added silently. "Back when Diana and I were in college, a student died after an overdose of drugs. Her parents came and they were so upset, neither of them could go into their daughter's dorm room. Diana and I volunteered to pack everything up and send it to them. Later, we talked about how sudden death makes facing the finality much harder than if the death is expected. College philosophy, I suppose, but after the car accident, and after I saw you, I knew you were too devastated to deal with the things that held so many reminders of Diana and Travis."

"You were a good friend to Diana, Adrienne. And when she was gone, you were a good friend to me."

Adrienne felt a rush of guilt. Had she been a good friend because she'd loved Judd? If that was a possibility, then she had to seriously look at all the motives that had followed—including why she had gone there to pack up Diana's personal things.

She shook off the dark possibilities and started for the stairway. "Would you rather I get the rattle and bring it down?"

"It's been three years. You don't have to protect me," he said, gesturing that she should go first up the stairs.

"I know this isn't easy."

"Hell, little in life is. Watch the third step. It squeaks."

She carefully stepped on the riser and predictably it sounded out its protestation. Laughing, she said, "Maybe the same carpenter worked on the building where I live. I have a floorboard in my apartment that does the same thing."

And in that precise instant, realizing the implications of her words, she damned her loose tongue. Since he was behind her, she couldn't see his expression, but the seconds of silence spoke volumes. Maybe he would just ignore it. Oh, God, please . . .

But he didn't. "Between the bed and the dresser, isn't it?"

Her face felt tight and her hands were suddenly cold. "Yes."

"Makes it tough for a guy to leave quietly."

Since she still couldn't see his expression, she didn't know if he was truly treating his exit that morning as "no big deal" or just another potential hazard of a one-night stand.

Clearing her throat and hoping she sounded breezily calm, she said, "Yes, it does."

"So you knew I was leaving before I was out of the apartment," he surmised, and she didn't miss the resigned tone. This time, she heard some regret and felt a rush of warmth.

Suddenly, she felt bad for him, sorry that he was shouldering all the blame for a night that she'd been as much a part of as he'd been. "I probably would have done the same thing if we'd gone to your place."

From the stairway, they walked down the carpeted upstairs hall. The second floor had a cool, sterile and empty smell, the silence of many seasons hidden within the walls giving off an eerie sense that life and noise would be harsh and careless and disturb the solemnity of the past.

Judd touched her arm and turned her so that she had to look at him. "*You* duck out of something sticky? I don't think so. Why didn't you say something to me that morning?"

"You mean try and stop you from leaving? Make you feel guilty?" She shook her head. "Judd, you don't duck the tough stuff, either. I figured you left because you were afraid if you stayed, I'd make assumptions about a relationship."

"No matter how you excuse it, Adrienne, it was a cowardly way out." He hesitated near the guest bedroom, where the boxes were. "I almost called you."

She froze. She shouldn't ask, she shouldn't want to know. "Why didn't you?"

"I don't know," he said wistfully. "Maybe I was afraid you'd say what I deserved to hear—go to hell, Judd."

She recalled too vividly how she'd felt not just that day but for weeks, even months to come. Hurt and foolish and disappointed and more determined than ever that he would never know how much that night had meant to her. She would not do as her mother had done: open herself up to unrelenting hurt by trusting her emotions and feelings as if they were a surefire gauge of love given and received.

But now, for reasons that escaped her, she was allowing all those past sentiments to storm back into her life as if they'd never been put aside. Well, they had been put aside— as they should have been. Judd wanted nothing from her and it was time she reminded herself of that.

"You're right," she said coolly. "I probably would have told you exactly that."

Adrienne walked ahead of Judd into the guest bedroom. Most of the room was filled with the stacked boxes she'd put there years ago. She'd placed them so a walkway between made them all accessible, but the close quarters made moving precarious, at best.

Adrienne had marked the boxes, but she didn't recall which one contained the baby rattle. Now squeezing between the stacked cartons, combined with feeling the frustrating anxiety of once again having to face the seemingly endless memories, had frayed her nerves.

Judd barely said anything. Whenever she glanced at his face, he either looked grim or so tightly controlled, she guessed it was taking just about all his willpower not to run from the room.

After twenty minutes of searching and no progress, he snapped, "For God's sake, Adrienne, are you sure you packed that rattle?"

"Yes."

"Maybe you threw it out."

"I would never have taken the liberty of throwing anything away before checking with you."

Judd had been moving the boxes they'd checked through and restacking them, but not too carefully. Adrienne steadied one that was about to tip over.

Leaning against one of the stacks of cartons, he surveyed the ones not yet opened. "Well, it's not in any of the ones you thought it was in."

Adrienne brushed a wisp of hair off her face. She'd discarded her jacket, as had Judd. He'd rolled his shirtsleeves up and she was too aware of the three open buttons on his shirt. Her blouse stuck to her and she wanted to blame the stifling August heat in the room, but knew it wasn't just the temperature getting to her.

She opened another box and as she began to go through its contents, she glanced over her shoulder. "Look, I know this is difficult for you. Why don't you—" But before she got the rest of the sentence out, the boxes that he'd stacked toppled.

He grabbed her and pulled her against him as a second stack of boxes teetered and finally fell around them, trapping them. In the sudden melee, she ended up sprawled across the sheet-shrouded bed, with Judd on top of her.

His leg was too intimately positioned. Her skirt had twisted up so that the garter and top of her hose pressed into the zipper of his pants. He'd managed to cushion her fall, but that, in effect, had sealed one of his arms beneath her and forced her face into his neck.

Neither moved.

Judd cursed and Adrienne forced herself to lie perfectly still, praying he couldn't feel her heart slamming into his chest.

In what felt like forever, he lifted his head and stared down at her. "You okay?"

"I think so."

"Guess box stacking isn't one of my talents," he said, making no effort to move.

"No, I guess not."

He stared into her eyes and she stared back, the heat between them searingly evident, the tension thick in the air.

Adrienne tried to look away, but couldn't. She was trapped by that smoky green gaze that had never lost the power to mesmerize her.

Judd murmured, "This is dangerous, you and me like this."

She drew a long breath, wishing she had the courage to slide her arms around him.

"You feel like you did that night," he whispered with seeming reluctance. His eyes seemed to say that this was the most logical and truthful admission he'd made all day. "Scared and nervous and not sure what to do."

"I wanted to make you happy," she said with a catch in her breathing.

"You made me hard."

She turned her head to the side, not embarrassed as much as unsure how to respond.

"Like right now, Adrienne."

"I'm sorry..."

"For what? For being a woman? Don't be silly."

"There's nothing between us except that one night."

"So if I kiss you, it won't mean anything."

"No, it won't mean anything at all," she said stiffly.

He cupped her chin and held her face steady while he lowered his mouth and kissed her cheeks. Then he brushed his mouth softly across hers. Adrienne was so rattled, she could barely respond.

Judd scowled and then lowered his head once again, this time taking her mouth fully. Adrienne felt something inside of her awakening, and without giving her actions any second thoughts, she slid her arms around him.

He shaped her mouth with his, gliding his tongue into hers on a foray of taste and sweet experiments.

Adrienne's heart raced and she started to panic. What was she opening herself up to? Hurt and disappointment were the only things her heart would gain as a result of this. Judd had said the kiss wouldn't mean anything and she agreed. So why was she lying here like some desperate woman hungry for something she could never have?

But before she could push him away, he rolled away from her. In one easy motion, he got to his feet and cursed again. Adrienne scrambled off the bed and frantically tried to straighten her clothes. She grabbed her jacket and there, in the corner amid the scattered boxes, lay the blue rattle.

She reached down and picked it up, calming her breathing with a force of will.

"Judd?"

He turned around and she showed him the rattle.

He stared at it as if it had been deliberately hiding until after they'd kissed. "Is it the same as the one you found at the hospital?"

"Yes ... I mean, it sure looks like it."

He didn't come near her or ask to look more closely at the rattle. Instead, he moved to the door, then gestured for her to follow. "Come on, let's get the hell out of here."

"But the boxes—"

"Forget them. With any luck, maybe we can forget what just happened between us as easily."

Chapter 4

By six the following morning, Judd was at his desk, a mug of strong black coffee at his elbow. Tired after a night of little sleep, he'd finally decided to come in early and check on any overnight developments in the Whitewell case.

Not a whole helluva lot, he thought in disgust as he went over what they knew. The police sketch of the suspect had been aired on the TV news shows and was to run in the newspapers.

Judd had stopped by the hospital late yesterday afternoon in the hopes that showing the sketch to the staff might prove lucky and someone might ID it.

"Gee, she looks a lot like my wife's sister," one employee had said stoically, "but she's not. This lady is too skinny."

Another was adamant that the sketch resembled a now-deceased woman who had appeared on one of the soaps. The others who had seen it either hadn't recognized it or had said the sketch was too plain and the woman too bland. Leo, the police artist, however, was too good to miss any salient details. In fact, he'd told Judd that Tanya had said over and over again that there weren't any distinguishing marks.

But when one of the nurses in maternity had looked at the sketch, she'd said something that had made Judd think twice.

"She looks too plastic," the nurse had remarked. "Like a generic picture. If I were asked to put together the features of an average middle-aged woman who was colorless and easily missed, this sketch would be a great example to follow."

"Easily missed" had stuck in Judd's mind. Maybe their suspect had gone to a lot of trouble to be perceived as plain—no makeup, uninteresting hair color, low-key personality.

Judd thought of Adrienne and how striking she was, but also how she didn't work at it. She drew second looks not just because of her spectacular legs that Fairfax had boldly noted, but because of her expressive eyes, her warm smile and the sense she exuded that knowing her would be a pleasant experience. It was one of the things that fascinated him about her.

Judd tapped his pen thoughtfully. Why in hell couldn't he shake out his thoughts about one Adrienne Trudell? He didn't want to be fascinated by her or curious or in any way preoccupied with her. But instead of firmly holding a spot on his not-interested list, she kept popping up as if she were an important part of his life. Like now, for God's sake, when he was supposed to be working.

Forcing his thoughts back to the case, he once again focused on what the nurse had said about the woman.

Easily missed.

Obviously, that was the reason the woman hadn't been stopped when she took the baby. She'd made herself practically invisible. What Judd wondered was whether practically invisible was the way she normally looked, or if she really had gone to a lot of trouble to make herself appear that way. Chances were, he was dealing with a very smart woman who didn't ignore appearances or perceptions. It was a tiny piece of insight, but he tucked it away in his mind for further reference.

An interview with Ronnie and Tanya Whitewell that one of the other officers had conducted revealed nothing in the way of new information about their missing baby or the mystery woman. But the biggest disappointment had been the fingerprint report on the blue rattle.

Finding the object in the bushes had raised his hopes. Professionally, he knew better than to count on such a quick break. Yet he knew carelessness existed in most crimes; the key was finding where the screwup was. Only on television did the culprit mess up on cue.

Judd read through the print expert's analysis, short as it was, but the conclusion left him with a dead end. The print was too smeared to be identifiable.

The lists of hospital workers and new mothers from the past five years would be in this morning, but he feared that even when they'd narrowed the lists to potential suspects, they could still pass over the woman because they didn't have a name to start with.

He shoved his chair back and stood. Moving over to the coffee machine, he poured himself his third mug. His head throbbed and his eyes were gritty from no sleep the previous night. He wasn't sure whether the cause was the worrisome case or Adrienne Trudell.

Kissing her, Judd decided, had to be the worst thing he could have done. Not that he hadn't enjoyed it or remembered all too clearly what the kisses on the night they'd shared a year ago had been like—that was the problem. He remembered too damn much. Still, he knew better than to allow himself to get tangled up in any kind of relationship—sexual or otherwise.

For one thing, getting involved personally with someone he was working with was bad news all its own. Not only did the department discourage such liaisons, but Judd had witnessed the inherent dangers when a former partner had allowed a personal relationship with a co-worker to interfere with work. Dan had been preoccupied and was eventually taken off a case when it was learned that some vital evidence in a homicide case was missing. Missing because Dan had been thinking about his date the night before instead of concentrating on his job.

Judd dumped a packet of sugar into the hot liquid and stirred. Not for a moment could he deny that he'd been thinking too much about that kiss, and worse, too much about Adrienne. But what bothered him was *why*. Kissing a woman was hardly a new experience for him, although he rarely did it impulsively. And he always kept himself under control so that no expectations were unknowingly created, no hope given to the woman that a kiss automatically meant moving to the next step.

Maybe he was overreacting. He'd been involved with damn few women since Diana's death, but then again one of those women had been Adrienne.

"Going to bed with Adrienne was one of your dumber moves Dillon," he muttered to himself as he stirred in a second packet of sugar. Sure, it *had* been only one night, but the rub was that—try as he might—he'd never quite forgotten it. However, he reminded himself firmly, his sharp and sensitized memory could claim extenuating circumstances. Adrienne had always had close ties to him because of her friendship with Diana. That automatically lifted her from

quick lay on a lonely night into another category altogether.

What that something else was, he didn't know. A friend?
An acquaintance? Should he act casual now? Distant? In-
different? It was like feeling his way through a dark alley
and not knowing which shadow hid the gun and bullet
aimed at his head.

Being assigned to work together on the Whitewell case,
plus going back to the house— My God, no wonder he'd
been unable to sleep last night. All the sudden and disturbing events had rocked him badly, the house especially. Not
only had the recollections of Diana and Travis shaken him,
but the growing certainty of Adrienne's effect on him had
knocked him for a loop. With Adrienne, even the memories of the past were more complicated.

He should, however, credit himself for keeping his distance from her ever since Child-Aid had created an office in
the police station. Wisely, he'd had nothing to do with her,
despite his being so aware that she was just upstairs. Ignoring her now, of course, was no longer possible, but he damn
well could keep his feelings about her under control. *Stay
focused on the job and get it successfully completed,* he told
himself. God knows the case was enough to deal with in the
days ahead.

Judd gripped his coffee mug and started to turn around,
when he sensed someone behind him. He swung just a little
too quickly and slopped the liquid.

"Damn," he muttered as he wiped his hands on some
napkins.

"I didn't mean to startle you," Adrienne said quickly.

Was she kidding? He was beginning to feel startled every
time she came within twenty feet of him. "I should have
heard you," he grumbled, hating that she'd caught him off
guard.

"I've been here a few moments. You were deep in thought."

About you, he wanted to say, but kept silent. He wasn't about to tell her that. He tossed the wet napkins into the trash and gave her a cursory glance. She wore slacks and a tailored blouse with a necktie and a jacket. She'd tucked her hair up in some complicated style that he guessed was to complete the professional look that began with the necktie. Instantly, he wanted to take her hair down and tell her to get rid of the tie. Women who wore them annoyed the hell out of him. He liked women to look like women, not like—he cut off his thoughts. *Dammit, man, get your mind on why she's here. What she wears is totally irrelevant.* He moved around her and sat down at his desk.

"What are you doing at work so early?" he asked in a gruff voice. "I thought your office opened at nine."

"It does, but I wanted to organize some information." She stood behind the chair beside his desk. "I might ask you the same question. Judging from the level of the coffee in the carafe, I'd say you've been here a while."

"Don't you know good cops never sleep?"

"I thought it was the city that never sleeps."

He sat back and gave her a direct look. Her eyes were bright, her skin dewy fresh, her attitude alert. Obviously, she hadn't dwelt on the effects of their kiss. Then again, maybe she hadn't been affected at all. "Well, you sure don't look as if you had a sleepless night."

She tipped her head to the side and frowned. "How do you manage to make what should be a compliment sound like it's not?"

"Practice. I stay up all night thinking them up." He indicated the sheaf of papers she held. "Is that the information you came down to organize?"

She placed the papers on the desk and hung her white leather bag on the back of the chair. "As a matter of fact, it is. Do you mind if I get some coffee first?"

"Sit down, I'll get it for you. How do you want it?"

"Black."

He went to the coffee machine and poured her a cup. "It's a good thing you did come in early. By late morning, drinking this stuff black is like consuming hazardous waste."

She crossed her legs and with a touch of amused sarcasm, said, "Hmm, and I've always been particularly fond of coffee that tastes like hazardous waste."

He grinned and she smiled back as he set the mug on the desk.

"You're quick, Ms. Trudell."

"Have to be, Detective Dillon. You tend to keep everyone on their toes."

He sank into his own chair, leaned back and planted his booted foot on the lower drawer. Adrienne sipped her coffee and then, with businesslike demeanor, she sat forward, her back straight, her hands busy with the papers. Judd noticed that her fingernails were a dark red today rather than the pink he recalled from yesterday. He also noted that one fingernail was broken. Had it happened at the house when he'd grabbed her to keep the boxes from hitting her? She'd been in the process of opening a box. Perhaps she'd snagged and torn...

Dammit, he was doing it again. He should be able to concentrate for more then five seconds on something besides personal knowledge of Adrienne Trudell.

"Are you okay?" she asked with an uneasiness in her voice. "I know I kind of barged in on you, but—"

"I'm fine," he snapped irritably. "You work here, for God's sake. How could you be barging in?"

Stiffening, she set her coffee aside, gathered the papers and stood. "I'll come back later."

Judd frowned. He sure as hell didn't intend to come across as some overbearing type of cop. "Sit down, Adrienne."

Instead, she slung her purse onto her shoulder, clutched the papers and gave him a withering look.

Judd sighed. He didn't need a battle of the wills. "All right, all right. I'm sorry I snapped at you."

She thawed, but not by much. "It's not that simple. You've made it clear you resent my having been assigned to work with you, but if you think I'm going to spend the time walking on eggshells or apologizing for being a female or..." She took a determined breath. "Or even for a one-night stand that means nothing to either of us, well, I'm not and you're wrong."

Judd shook his head, not even attempting to sort all of that out. He held his hands up, palms facing her. "Truce, okay?"

After glaring at him one last time, she nodded.

"Now, would you please sit down?"

She did, but gingerly, as if she intended to get up if he did or said one thing she didn't like.

He took a swallow of coffee, feeling a little as if he'd survived round one of what he now knew with certainty would be a strained and very tense working relationship.

He nodded toward the pages she'd once again placed on the desk. "What have you got?"

"Information on the blue rattle."

Suddenly, he was damn glad she was here. "That was quick work."

"I told you I was going back to the hospital to check on it."

"Yeah, you did."

"Well, I found out a few things that might be useful."

"I'm listening."

"For one, the blue rattles were in newborn packets for the baby boys. Pink, obviously, for the girls. The hospital orders the packets from a company that sells them wholesale. Maternity started using the packets from this particular company a few months before Travis was born. About a year ago, the supplier discontinued the rattles. Now they use soft rubber ducks. Tanya had one of those on her night table."

Judd nodded. "How did you find out all of this?"

"Once I learned where the packets came from, I called the company." She lifted one of the papers where she'd scribbled some notes. "It's the Lambert Supply Company, located west of Boston off 128. It's a family-owned business, and as of now they only distribute in New England."

"Then at least we have a manageable starting point."

"Yes."

"Good work, Adrienne." Judd was impressed. He knew she handled a lot of the probing and leads when Child-Aid dealt with their major area of expertise—missing children—but admittedly, he'd never considered the similarities between what she did and good investigative work. And because the police were always involved with finding the missing kids, he'd assumed the agency was more of a feel-good operation for the parents than anything else.

Now for the first time, he understood why the chief had pushed to bring Child-Aid in-house. Obviously, the agency was an asset, as well as a valuable resource. Studying Adrienne now, Judd didn't miss the sparkle of excitement in her eyes.

"There's more," she said, shuffling the papers.

"Okay, let's have it."

"About a year ago, a bunch of the packets were stolen from the hospital supply room."

Judd's cop-radar immediately shot up. "Packets were stolen? Are you sure?"

She leaned forward, and her blue eyes were as dazzling as her enthusiasm. "I'm sure. The reason the theft was noticed was that they—the hospital, I mean—unexpectedly ran short. When they reordered from Lambert, they were told the rattles had been discontinued, and replaced."

"With the ducks."

"Yes. At first, they thought the inventory shortage might be due to an upswing in births, but births were actually down in that month."

"That month being?"

"September of last year. Since they don't want to stock-pile the packets and because Lambert is so accessible, the hospital orders on a monthly basis."

"Theft problems any other months?"

"Nothing of that magnitude."

"They ever catch who did it?"

She shook her head.

"Okay, so you've narrowed down the theft of the packets from the supply room to only last September."

"That's what I concluded, so I got a list of all the people who worked that month." She passed him a paper with about three dozen names on it.

"How many of these are full-time?"

"About half. I thought if we compared it to the list that Fairfax is sending over, we might have some names worth looking into."

"Very impressive. I should have been using you on investigations a long time ago."

"Really?"

"Yes, really."

For a few seconds, they stared at each other in an unintentional silence that caught both looking too long and sitting too still. Aware and yet tense, as if each were mesmerized by the other.

Finally, Adrienne looked away. "It was fun," she said in a husky voice. "Finding the information, I mean. A lot like putting together a puzzle."

"You do this kind of thing for Child-Aid, don't you?"

"Some, but not as much as I'd like. The police handle most of the questioning and footwork, as you know, but I think—" She stopped herself. "Never mind, it's just my own personal opinion."

"Tell me. I'm really interested."

"Well . . . I'd like to see the agency be more aggressive on the investigative side. We need to be aware of the machinations people concoct to take a child they have no right to. That helps to define their motives, as well as make us more diligent in protecting the children *before* they are missing."

"Valid points," he said. "And the head of the agency—what's her name?"

"Evelyn Hudson."

"Oh, yeah. One of the guys upstairs says she's cold, tight-faced and probably tight—" He stopped himself just in time. "Sorry."

"I will agree that Evelyn can be intimidating. She feels she has to be in order to get the funds the agency needs from the state budget, as well as deal with the police." She paused a moment, giving him a measuring look. "Some of them aren't always as sensitive and cooperative as you are."

He raised an eyebrow. "Was that a shot?"

"Of course."

He chuckled. "You're a tough lady." He paused a moment. "So, do you think a more aggressive investigative operation would increase the success ratio for Child-Aid?"

"If by success you mean getting children found quicker, then yes. Child-Aid doesn't care about applause from the governor or news profiles on how dedicated we are, but we do care about finding children in the fastest and most efficient way possible. Working with you is a good start."

"Working with me?" he asked, feeling ridiculously flattered and reminding himself not to get all soft over a few pleasant words. "You see me as a step toward fast results?"

"You're very good at what you do."

"What am I, some sort of test case?"

"Certainly not, but getting the best detective to solve a tough case is valuable for all concerned. Especially for the Whitewells and, of course, little Caleb."

For reasons Judd didn't want to think about, he suddenly felt as if he were doing his job not only to solve the case, but to stay in Adrienne's good graces. So much for a few exchanges of soft and pleasant words.

Scowling, he pushed his chair back and opened one of his desk drawers. "No question you've made a good start. However…" Judd took out Travis's rattle and then dumped out an envelope containing the other rattle that had been returned after the print check. He placed the two rattles side by side. "Let me ask you some questions. When you talked to the packet supplier, did they say they made the rattles or did they buy them somewhere?"

She stared at the two identical toys and then took a third blue rattle from her purse. "Inventory at the hospital found this for me. I brought it along to double-check that they're all the same. They are." She glanced up at Judd after she returned the rattle to her purse. "The supplier didn't actually say where the rattles came from originally, but I got the impression they just assembled the packets. I mean, each packet contains a variety of items. Disposable diapers, baby formula, small boxes of infant cereal, powder and lotion, that sort of thing. I would think the rattles are like the other things—bought from yet another supplier."

"Yeah, look at this." Judd showed her the origin imprint on the rattle. "Made in Japan."

"Guess that answers the question."

"But raises another one. Is the rattle sold in stores as well as to this company?"

Adrienne's shoulders sagged and she sat back in obvious disappointment. "In other words, thousands of them could be around."

"Exactly."

"Damn. And I thought this was such a good lead."

"It's an excellent lead, but like the puzzle you talked about, we don't want to assume that this is the piece that leads to the kidnapper. Easy and quick assumptions make for carelessness or worse, sloppiness."

"But don't you think it's awfully coincidental that we found the rattle outside the hospital? After all, since they no longer distribute them, it's unlikely it would just be lying there unnoticed for a year. Besides, it would have been dirty, probably broken and at the very least faded from exposure to the weather. And what are the chances it was just casually dropped by a passerby on the same day little Caleb was taken and Tanya saw the woman with a blue rattle?"

Judd nodded. "I can't argue with your logic, and your questions are dead-on."

"So you think the rattle was dropped by the woman and perhaps..." Adrienne hesitated, as if sorting out her thoughts. "If she worked at the hospital a year ago, she could have stolen the packets from the supply room and that would account for how she had the rattle."

"Possible, but why did she wait a year?"

"To give the hospital time to forget her?"

"Maybe. But why this hospital? I mean, if her sole motive was to take a baby, Seapoint Hospital is one of many in the state and hundreds in New England alone. Why chance going back to where someone might recognize her?"

She slumped deeper in the chair. "I'm getting a headache."

"I know the feeling. But it's just a lot of questions that we don't have answers for yet." He shoved his chair back and stood. "What you have gotten, however, is terrific. And I agree with your 'too coincidental' theory, but just in case, I'm going to get a couple of officers to check around the local stores. If the rattle is sold nationally, it's bound to be available in Seapoint."

He glanced up at the clock. "Those lists from Fairfax are due here a little after eight, so we have some time to kill. I'm starved. How about taking me out to breakfast?"

She didn't move, staring down at the pages scattered on his desk.

"Adrienne?"

"I just thought . . . we might have gotten really close to a solution," she said haltingly. "So close that we would find Caleb very soon. Maybe even today."

He tipped her head up and saw the discouragement in her eyes. "Listen, thanks to you, we're closer than we were. You can't let the unanswered questions throw you. Believe me, if I had a nickel for all the questions, dead ends and hours of waiting in any one case, I'd be richer then the last lottery winner. It's slow and cumbersome and usually frustrating. But it's also damn rewarding when it all works out and the case is closed."

"What happens when the ending isn't happy?"

"You deal with it, but you can't work on the premise that it will be tragic."

"And you stay out of it emotionally and personally."

"Yes."

"I have to learn that."

"Sometimes it's damn tough, Adrienne. And I think you might have a point on cops being more sensitive. Sometimes we give the impression of being coldhearted and detached. I guess the ideal is to be professionally compassionate."

She sighed and nodded. Judd stepped back and she rose, gathering the papers.

Judd said, "I can put those in my desk."

"All right."

He did so and after she'd retrieved her purse, he took her arm. They were almost down the stairs, when she stopped.

Judd halted, studying her. "What's the matter?"

"You said *I* could take you out for breakfast?" she asked, obviously just realizing what he'd said earlier.

He grinned. "Hey, I don't want to be accused of sexist assumptions. Since we're partners on this case, we can trade off."

They continued. "Hmm, I think I'm going to get the best of the deal. I never eat much breakfast, but I adore dinner."

"Today, you're going to eat breakfast. Macko's Diner makes the best eggs and home fries you'll ever eat."

"Macko's?" Adrienne grimaced. "Not that dilapidated old diner on Winkler Steet?"

"That's it."

"I thought the health department closed them down."

"As of yesterday, they were still open."

She shuddered. "Why doesn't that reassure me?"

Outside the sun was bright and promising another hot day. Judd unlocked his car and gestured her inside.

Once they were in traffic, she said, "Thanks."

"For what?"

"For listening and understanding some of the things I want to see Child-Aid accomplish."

"You're idealistic, Adrienne, and by any stretch of the imagination, the world can use more like you."

"What a nice thing to say."

"Hmm, well, you better treasure it. I try never to say more than one nice thing a month."

As they pulled into the crowded parking lot at Macko's, Judd decided that maybe she wouldn't be so tough to work with, after all. It probably wasn't a particularly safe conclusion, given how close they would have to work together for the duration of the case. But as long as he stayed on his toes, kept his thoughts away from that night he'd spent with her and didn't take up a lot of time remembering that kiss they'd shared at his house, he'd be okay.

After all, they would be in public ninety-nine percent of the time. It wasn't as if they had to live together to get the job done.

Yeah, handling a few days would be okay.

He hoped.

Chapter 5

Macko's had the unerring smell of coffee and grease collected under a permanent cloud of hazy, smoky blue air. The diner, converted from an old train car, had become a haven for workers not given to suits and ties. Jeans, T-shirts, heavy boots, a few tattoos and enough noise to assure any patron that quiet conversation would be impossible, were its mainstay.

An upcoming Red Sox game was among the morning topics, as were complaints about a rumored pay cut planned for state workers and, of course, the missing Whitewell baby.

To Adrienne's surprise, she wasn't the only female in the place. Two women sat at the counter and another one in a booth. Most of the customers spoke to Judd and a few asked about the kidnapping. Adrienne concluded he was more than an occasional customer.

He took her arm and led the way to a booth that had just emptied.

She slid in and immediately noticed the lumpy seat. She'd never been in Macko's, although it was considered a Seapoint landmark. Despite attempts to sanitize its image and endless warnings from the health department, Adrienne knew Judd was among a large percentage who praised the diner for being homey, generous in its portions and cheap.

Across the street was another restaurant with plants hanging in the windows, but their business was half that of Macko's. And looking around, she had to admit the place had a sort of frantic charm.

She tried to imagine Judd bringing Diana to Macko's, but she knew even the idea would have been preposterous. Diana simply wasn't the diner type and would have been appalled by the rugged atmosphere. The fact that Judd had brought her here raised some questions in Adrienne's mind. Did he think she was less fastidious than his late wife? Or was she of such little importance to him personally, he simply didn't care if she liked the place or not? The latter seemed the most likely, she decided and winced a little at the revelation.

Perhaps he viewed her as one of the boys. Well, that was what she wanted, wasn't it? To be treated as a co-worker? As someone assigned to him to help find a missing baby? After all, they had both determined that this was a working relationship. She'd also been the one accusing him of putting too much emphasis on the night they'd made love.

Now to sit and wonder why he wasn't treating her the way he would a woman who was a real date or a woman he loved was neither logical nor wise.

Obviously, she couldn't have it both ways. She didn't want personal attention from him, she reminded herself. He'd made it quite clear numerous times that she meant nothing to him. And she absolutely refused to allow her own heart to weave dreams, as it had done that night. Dreams and wants that had shattered.

Judd peered at her, his gaze steady. "Is this long silence because of the noise or are you still trying to put pieces in the Whitewell puzzle?"

She found a clean spot on the table and propped up her elbow. Resting her chin in her palm, she said, "I was trying to figure out why that lovely restaurant with the hanging plants across the street isn't as busy as this one."

"Are you kidding?" His tone sounded as if she should know the answer.

"It seems to me it should be. There's lots of parking, the windows are clean and no doubt the cholesterol level is half what it is here."

"Lousy service, lousy food," he said bluntly. "I took Diana there a couple of times. But even she agreed it wasn't worth a third visit."

"Did you ever bring her here?" she asked.

Judd raised an eyebrow as if she'd presented an outrageous notion. "Be serious. Diana wouldn't have come in here if it was the only eating place left in the state."

Adrienne silently admitted that she wouldn't have chosen Macko's herself unless really desperate, but she also sensed something in Judd's words she couldn't put her finger on. A touch of resentment? Had he tried to bring Diana here and she'd balked? Adrienne dismissed the thought quickly. She had an overactive imagination when it came to Judd.

Besides, one didn't need to be particularly insightful to realize that the crowd at Macko's was working-class. Ambience and soft music would be disposed of early on in the fray of salty language and country music.

After a few minutes, the table still hadn't been cleared. Judd glanced at his watch and then stood. Adrienne started to slide from the booth, too, assuming they were going to leave.

"Sit still. I'm just going to hurry Glenda along."

Then, to Adrienne's amazement, Judd stacked up the dirty plates, cups and silverware and carried them to the counter. He returned with a wet cloth and wiped the table, then brought two mugs of coffee.

Once he was seated again, she commented, "That was very impressive. Maybe that's why the place across the street isn't doing so well. They don't allow you to clear your own table."

"Now there's a thought," he said, matching her sarcasm. "Actually, it's less complicated. Glenda is busy."

"The waitress, right?"

"Yeah. She's also part owner with Macko. It's a two-person operation. They've hired people in the past, but none of them are fast enough. Guys who come in here are usually pressed for time, so they all sort of pitch in and help."

Looking around, Adrienne said, "I have to admit, it does have the feel of everyone being equal. No doubt, that's part of its charm."

Judd sat in the corner of the booth, the morning sun revealing lighter streaks in his sable hair. After studying her silently for more than a minute, he said, "So which Adrienne is the real Adrienne? The one with the sarcastic bite or the one who just admitted Macko's has some appeal?"

Somewhat taken aback by the unusual question, she said, "Perhaps both . . . or neither."

"Ah, the mysterious woman. Is that it?"

"Maybe."

"Or are you just indecisive?"

Adrienne sipped her coffee. She was unsure where this was going and already not liking it. Carefully, she said, "I can be very decisive about certain things."

"Such as your job."

"Definitely."

"No second thoughts about our working together?"

She almost said no, but changed her mind. Why not be honest? Judd was too perceptive for her to pussyfoot around any unresolved intimate issues that could wreck a working relationship.

"Of course I've had second thoughts," she said. "Third and fourth ones, too. But I'd like to think we're both adult enough to step away from anything personal, or at least handle it in a strictly professional way."

"Neither occurred with that kiss," Judd said in an even voice.

"Is that what this is all about? Did you expect me to get huffy over the kiss? Or refuse to work with you?"

"Hell, I don't know what I expected. I'm still trying to figure out why you didn't at least resist."

"Why I didn't resist!" she said, more than a little outraged. "Why didn't *you?*"

He scowled as if she'd presented him with an unheard of question. Finally, he muttered, "Point taken."

Adrienne found his easy compliance refreshing and interesting. But knowing that Judd rarely conceded weakness, she decided to take this tiny amount of insight into him in the broadest way. After all, he could hardly argue that she should have stopped the kiss and not come off as a total sexist. Then again, his admission also revealed another truth. He'd have no trouble resisting her in the future; in fact, he'd probably make a point of it just to show her he could. Well, she didn't want to be kissed by him, she concluded firmly. She absolutely did not.

"We better order," Judd said and indicated the menu on a nearby wall. Adrienne read the items and didn't know whether it was the enticing smells coming from the kitchen or the fact she'd been up for hours and had only coffee, but she was starved. Maybe the rush of going one-on-one with Judd had stirred her adrenaline.

"What's good?" she asked, then held up her hand. "Don't tell me. Sausage, eggs and home fries."

"And Glenda's homemade bread."

Adrienne's mouth watered. She hadn't had homemade bread in years. "Sounds wonderful."

But instead of Glenda appearing and writing down the order, Judd called her name. A sixtyish woman with red cheeks and a dazzling smile glanced up from the far end of the counter. Judd called out the order, she nodded and within six minutes, she delivered two heaping plates of steaming food.

After setting the hot plates down, she glanced at Adrienne but was obviously still speaking to Judd when she said, "Well, she's sure a sight for sore eyes."

Judd sprinkled pepper on his eggs. "Glenda, you're wrong."

"Now, Judd Dillon, don't you go and try to pull any fast ones on me. You come here with a gorgeous thing like her, I know more is goin' on than just a cheap date."

He ate a piece of sausage. "This is great, Glenda."

"Don't you go and try to change the subject, neither."

He grinned. "Sorry to disappoint you, but Adrienne works with me."

Glenda looked at her as if Adrienne had been beamed down from Mars. "She's a cop?"

"Not exactly. She's with Child-Aid."

Adrienne felt as if she were watching a Ping-Pong game. It was the most bizarre feeling, listening to two people discuss her as if she weren't there.

At the mention of Child-Aid, Glenda gave Adrienne a wide smile. "Why, honey, you should have said so. Are you shy or have I been runnin' my mouth so much, you don't know what to say?"

"I—"

"You've been running your mouth," Judd said so smoothly that Adrienne guessed these two were old and good friends.

Glenda planted her hands on her hips and scowled at him. "Well, if you'd find yourself a woman and settle down like I've been tellin' you to do for the past year, then I wouldn't have to be askin' all these questions." She leaned closer to Adrienne. "He really is in a bad way, you know. Livin' alone in that apartment and refusin' to let himself care about a woman again—"

"Glenda," Judd warned.

"Okay, okay, so I mother you too much, but you know I like to see all you guys married and happy, like my Macko and me."

"Glenda's a romantic," Judd said in a tone that made it sound more like a disease than a pleasant quality. "She's determined to believe that love solves every problem."

"Well, it sure doesn't hurt," Glenda said.

Adrienne sensed Judd's irritation and quickly swallowed her fourth bite of eggs. Changing the subject, she remarked, "Judd raved about the food here, Glenda, and he certainly was right."

"Well, thank you mightily, honey. We don't get too many dressed-up ladies in here. Mostly they want to eat across the street." She peered out the steamy window. "Gee, it's too bad how their business is so slow."

Judd and Adrienne and Glenda looked at one another and then all three laughed. Adrienne went back to her food, but Judd pulled the sketch of the woman from his pocket.

Glenda lowered her voice to a hush. "When I saw you come in, I figured it would be about that poor missin' baby."

Judd nodded. "I thought you might have heard something."

"A lot of guys were talkin' about it this morning. Elmer, from over at the hardware store, thinks the woman is a kookoo. Scary, huh? Saw that there sketch in the mornin' paper. I tacked the picture up on the mirror there by the doughnuts and I been pointin' it out to anyone who hasn't seen it."

"Thanks, Glenda."

"Sure. Always glad to help the cops. Hope they get that woman and string her up," she said forcefully, obviously unable to comprehend anyone's kidnapping an infant.

Adrienne couldn't understand it, either, but she wasn't quite as quick to lash out. One of the things she'd learned at Child-Aid was that every terrible act didn't always have a sinister motive. There'd been one case where a woman had hidden her children and refused to reveal where. She'd gone to jail and as a result, her motivation for secreting her children had turned into the very real reality of her ex-husband abusing the kids.

Adrienne didn't believe the Whitewell case was as straightforward, but then, as Judd had said, there were still too many missing pieces.

Glenda gave Judd a curious look. "So how come they gave the case to you, Judd? I know you have a hard time around kids since Travis—"

Immediately noticing Judd's discomfort, Adrienne intervened and asked, "Glenda, could I have some more coffee?"

"Why, sure." Glenda turned away and Judd sagged back in the booth.

"I know she means well, but sometimes she stumbles onto topics—especially about Diana and Travis—that make me want to tell her to back off. Usually, I just shrug it off, but after yesterday at the house..."

"She *is* very blunt," Adrienne commented, although, to be honest, she was as curious as Glenda about why he, specifically, had been assigned to this case. His thoroughness and professionalism were obvious reasons, but she knew that the Seapoint Police Department had received commendations for its array of very skilled officers. Why hadn't one of them been assigned to the case, instead?

"Going to get the rattle was rougher than I thought it would be."

"Judd, that's understandable."

"Is it? Three years is a helluva long time. What's odd is that some days Diana and Travis are like faded memories. Then some tiny incident or an unexpected comment will bring the memories back, make them as clear and tragically real, as if the accident happened just yesterday."

"I should have gone to the house by myself," she said.

He sighed. "No, it's long since time for me to put the past where it belongs. And for the most part, I have." He paused as if just figuring something out, then he muttered, "Maybe that accounts for the kiss."

Adrienne's pulse sped up. Her mind leapt in two different directions at the same time. Did he consider her a part of the past that needed to be set aside? Or did he mean that the kiss obliterated the past? Either conclusion was hardly flattering.

Instead of expanding on his comment, he pushed the food around on his plate.

Adrienne's own appetite was suddenly gone and she moved the half-finished plate aside and touched her mouth with her napkin.

Glenda came back with a pot of coffee. She refilled both mugs and dropped a handful of cream packets on the table.

"Guess I better let you two finish before the food gets cold." She gave Judd a mercurial look and then bent toward Adrienne and said, "You'd be perfect for him, you know. I feel it in my bones."

"Glenda, for God's sake," Judd growled.

"I'm just sayin' it like it is," she said, clearly not at all disturbed by Judd's harsh tone. "I'll even make a prediction." At Judd's cold glare, she closed her mouth, but she gave Adrienne a brief smile before going back to her other customers.

He opened two packets of cream and dumped them in his coffee, then pushed his plate aside. "Maybe bringing you here wasn't such a good idea. I forgot Glenda's ongoing campaign to find me a woman. Not just any woman, mind you, but the 'perfect' woman."

A woman like Diana, Adrienne concluded. For she certainly had been perfect. Beautiful, classy and she'd adored Judd. "Glenda obviously cares a great deal about you."

"I suppose, but sometimes she steps over the line. Even my own mother isn't as dogged in getting me hooked up with someone. I'm sorry if she embarrassed you."

"She didn't. I don't embarrass easily."

"No, you don't, do you?"

Adrienne managed a smile. "It was my mother who did the embarrassing things. I think I became sort of immune to it."

Judd watched her a moment, unsure how to continue or what to say. Cautiously, he finally said, "I remember that Christmas you spent with us when she went off to Vegas with a boyfriend."

Adrienne shuddered. "Five years ago. That was boyfriend number ten, I think. I kept losing track." Adrienne

heard her own bitterness and silently chastised herself for it.
Her mother hardly needed to clear her life-style or her boyfriends with her daughter, but back then, Adrienne had
desperately wanted her mother to find someone who was
more permanent than two weeks.

She blamed her own lack of trust in the motives of men
on having observed the parade in and out of her mother's
life.

The night Adrienne had spent with Judd, the night she'd
thought was so wonderful, so perfect—a night she'd desperately wanted to be a beginning for them—had instead
been little more than a night of sex for Judd. Rather than
just accept that, as her mother would have, Adrienne had
taken the rejection as proof that she had poor judgment
when it came to men.

The alternative was that *all* men were as untrustworthy as
her mother had claimed, an assertion Rhoda Trudell had
embraced since Adrienne's father had deserted them.

Well, she thought with a sigh, she needn't worry about
anything happening with Judd again. She certainly didn't
need her life shattered by him; trusting him with her heart
was not a wise idea. In a way, she was proud of her honest
evaluation of their relationship. It made her aware and
guarded and convinced her that whatever sexual attraction
might exist meant nothing more than just that. It wasn't love
and never would be.

Glancing at Judd, Adrienne added, "You and Diana were
great that Christmas, by the way. I don't think I could have
gotten through the holidays by myself."

"Sure you would have. Diana always said you were the
most independent and the most stable woman she'd ever
known. My guess is that's one reason why you're so valuable to Child-Aid."

A young man in his mid-twenties with shaggy hair, dressed in jeans and a blue work shirt, stopped at Judd's table. An oval patch on his pocket read Keith.

A crumpled bill cap was in one hand. He looked nervously at Adrienne. To Judd, he muttered, "Sorry to interrupt, but Glenda said I should talk to you."

Judd straightened. "Sure, Keith."

The young man looked even more uncomfortable, his eyes darting in Adrienne's direction again. A few beads of sweat slid down his temples.

Concluding from his obvious nervousness that whatever Keith wanted to say to Judd, he wanted to say privately, Adrienne said, "Let me take care of the bill and I'll meet you in the car."

Judd nodded. "Thanks. I'll take care of the tip. Be out in a few minutes."

Adrienne slid out of the booth and Judd indicated for Keith to sit down.

Judd watched as Adrienne walked to the cash register, noticing all the appreciative looks she received. He wondered if Glenda had put the word out that Adrienne "belonged" to Judd and that accounted for the lack of whistles. Probably, Judd decided, making a mental note to totally squash any of Glenda's lingering romantic notions by not bringing Adrienne here a second time.

Adrienne paid Glenda and the two women began talking. Judd wondered briefly about what, but immediately he didn't like what he came up with. He'd always hated being discussed and dissected as if he were some dimwit who didn't know what was good for him. He sure as hell didn't need Adrienne joining in with Glenda on some crusade to find him a woman. Adrienne, he observed, glanced back at him for a moment before going out the door.

In that fragment of time, he realized she was the first woman he'd ever brought to Macko's. Just as quickly, he dismissed any significance he might attach to that fact. After all, they were working on the same case. It was only logical they were going to end up sharing a few meals. Besides, if he had any interest in her beyond her working on this case with him, he sure in hell wouldn't have chosen Macko's as a romantic starting point.

Keith lit a cigarette and Judd noted the man's hands were shaking. "You look as if you're about to freak. What's going on?"

"God, Judd, I'm in a helluva mess."

"Why am I not surprised?" Judd murmured wearily. "You've been in hellish messes since you were a kid."

"Man, I been out of trouble for more than six months," Keith said defensively.

"Practically a lifetime," Judd said sagely. "So what is it now? Drugs? Shaking down some poor store clerk for money? What?"

"I ain't done none of that. I've been clean, I swear."

"Okay, Keith. You're usually pretty honest with me, so what's the deal?"

"Late last night, I was upstate and..." He dragged on the cigarette as if to gather courage. "You see, I'd already told Janet I was goin' to a union meeting, but that's always held over at the hall on Downing Street so she assumed that's where I was... Oh, God..." His face was flushed and he crushed out the cigarette. "Man, I could use a drink."

Judd sat back and said, "In other words, you weren't where you told Janet you'd be."

"Yeah."

"And she found out."

"No! No way, man. She don't know nothin'."

"Keith, look, whatever the problem is, it sounds more like it's with Janet than with me."

"I'm gettin' to it."

Judd glanced out the window, where he could see Adrienne waiting for him by the car. The sun spilled over her and he found himself staring.

Quickly he averted his eyes and looked at Keith. In a toneless voice, he said, "Three minutes, kid. Then I'm gonna split, so let's have it."

Keith swallowed and lit another cigarette. "I was workin' upstate back in June and this woman—named Crystal—well, Crystal and me, we sort of got to know each other..."

"You're getting it on with Crystal."

"Oh, God, she's good, Judd," he said with a kind of goofy grin that almost made Judd smile. Keith leaned forward, his voice low, "I mean, she does the kind of stuff I ain't never had at home." Suddenly, he let his head fall forward and whatever pleasure he'd derived from the memory immediately evaporated. "Janet will kill me."

"Probably." Judd put some folded bills for a tip under the ketchup bottle. "Look, your getting involved with women other than your wife isn't something I can help you with. Although I can tell you, it has trouble and disaster written all over it." He glanced at his watch. "Keith, I have to get going. My advice is decide if it's worth losing Janet over Crystal."

"But Janet wouldn't have to know if—"

"If what?" Judd said impatiently.

"Glenda said I got to do my civic duty, but you got to promise to cover my ass so Janet won't know the real reason—"

Judd frowned. "Keith, what in hell are you talking about?"

He took a deep breath and crushed out the cigarette. "Last night around ten o'clock, I was leavin' Crystal's and there was this car with a flat tire. The woman was trying to change it, but she didn't even know how to set the jack. I wasn't goin' to do nothin'. I told myself to mind my own business, but I—"

"Couldn't just leave her there." Keith had always had a kind streak, which Judd had concluded long ago had kept the kid from getting into the serious trouble that meant prison time.

"Yeah, but I should have..." Then his expression crumpled. "And if I was smart, I wouldn't be sittin' here tellin' you all this." He gave Judd a pained look. "I think it was the broad who snatched the kid."

For a few seconds, Judd stared at him, dumbfounded. "Say that again."

"The kid who was grabbed from the hospital."

"Yeah, I know, but how did you know it was the woman?"

"Crystal and me, we were so hot, uh, well, we forgot the TV was on. So after we finished, we were layin' there and, well, you know—"

"For God sake, Keith, get to the point."

"When I got home, I saw her picture on the late news."

"You're saying the woman with the flat looked like the picture they flashed on the news?"

"Well, sort of, but then I also heard the kid cryin'. There in the back seat in one of those baby seats. It was wrapped in a blanket and she—the woman, I mean—was really ant-sy. She kept sayin' her son was hungry and she needed to get home and would I please help her."

"So you changed the tire."

"Well, hell, I couldn't just walk away. Besides, Crystal was standin' on her porch askin' the woman if she wanted to come inside and wait."

"Okay, slow down," Judd said, frantically trying to put it all together. "Did she take the baby and go into Crystal's?"

"No. She stuck one of those plastic plugs in the kid's mouth—"

"A pacifier."

"Yeah, that's it. Then she stood there and watched me change the tire."

"You said upstate. Where?"

"Louiston."

"So what happened after you changed the tire?"

"Nothin'. She got in the car and drove away."

"Did she pay you?"

"No. Didn't offer, either."

"What kind of car?"

"It was a small station wagon. Not very new. Had a bumper sticker. Rhode Island plates. I asked her where she was from and she wanted to know why I was askin'. Weird, huh? I mean, that's not some personal question, is it?"

Judd said, "I want you to think. What was her plate number?"

"Oh, God, you had to ask."

"Think, Keith."

"I looked at it, but..."

"Was it a vanity plate?"

Keith shook his head. He glanced down at the folded bills Judd had left as a tip for Glenda. "One of the letters was a 'G' and the number was..." He rubbed his fists in his eyes. "There was a six and a nine and a four. That's it! I know that's it."

Judd slid from the booth. "Keith, you're a godsend."

"Wait. You gotta make sure no one knows I told you. I mean, Janet can't know anything about this."

"Okay. Since you didn't come down to the station and file a report, I can treat it as an anonymous tip, but you want some advice?"

"Lose Crystal," he said, dejected.

"Or you'll definitely lose Janet."

"Yeah, I'll have to think about it."

Judd squeezed the young man's shoulder. "Thanks, Keith. This might just be the break we need."

Chapter 6

Hot, sticky and irritated summed up Adrienne's disposition when Judd stepped out of Macko's.

She'd shed her jacket and tie and had opened the buttons of her blouse, wishing she could release the catch on her bra. In fact, at the moment, she wished she were home standing naked in her air-conditioned bedroom. The plastic of the car's seat stuck to her legs, adding to her discomfort.

It was August, so she couldn't expect cool breezes and low temperatures, but as much as the weather bothered her, the heat only exacerbated her annoyance with Judd.

She'd had no idea who Keith was when she'd realized he wanted to talk to Judd alone. Sure he'd looked nervous and jumpy, but she'd just assumed he was some poor guy who'd been helped by Judd in the past or had gotten into some minor trouble and needed some advice. Adrienne understood he wouldn't want to bare his soul in front of a stranger.

That was fine. She was perfectly willing to accommodate Keith and Judd. In fact, she'd even been proud of herself for having taken the initiative before Judd had to ask her to excuse them.

But then she'd talked to Glenda as she was paying the bill.

Casually, the older woman had commented, "Thought you were helpin' Judd with that poor missin' baby case."

Adrienne had scowled. Of course she was and Glenda knew that. Shrugging, Adrienne had said, "Didn't I make it clear earlier that I was?"

"Then how come you're leavin' just when I send someone who might know somethin' over to talk to the two of you?"

"You mean Keith?"

"Well, honey, I sure didn't hide any information in those last mugs of coffee."

Adrienne had felt like an ignorant fool, but she smiled and tried to act as if she wasn't in the dark when it came to Judd's motives. "Judd will fill me in later. You know how men are. I noticed that Keith was uptight and so I excused myself."

"And Judd didn't stop you?"

Should he have? Adrienne had wondered instantly. Glenda's question certainly made it appear that Judd should not only have urged her to stay, but insisted upon it. She hadn't gotten any signal from him, and had in fact seemed to appreciate her quick assessment of Keith's mood. "Judd probably wanted Keith to be comfortable enough to talk."

But despite Adrienne's putting such a good face on it for Glenda, she felt a slow-burning fury at Judd. Not once had he tried to discourage her from leaving. Nor had he simply said, Keith was uncomfortable and he, Judd, would fill her in on the details later. No, he'd let her get up and walk away with nary a word.

"Humph," Glenda had said as she separated the bills and put them in the correct register slots. "Never seen that sort of thing bother Judd in the past. Then again, he don't usually work with a woman." She flashed Adrienne a knowing grin. "Maybe this is a sign you two are fixed in the stars."

"I beg your pardon?"

"You two are meant to be, honey. I just feel it in my bones. Destined, just as I was about to predict before Judd told me to mind my own business."

Adrienne had glanced back at Judd. From where she stood, it looked as if he was intensely questioning Keith. She immediately wished she'd been able to complete that assertiveness course she'd begun last spring. Then she would probably feel confident enough to march back to the table, plunk herself down and demand to know what was going on. If the situation were reversed, she had little doubt Judd would do just that. Then again, she decided irritably, Judd would never have excused himself, in the first place.

Telling Glenda again how good the breakfast had been, Adrienne had added, "As for your prediction, I think it's safe to say that the only thing Judd and I are destined for is getting through this case as quickly as possible."

Before Glenda could say anything more, Adrienne had turned and left the diner. That had been fifteen minutes ago.

Now, between the August heat and her own expanding anger, she told herself to get her emotions under control. By losing her temper and railing at him, she would only prove the worst stereotype about women—they got too emotional about things they should just shrug off.

She tried to calm her rising anger as she saw Judd approach the car. He walked to the passenger side and planted his hands on the open window edge. Dark glasses covered his eyes. "I'm gonna make a quick phone call to the station. Be right with you."

"Why don't you use the radio in the car?"

"Too many people with police scanners."

"Oh." That made sense if the information he needed to impart was sensitive. "I presume the call is about the case."

But he was already hurrying across the lot to a pay phone.

Adrienne sighed. As always when he was so close to her, she was too aware of him. Of the sense of power and control he wielded so naturally that it seemed to be an intrinsic part of his character, the leanness and agility of his body, the slight messiness of his saddle brown hair, the hard lines in his face.

She reminded herself that beyond his ability to throw her insides into a jumble, he had also hurt her. It hadn't been a minor relationship gone awry, nor had it involved a decision that *she* didn't want to be involved, as had been true of Hugh Potter, a foreign car salesman she'd been dating before the night she spent with Judd. In fact, Hugh's canceling their dinner date that night had been the catalyst that had set her life on the course she'd taken.

Not only had she let her guard down and done what she'd never done before—slept with a man because of a seething sexual chemistry, but she'd totally opened her heart. Although she hadn't been courageous enough to say the words out loud, to herself she had finally admitted that the reason Hugh had never really excited her was that she'd been in love with Judd Dillon. Not the secret crush she'd had on him when he was married to Diana, but real love. Adrienne had taken that night with him very seriously.

Yet her love had been wasted. He'd shown her beyond any doubt that he'd had none of those same feelings for her.

She couldn't even soothe her wounded pride by believing he'd rejected her. As painful as that would have been, rejection would at least have carried some core of emotion, but Adrienne didn't even have that to make her feel better.

They'd spent the night making love, and then he'd walked out of her apartment without even a goodbye, let alone a verbal brush-off.

For days, her feelings had gone from hate to tears to self-imposed contempt at her own stupidity. Why had she let herself expect more? She'd actually allowed herself to believe that he just might care a little about her.

The only plus now, she concluded, plucking at her blouse where it stuck to her skin, was her vow. Never again did she intend to be so foolish. One major heartbreak in her life was enough.

"Hell, it's hot in here," Judd said a few moments later when he slid behind the wheel. He shoved a hand through his hair and then rolled all the windows down.

Adrienne sat stiff and stared straight ahead. "I hadn't noticed."

"Hadn't noticed?" He glanced in her direction before starting the vehicle. "Is that why you took off your jacket and that dumb tie?"

She swung around, her eyes snapping with anger. "Dumb tie?"

He checked the rearview mirror, then backed out of the parking lot. "Yeah, it makes you look like you're trying to prove something."

Adrienne folded her arms. "And just what do you and your vast store of wisdom about me think I'm trying to prove?"

Obviously, he heard the edge in her voice. "Look, I'm sorry you had to wait out here, but Keith—"

"I'll get to Keith in a minute," she said, realizing she shouldn't be so touchy. Keith and what he'd said was more important than an argument over what she wore. Yet his comment about the tie irritated her. Maybe it was the heat or an accumulation of annoyance with him or just her pride, but this was one topic she would *not* let slide. "Exactly what do you think I'm trying to prove?"

"Forget I mentioned it."

"Wait a damn minute. You started this and I think I deserve an explanation."

"I started it? The last time I looked, we were getting along pretty well. You're the one who's all in a flurry about something. As for the necktie, I just don't like women who dress like men. Hell, *I* hate wearing them, and looking across a table at you in one just rubs me the wrong way."

"Since I'm neither your wife nor your girlfriend, what I wear shouldn't bother you at all."

"True." And without any second thoughts, he added, "Just as I won't let it bother me, either, that your blouse is unbuttoned enough that I can see the swell of your breasts." He said it so easily, she was certain that he wasn't fazed.

She glanced down and her heart sank. She hadn't noticed, but her blouse was open to the tune of five buttons, and too much of her breasts *did* show. Since she knew she'd only deliberately opened three, the last two must have been an unconscious reflex to the stifling heat in the car.

Good grief, she hoped that was all it was. The last thing she wanted was to give Judd the impression she was playing some flirtatious game.

She started to close the buttons, but he set his sunglasses on top of his head and reached over and took her wrist. "You don't have to do that."

"I didn't realize I'd opened so many. It was hot and I felt so sticky and uncomfortable that I . . ."

"Adrienne, it's okay."

"I don't want you to think I was being unprofessional." One of the things she'd learned in her unfinished assertiveness class was not to dress in a provocative way if you wanted to be taken seriously in the workplace.

"Because you were hot and took some clothes off? It's not as if you'd stripped down to your panties." His eyes were so sincere that she relaxed. He hadn't teased, and even the comment about seeing the tops of her breasts hadn't been all that bad. He *didn't mind*. Then again, what did she expect from him? Flirting and cavalier remarks? No, his assurances were at the same level of his interest for her. Zero. She should have been relieved. But she wasn't.

"So is the reason you wore the necktie really to prove your professionalism?" he asked as he came to a stop at an intersection and settled his sunglasses back in place.

Adrienne had always strived for professionalism, in dress and in conduct. It was one of the things that some of her coworkers in the past had never quite learned. Not that it was wrong to date someone you worked with, but Adrienne had always avoided blurring that line between work and fun. Wearing ties gave her a sense of... what?

She thought for a moment. Power? Maybe. Wearing them, she hoped, carried the message that she would not stand for being mistaken for some empty-headed flirtatious female, as her mother had been.

When Child-Aid had moved into the police department, being surrounded by men had made her doubly careful. In an even tone, she said, "Women working in the police department have to present a certain persona."

"Is that a nice way of saying cops are sexist?"

"Some are."

"So are some plumbers, some druggists and even women when they giggle over a guy in tight jeans."

She glanced over at him, not wanting to recall the times she'd seen him in snug jeans. "Some women find that very sexy."

"How about you?"

She shrugged.

"I rest my case."

"All right, but I don't stare at—" she swallowed the "you" just in time "—at a guy the way men stare at women. They give women *head-to-toe* visual strips."

To her surprise, he didn't deny the description. "It's the primal side of our nature," he said in an amused tone. "We're checking out the merchandise to see if she can cook and clean and still be sultry enough to keep us interested in bed."

"Very funny. Did it ever occur to you that women might be checking a guy out for the same reasons?"

To her disgust, he didn't miss a beat. "Guess I'll have to work on my cooking and cleaning, when it comes to you, Ms. Trudell. We both already know about the good sex."

Adrienne sighed. If she hadn't taken her tie off, none of this conversation would have taken place. But what was even more unnerving was how she'd progressed from being angry at him to talking to him so easily about how each viewed the opposite sex.

Finally, in her best crisp and cool voice, she said, "Detective Dillon, I suggest we change the subject."

"You're sure, Ms. Trudell?"

"Very sure."

"Damn. And here I was about to expand on how great you were in bed." He pulled into the police department's main lot and found a parking place on the shady side of the building.

She peered at him. "Is this the same guy who was so uptight and worried that our working together would be a problem? Now you're talking about us having good sex as if it were something as ordinary as sharing a cup of coffee."

He turned, but because he wore the dark glasses, she couldn't see his eyes. "It was the necktie that changed my opinion. I think that's called getting enlightened, isn't it?"

"You know, I'm not sure whether you're serious or—"

He cupped the back of her neck and then dipped his head and kissed her. Adrienne was so stunned, she forgot to close her eyes. His mouth was surprisingly cool, but her body broke out in a sudden flush of new heat.

He coaxed her mouth open—actually, it took little encouragement. Adrienne felt as if she were reeling under an onslaught of sensation. The deepened kiss made her shiver, and when he tugged her a little closer, she went willingly.

Then he lifted his head and looked at her for a long time. She guessed her cheeks were red and her eyes were too wide. On the one hand, she knew she should show some annoyance, but on the other, she wanted him to kiss her again. Her lack of courage in not berating him and her obvious compliance made her angry with herself.

Judd grinned. "Sex with you, angel, was definitely not even close to ordinary. And before you get huffy, I know that comment crossed the line, and I apologize. You don't need to go into some fit of outrage. I meant it as a compliment."

Adrienne wanted to ask a dozen questions, but instead she concentrated on getting her blouse all buttoned. What was wrong with her? Judd Dillon was the *last* complication she needed in her life.

"Need help with the tie?" he asked helpfully. "I tie a mean knot."

"Go to hell, Judd Dillon," she said in her sweetest voice.

He chuckled, shaking his head, deciding that now was not a good time to continue pushing her. Inwardly he smiled, ignoring the strange warmth teasing her gave him. Who knew it would be so much fun? Getting out of the car, he watched as she followed suit.

They walked together into the police station, where he stopped near the stairs and said, "One more point about the necktie."

"I don't want any more of your advice," she said firmly, keeping her back straight and wishing she could snap her fingers and instantly be in the cool privacy of her office.

"This isn't advice. Just an observation. You don't need to prove anything by wearing a damn tie. You're a professional and you've already proved it by the quality of the work you do and the responsibility you take on. You honestly think the chief would have okayed and assigned you to work with me if he didn't know that your credentials were impeccable?"

She had begun to ascend the stairs, but halted a few steps up from him. Looking down at him, she asked, "Are you saying that to make up with me?"

"Such a suspicious mind."

"Words, like actions, aren't always reliable, Detective Dillon."

"And you, Ms. Trudell, are too willing to assume the worst motives. Lighten up."

As they climbed the stairs, Adrienne frowned. Maybe she *was* taking herself too seriously. If she really wanted him to know he didn't mean anything to her, then she wouldn't get indignant so easily. However, he did do things that threw her off stride. The "dumb" tie comment and, of course, that kiss.

She pressed her lips together and reminded herself she was supposed to be keeping her head straight about him. She definitely should not be allowing these unexpected kisses to just happen without cutting them off. Twice now, she'd simply caved in. That, she concluded, was hardly a professional response.

As they wound their way past the desks, she looked around her. Already the police department was so much more familiar to her. Everywhere phones rang, and nearby a man was being taken into an interrogation room by two officers. Judd signaled across the room to another officer and she snapped her attention back to the situation at hand.

At his desk, Judd indicated the chair where she'd sat earlier. "Sit down and I'll fill you in on what Keith had to say."

Adrienne sat down and Mike Shelby wove his way between desks, loaded down with computer printouts.

"Hi, Adrienne."

"Hello, Mike."

"Those the printouts of names from the hospital?" Judd asked.

"Yeah. Thank God, Seapoint is a small hospital. One of the guys said Providence did this kind of check a few years ago and the list of names was endless." Mike laid the sheets on Judd's desk. "We've already checked out and eliminated a lot of these names. A few have died and those who still reside in Seapoint have checked out okay. The DMV is still working on the plate number Cokeburn gave you, and we should know something within the hour."

At Adrienne's scowl, Judd explained, "Keith Cokeburn, Adrienne. He changed a tire for a woman with a baby late last night. He remembered part of the license plate number. I called it in to Mike and he got in touch with the Department of Motor Vehicles."

"The phone call you made."

"Yeah."

She waited for him to reveal some piece of information that would support his not having insisted that she stay while he talked to Keith—as Glenda had suggested he would have done with a partner—but Judd turned to Mike.

"Good work, Mike. How about the rattle? Any of them sold locally?"

"We've checked baby stores and drugstores and the chains, but nothing that matches that particular rattle."

Adrienne said, "Lambert might know."

Judd quickly explained who Lambert Supply was, then took Adrienne's papers from the desk drawer. He shuffled through the pages and showed Mike the one with the information on the company.

Mike nodded and made a note of the name, location and phone number. "I'll get someone on this. We're also checking on the women who gave birth."

Mike then indicated the names on the printouts that were still in question. There were about ten and Judd knew that each would have to be checked out individually.

He pushed the list of former employees toward Adrienne. "Make me happy and tell me you know who all these women are."

She glanced at the list, running her finger down and then stopping at the sixth name. "I know Opal French. She's a friend of my mother's. She had some asthma problems and the hospital odors made it worse, so she quit. She lives down in Jamestown with her second husband."

"What happened to the first one?"

"Mom said he died after a stroke a few years back."

"Know the name of the second one?"

Adrienne thought for a moment. "No."

Judd lifted an eyebrow. "Mike, run a computer check on an Opal French."

"Already did Opal. Nothing."

Judd nodded. "Okay. Thanks. Let me know when DMV has some plate numbers."

Mike walked away and Judd sat down, leaning back in his chair. "What about Opal as a possibility?" he asked Adrienne.

Adrienne tried to picture Opal as a baby snatcher. "My immediate reaction would be no, but honestly I couldn't be positive. Frankly, I haven't seen her in a while. And you said at the hospital that the woman who took the baby is probably someone not easily suspected. That's how she pulled this off. Knowing her name might show up on hospital records seems careless on her part, if she was trying to get away with something."

Judd tapped a pen on the desk, his face thoughtful. "How well do you know Opal?"

"In the past, I knew her pretty well. As I said earlier, she and my mother used to barhop together back in the days when that was a novelty for women."

"Opal met her second husband in a bar?"

"I think so, but I'm not really sure."

"Does Opal know what you do? Child-Aid, I mean."

"She may. I don't know."

"Then this would be a good time to catch her up on your life."

"Judd, what are you talking about?"

"You're going to pay her a visit."

"But what excuse will I use?"

"Do you have to have an excuse to stop by for a friendly visit?"

"Well, no, but since I'm not in the habit of driving down to Jamestown and casually dropping in on her, won't she be suspicious?"

"If she's the kidnapper, she'll be suspicious. If she's not, she'll be curious at first and then delighted to see you."

"Listen, I can see the direction you're going in, but I'm not very good at deliberate deception. I'd probably blow the whole thing."

"You'll do fine," he said, dismissing her concerns. "Here comes Mike."

"Just to make sure, I checked the Outstanding Warrants, but nothing on Opal French. Looks like this one is gonna be slow going."

"Damn."

"Yeah, a prior warrant on Opal for kidnapping would have been a real plum."

"We should be so lucky."

"Oh, had a call from DMV. They're having some computer problems, so it's gonna be a while before they can run that plate number."

"Why in hell didn't they tell you that when you called it in?"

Mike shrugged. "Who knows. Probably hired some broad more interested in polishing her nails than doing her work."

Adrienne narrowed her eyes and glanced at Judd.

"Mike, there's no shortage of guys who screw up, either," Judd said.

"Hey, I've heard you blast some of those women over there."

"I'm trying to turn over a new leaf."

"Why would—"

Adrienne interrupted smoothly, "I've been giving him a lot of grief about sexist attitudes, Mike."

"Sexist? Who's being sexist?"

Judd got to his feet. "Never mind. Adrienne is going to pay Opal and her second husband a visit. Keep on the DMV. I want an ID on that plate by tonight."

Outside, Adrienne stopped. "You're going with me?"

"You didn't think I was going to send you alone, did you?"

"Judd, it's going to be difficult enough convincing Opal I just happened to be passing by and decided to drop in. You being with me will only complicate matters."

"Why? Does Opal think you hate men?"

"Of course not."

"Then what's the problem?"

"Oh, I can see it all now. 'Hi, Opal, Just thought I'd stop in out of the blue and say hello, and by the way, this is Judd Dillon, a detective who tagged along for the ride.'"

"Haven't you ever heard of undercover work? We're going to apply the same principle. We're not going to be what we really are. Since Opal probably considers you to be a nice young woman, then it seems reasonable that the man you're with would be a nice guy, a guy you're getting serious about. And since it's such a beautiful day, we decided to take a ride down to the shore and walk on the beach. You recalled that Opal lived in Jamestown and so you decided to stop in and say hello."

"Pretty flimsy."

"Trust me, it'll work."

"And just how serious am I supposed to be about you?"

"Some adoring looks would be good."

"And should I hold your hand, hug you every few minutes and generally look as if my life is meaningless except when you're beside me?" she asked, an edge of sarcasm in her voice.

He slung an arm around her neck and gave her a gentle squeeze. "Hey, that would be great, Ms. Trudell."

"Hey, that would be only in your dreams, Detective Dillon."

He grinned and she scowled.

A few minutes later, he pulled into the morning traffic. "We'll stop at your apartment first and then mine." At her puzzled look, he added, "Neither of us is wearing beach-walking clothes."

On that point he was right.

He drove into the parking area beside her apartment building and she was caught by a sense of déjà vu. That night, he'd parked in almost the same place. Except then, there had been long kisses in the car before they'd gone inside the building. She'd been aroused and hot and she remembered all too well how he'd lowered the bodice of her dress and kissed her breasts. She'd arched into him, tunneling her fingers through his hair, sighing his name as if it were the sweetest word on earth. . . .

He touched her arm, and she jumped, her eyes flying open.

"Adrienne, you okay?"

She refused to look at him, scrambling to undo the seat belt. "I'm fine. I was just thinking about...about how this will all work . . . with Opal, I mean."

"Look at me."

With the belt opened, she reached for the door handle, keeping her eyes averted.

"Adrienne, for God's sake, will you look at me?"

"I can't."

"All that stuff before about how we should act at Opal's wasn't some attempt to turn our working relationship into anything else."

"I know that."

"Then you're angry about my having kissed you at the station, aren't you?" He shoved a hand through his hair. "You sure as hell have a right to be. Especially since I'm the one who complained the loudest about our working together, considering what happened between us in the past."

"I shouldn't have let you. Kiss me, I mean."

Just as she shouldn't have let him make love to her a year ago.

She pushed open the car door, then turned. "Do you mind waiting down here for me?"

Judd stared at her, searching her face and seeing exactly what worried her. Wanting to reassure her and not knowing why it suddenly felt so important, he said, "We wouldn't wind up in bed, Adrienne."

But instead of addressing the obvious source of tension between them, she said, "I'll be only a few minutes."

Leaving the car without a backward glance, she hurried up the steps of her building. He watched as she unlocked the security door and disappeared inside.

Judd slumped low in the seat, his own memories of that night too vivid, too damning. Hell, he'd paid the price of commitment and involvement with the untimely and unnecessary loss of his wife and son, a wrenching disaster that still clutched at him. He didn't want another woman, he didn't want any of the ties and promises that went with a serious relationship.

The problem with Adrienne was that Judd wasn't sure exactly where she belonged in his life. She'd been a friend and, briefly, a lover, but unlike any friend he would normally remain in contact with, he'd deliberately ignored Adrienne. Unlike a satisfying lover who he would have revisited time and again, he'd fled her place in the breaking dawn and had never gone back, trying like hell to wipe away every memory of her body, her mouth and the thousand sensations she'd caused within him.

Twice now, he'd kissed her in defiance of his feelings that it would be dangerous, and twice he'd gotten more than he wanted. Maybe it was just leftover memories of past kisses—he knew what she liked. He knew the tiny sounds she made, arousing sighs that excited and inordinately pleased him. Unfortunately something told him the past—and what they'd shared—was only the beginning.

Judd scowled into the hot morning light and tried to ignore the incessant stirrings of interest in Adrienne.

"Dammit, it was one night. And now it's just the memories of great sex haunting me. *That's all it is,*" he muttered out loud as if doing so would make his pronouncement more valid.

Nothing more. And the best way to prove that was to keep himself in check.

He glanced up when she opened the car door and slipped inside. She wore loose-fitting shorts and a long terry-cloth top with a huge sailboat on the front. Sunglasses rode atop her head and her earrings were big red plastic hoops.

"All set," she said, giving him a bouncy smile.

Judd scowled. God, he'd forgotten just how spectacular she looked in shorts.

Then again, he was beginning to think there was little about Adrienne that wasn't spectacular.

Chapter 7

Twenty minutes later, Judd came out of his apartment and slid into the car. He, too, had gone to change into what he called grown-up play clothes. Just the way he grimaced reminded Adrienne that he had little time for play, and she doubted he'd spent any time in the recent past even close to the beach, unless it was to find some culprit.

After a quick glance at him, however, she was reminded of their conversation earlier about her wearing a necktie and guys looking sexy in tight jeans. Actually, she wouldn't have described his jeans as tight, she decided, mulling over why she, like many women, was so fascinated by the sight. Judd's were more like comfortably snug, but they were still far too dangerously thought-diverting. His soft blue T-shirt exposed the cords of muscle in his arms and brought back too many memories of the night, when she'd fallen asleep in those arms. Altogether a sexily unsettling image that she firmly reminded herself would only affect her if she was foolish enough to allow it to.

She sighed. Thinking about Judd in any way except as the man she was working with to find Caleb Whitewell, had become a mindless seesaw of ill-defined logic.

She no longer loved him. She'd settled that in her mind a long time ago. Yet, in the past twenty-four hours, she admitted that she'd been gripped by anticipation at seeing him, filled with a kind of kinetic energy and, worst of all, had allowed her thoughts to stray into areas best left untouched. Thoughts that were uncomfortably close to fragments of her desire for him years ago.

All of that and this last—feeling desire for Judd—only proved to her that her good sense wasn't sensible at all. She couldn't let herself be sucked into the throes of some silly out-of-control emotion that would lead her into getting hurt all over again.

And just what did any of those thoughts and feelings have to do with her job? she reflected grimly. Nothing. She'd always been focused solely on her work when a child was missing, at times to the point where she didn't eat or sleep very well. Some might call it an obsession and getting too emotionally involved, but Adrienne called it caring and dedication. How anyone could deal with missing children as if they were objects, to be sought as one searched for a stolen car, smacked of being cold and chillingly inhuman. Of course, getting immersed in a case held another risk. Even Evelyn, her superior, had chastised her a number of times in the past year for risking burnout.

Adrienne, however, had found her work required just the kind of dedication and concentration that didn't leave time for much perspective on her personal life. In fact, if she were totally truthful, she'd had no personal life in the past year. Not since—

No personal life since that night with Judd? Was that possible? Her eyes widened at the tiny revelation. She hadn't thought about it in that light, but it was true. Sheer coincidence, she decided firmly, dismissing the thought. One thing had nothing to do with the other. Working hard and not having much of a social life *did* not have anything to do with old feelings for Judd Dillon. It did not.

Not at all pleased by the path her thoughts had taken, she pushed the uncomfortable insight aside. She adjusted her sunglasses and looked straight ahead.

"I hope you're thinking about how all this will play out," Judd commented as he drove through town and into the summer beach traffic, on their way to Opal's.

Sighing and glad to train her thoughts on the real reason they were together, she said, "I'm afraid I can't quite picture Opal as someone who would steal an infant from a hospital."

"Even though you said she resembled the sketch?"

"A lot of women could look like that sketch. Maybe the woman who took Caleb deliberately distorted her looks."

"Maybe," Judd murmured. "Frankly, I'd like Opal to be it. To walk in and find the kid would be a lucky break."

"Well, you don't have to make it sound like I'd be disappointed. I want to find Caleb, too," she said with more irritation than she intended. The truth of it was that the sooner they found Caleb, the sooner they would no longer have to spend so much time together. So a quick end was exactly what she wanted. Wasn't it?

In a less strident tone, she asked, "What kind of ruse are we using?"

"I thought we'd park the car a few houses from Opal's. Then we'll walk to her place, knock on the door and after she expresses surprise at seeing you, you can say the car broke down and would she mind if I used the phone. While I'm doing that, you can visit and learn what you can."

"Sounds awfully easy," she said skeptically.

"Since we don't know if she's the one we're looking for, I'd rather not be too tied down as to how we play it. Instinct is a big factor."

"Play it by ear, you mean."

"Yes and no. It's cop thinking, Adrienne. When you're with another cop certain instincts kick in. You end up sensing what to do and how to act so that you get a lot more information than it might appear, to a casual observer. I'm counting on you to know the baby stuff. You know any special smells associated with infants or baby things like a bottle or diapers. In other words, keep your eyes open." Then, as if he'd explained the plan fully, he added, "By the way, I called Shelby to see if anything on that plate number had come in. Nothing yet."

"Which reminds me," Adrienne said, turning in the seat and peering at him. "You still owe me an explanation regarding your talk with Keith."

"Why does this sound like I'm in some kind of trouble?" he asked, bracing himself for an onslaught of criticism.

"I just have a few questions."

He sighed. "Go ahead."

"You don't have to act like this is an inquisition."

"Adrienne, in my experience with you—the most recent being the necktie conversation—you tend to get all hung up on what you *think* I mean rather than what I really mean."

His comment immediately bothered her. Was he making some vague reference to the night they'd spent together? That she'd given it more meaning than he'd intended it to have? Certainly no argument there, she concluded grimly. Not that she would let *him* know that, of course. "Perhaps because you don't make yourself entirely clear."

"I'll work on my approach," he said sagely. "Ask your questions."

"At the diner, since Keith obviously wanted to talk to you about this case, and since I'm supposed to be working with you, why didn't you insist that I stay?"

"I didn't tell you to leave."

She scowled. That was certainly true. In fact, she hadn't given Judd much of a chance to say anything, she'd just read Keith's body language and made an assumption.

"Well," she said. "I wouldn't have left if I'd known he might have had information on the woman we're looking for."

"I didn't know he had information, either."

She stared at him. "But he looked so jumpy and fidgety, I thought—"

"That he had experienced some dark trauma he wanted to tell only to me?"

"Yes, I guess I did."

"You aren't all that far wrong. The gist of what he told me was that when he helped this woman change her flat tire, it was outside his girlfriend's house in Louiston. Keith told his wife before he left home that he was going to a union meeting here in Seapoint." Judd glanced at her before snapping on his directional signal and turning onto Beach Rock Road. "So now you know the dilemma he found himself in."

Adrienne thought for a moment. "If he'd come to the station and given a report, there's the possibility his wife would find out he wasn't where he should have been. She would find out he was a liar and a cheat."

"You got it."

Adrienne considered her own feelings on deceptive men. Her father, who'd walked out and never returned, her mother, who refused to trust a man for anything but a good time because she was sure they were all liars.

Even her own experience with Judd hadn't been what she'd expected. She'd thought she loved him and he'd certainly given the impression he'd felt more than just a sexual attraction, but in truth, she'd often wondered if he'd felt even that. At least the men in her mother's life had stuck around for a few months. Judd had barely stayed one night.

Now Adrienne folded her arms and said coolly, "Well, in my opinion, your friend Keith deserves to get caught."

Judd shrugged.

"You think it's okay for him to cheat on his wife?"

"I think it's none of my business and not my problem. I'm glad he came to me when he did because if I found out later that he had pertinent information and didn't come forward, I would have hung his— Never mind..." He shook his head, clearing it from a cloud of dark thoughts. "Keith did come forward so it's not an issue. And if his information gets this case solved quicker and brings the baby home safe to Ronnie and Tanya, then Keith may not care if he has to take some heat from his wife."

"Wait a minute," Adrienne said, still thinking about what Judd had started to say about Keith if he hadn't come forward. "You're a police officer. You're not supposed to hit on a citizen just because he didn't do his duty."

If Adrienne hadn't been staring at him, she knew she would have missed the bunched cords of muscle in his arms that suddenly went taut. It lasted less than five seconds, but there was no doubt in Adrienne's mind that Judd was furious but determined to hide it.

"Let's change the subject," he said.

The better part of wisdom told her to leave the issue alone; obviously, it was a sore subject with Judd. But whether it was curiosity or genuine interest on her part, she wanted to know why a police officer who was seen by the department as one of the best could so arbitrarily consider strong-arm tactics a viable option when a citizen didn't co-operate.

She took a deep breath and, before she lost her nerve, said, "I don't want to change the subject, Judd. This is important. From what I read and see on the news, there's entirely too much police brutality. The very idea that the Keiths of this world should live in fear that a cop will physically hurt them if they don't cooperate is frightening."

"In the first place, you don't know what in hell you're talking about, so please spare me the idealistic crap."

"You're denying that there's police brutality?"

"This has the same feel as that sexist stuff we discussed earlier. Yeah, there probably are a few bad cops, but using some broad brush to paint every police officer who departs from some civilian code of decorum as a brutality-obsessed cop is ridiculous."

"All right, I'll concede your point. And for the record, I don't consider you a brutality-obsessed cop."

"A vote of confidence. How encouraging and generous of you," he snapped.

"You're being sarcastic."

"And you're about to ask some nosy questions."

"Because you're scaring me," she said, not about to let his sudden reserve and distance discourage her. "It's obvious you're angry. Not just surface anger, but deep and deadly."

Then, as if he'd revealed too much, he drew in a long breath, obviously forcing himself to relax. If Adrienne hadn't known him very well, she might have bought it. But she'd known Judd a long time, and not just on a personal level, either.

From the day Child-Aid had moved their offices onto the third floor at the police station, Adrienne had heard that Judd's reputation in the department was exemplary. Skilled, precise and professional, he was thoroughly respected. In fact, she'd seen cold deadly fury in him only once.

The day the police had found the drunk driver who had hit Diana's car.

"Let me put it this way," Judd said with obvious exasperation. "If we don't find the baby or the woman, or if we do and the ending is tragic, how would you react to the news that some guy had had information that could have helped and he didn't come forward?"

"I know what you're getting at, and of course, I would be angry and upset."

"Angry and upset? Please spare me the textbook reactions. Let's make it a little more personal. Let's say it was your baby. How would you feel about Keith then?"

Adrienne was amazed at how swiftly her inner body reacted. It tightened and she felt a rush of pure horror, followed by dark fury.

He gave her an assessing and derisive look. "Ah, the lady has a lethal streak."

Adrienne took a deep breath, scowling that she'd revealed herself so easily. "All right. I admit I wouldn't be anywhere close to calm and objective, but the police are supposed to be."

"Cops are human. They have wives and kids and feelings of inadequacy and anxiety, and sometimes they take things personally."

Adrienne stared at him for a long moment. His mouth was set in a grim line and his hand was tight on the steering wheel. He passed 29 Beach Rock Road, drove past a few houses and then stopped.

"You mean Diana and Travis, don't you?" she asked softly.

For long tense seconds he simply stared straight ahead and said nothing.

"Judd?"

"Yeah, I mean Diana and Travis."

"Somebody saw something and they didn't come forward?"

His hands clenched and he looked as raw and hard as she'd ever seen him.

Bitterly, he said, "A guy with a string of drug-related arrests saw the drunk hit Diana's car. He didn't call it in because he was making a delivery to some dealer and he would have been late." In the coldest voice she'd ever heard, Judd added, "He just left them there to die while he made his damn coke delivery."

"Oh, Judd..." She didn't know what to say. She didn't know any words that would change anything or make him feel any less angry.

With only the intention of offering a scrap of human understanding, she reached over and took his fisted hand in hers. It was hot and clammy and totally unresponsive. She folded her fingers around his, soothing out the tension and not letting him go when he tried to pull away. To her amazement, he began to relax, and Adrienne felt a deep sense of well-being that she could offer him comfort on at least some level.

In a low voice, she asked, "How did you find out about this guy?"

"Street contacts."

"Oh." She'd seen some of those contacts at the station. In her opinion, their reliability was questionable, but admittedly, those who blended in with the street would probably be privy to a lot more passed-around information than an ordinary citizen.

Finally, he said, "It was a long time ago. I should be over it by now. At the very least, I shouldn't be bringing it up and dumping my less than professional feelings on you."

"I'm glad you did. Especially since I know you're usually careful when it comes to talking about your personal feelings."

He shrugged. "There's nothing that can be changed about the past. They're both dead and no matter how much I want to think that might not be true if that piece of human debris had called 9-1-1 or if the bastard who'd been drunk had stayed out of his car and taken a cab, instead . . ." His voice trailed off as he pulled his hand from hers and opened the door. "Come on, we have a case to solve. Spending the time going back where neither one of us can change a damn thing is futile."

Adrienne got out of the car and closed the door. As the two of them walked toward Opal's, Judd put his arm around her and squeezed.

She nestled against him for a moment, slipping an arm around his waist and feeling a sense of connection, friendship. Suddenly she was struck by the multiplicity of emotions that didn't need words. Sometimes, she realized, silence was very much the right choice.

Adrienne wasn't sure what it all meant, but she felt as if she'd seen a tiny window open inside of Judd. Maybe, just maybe, his coldness and his determination to close off emotional reactions—his reputation of having no heart—were justified as much by what hadn't happened as by what had.

She couldn't imagine the deep fury and layers of frustration Judd must have felt when he'd learned that there was a witness who hadn't bothered to stop. To know that his wife and son might be alive today . . .

Adrienne felt a sudden painful lump in her throat the size of a tennis ball. This tiny window Judd had opened was important to her because he'd allowed her to see inside. Maybe not in a totally agreeable way and not without some prodding, but he'd permitted her to be a friend and that had a great deal of meaning for her. Adrienne had always been good at friendships.

"Here we are," Judd said, letting her go and then pausing before knocking. He glanced to the side, where a view of Narragansett Bay spanned out in the distance. "Opal into boats?"

Adrienne cleared her throat. "Boats?"

"Yeah, that sure looks like a dock beyond where the yard banks down."

"Maybe. I don't ever recall her mentioning boating, but this *is* coastal Rhode Island."

Judd raised his hand to knock. "Ready?"

"I hope so."

Opal opened the door on the third knock. A slender woman, her hair was peppered gray and she wore it tied in a ponytail low at the back of her neck. Her facial skin sagged, and where most people who lived so close to the water would have had at least some tan, Opal was as pale as white bread. She wore a shapeless dress in a forgettable shade of gray and an apron that advertised a local grocery store.

Looking at Opal now, Adrienne saw little resemblance to the sketch, beyond the shape of her face and body. Then again, with some makeup, perhaps a wig, it was possible.

"Opal, I know you may not remember me. I'm Adrienne Trudell."

Opal peered at her, her hemp brown eyes squinting then rounding in recognition. "Why, glory be, it is you, Adrienne." Then immediately, her face broke into a worried look. "It's not your ma, is it? She's always runnin' off hither and yon. Why, last time I talked to her, she was whoopin' it up in Texas."

Adrienne shook her head. "She's still in Texas. Last I heard, she was seeing some retired rodeo star."

Opal didn't exactly laugh, but Adrienne sensed she was trying to be polite. "That ma of yours, she sure does like variety in her men, don't she?" She didn't open the door wider or invite them in.

Judd said, "Sweetheart, we shouldn't keep the lady wondering what we're doing here."

Adrienne was so taken aback by the endearment that she almost forgot why they were there. "Oh, uh, yes. And I should introduce you. I already told Judd about you, Opal. Judd's my fiancé. Our engagement isn't official, I don't even have a ring yet, so you're the first to know. We came down here to enjoy the beach and make some plans, when our car broke down a little way up the street. I was wondering if Judd could use the phone to call his mechanic."

When Adrienne smiled at Judd, she saw he was staring at her as if she had three heads. Had she said something wrong? Opal's grin certainly indicated she believed the far-fetched tale.

Then, just as quickly, his expression lightened and he tugged her close to drop a kiss on her forehead. "I don't think Opal wants to hear our entire history."

Adrienne snuggled closer to him, wondering why this ruse wasn't more difficult for her to believe. If she closed her eyes, she could really believe Judd took her words seriously. Gluing themselves to each other, along with Judd's little kiss, sure made it feel real.

She gave him a tender glance. "Of course, you're right. If Judd could use the phone, Opal, we'll be on our way."

Clearly, Opal couldn't reasonably say no, but Adrienne and Judd both noticed a certain reluctance.

She glanced furtively behind her and then with a hesitation that had Adrienne and Judd looking at each other, she nodded.

"Phone's in the kitchen."

Adrienne said, "Go ahead, honey, I'll wait here and catch Opal up on what I'm doing."

Judd gave her a direct look and their eyes met, with each understanding exactly what was going on and what they needed to learn.

Judd went into the empty kitchen, a rather dismal room with little to show that Opal was much of a cook. He looked around for any sign of baby formula, then surreptitiously checked the trash for disposable bottles, but found none.

Taking a long-handled spoon from the counter, he moved the discarded plastic wrap in the trash to look beneath it and found more plastic. Carefully, he lifted one of the scraps and took it over to the window.

"Well, I'll be damned," he muttered. Quickly, he found a clean plastic bag and put the pieces of plastic inside. He glanced out the window and saw a speedboat bobbing from a line tied to the dock. When a man walked down the dock, said something to someone in the boat and then walked back, Judd recognized him. Boris Skodie, a con man who'd gone into cutting coke for the street. He was cruel and ornery and was known all along the East Coast as a slippery SOB who always beat the system with the help of a smart lawyer. Hardly able to believe the stumble of good luck, he went to the phone and then hesitated. No, the first thing he had to do was get Adrienne out of here. Judd had counted Boris plus two men with him. And there could be more. An attempted arrest without backup could be dangerous.

Judd moved quickly back to the room where he'd left Adrienne with Opal. But Adrienne wasn't there.

Then he heard voices and realized they were in the bed-room. For a moment, Judd blinked in confusion, but then realized that Adrienne had probably talked Opal into tak-ing her into the bedroom. Obviously, that was where there might be signs of a baby. He was about to go and find her, when she returned.

The disappointment in her face said it all.

"Thanks for the use of your phone," Judd said as he moved forward and took Adrienne's arm.

She looked surprised by his obvious rush, but didn't ob-ject.

"It was so good to see you again, Opal."

"You be sure and say hi to your ma for me the next time you see her."

"I'll do that."

Judd hustled her out the door as Opal called out from behind them, "And good luck. Hope you both will be real happy."

When they were out of sight of Opal, Judd let Adrienne go and ran to the car. Inside, he used the radio and issued a scrambled code of messages that alerted the Coast Guard. Next, he called Mike, using another set of coded messages. By the time Adrienne was in the car, Judd had the vehicle in gear and was pulling away.

"*What* is going on?" she asked as he careened around a corner toward a small shopping area. He swung into the parking lot, braked and was almost out of the car, when Adrienne reached over and grabbed his arm. "Judd, what is it?"

Instead of answering, he asked, "No sign of the kid, huh?"

She shook her head. "I even used the ruse of going to the bathroom so I could check for any sign of diapers or baby things in case she'd hidden little Caleb when she went to answer the door."

"Good thinking," he said hurriedly. "Stay here. I'll be right back."

She watched as he zigzagged across the parking lot, literally leaped over a small rock garden and headed back toward Opal's.

Adrienne scowled. Had Judd found something in the kitchen that would lead him to think Caleb was there? Or had been there? But if he had found something, then why had he ordered her to stay here?

She reminded herself that if he had found Caleb or some sign the baby had been there, the most important thing was the safety of the infant not making sure she had a part in the arrest process. But this was a little too bizarre; the least he could have done was tell her what was going on. She'd certainly seen nothing amiss, and all he'd done was spend less than five minutes in the kitchen. Besides, she was more inclined to think he just wanted to get her out of the way. If she were his partner or if she were Mike Shelby, she wouldn't be cooling her heels, she would be right beside him. As much as she hated to admit it, he definitely left little doubt that he still disliked the idea of working with her.

"Well, that's just too damn bad," she decided as she opened the door and got out. Slinging her canvas bag over her shoulder and putting on her sunglasses, she hurried in the direction that he'd gone. As she got closer, some second thoughts slipped in, but she dismissed them. Stop giving him the benefit of the doubt, she scolded herself. You did that at Macko's and later found out the real truth—that Keith might have seen the woman who took Caleb.

Adrienne was positive the woman they sought wasn't Opal. There were no signs that a baby was in Opal's home or ever had been. And there was no way Opal would have had time to remove every scrap of evidence. Adrienne was trained to look for the obvious things a baby would need—the diapers, disposable bottles, powder—but there were also the smells of a baby and Adrienne hadn't smelled any air freshener that might have been used to cover that. Nor had there been any sounds. Not a one.

And yet, Judd had reacted as if something was wrong.

As Opal's house came into sight, Adrienne halted, her mouth gaping in astonishment. Three police cars were parked in a way that the street was blocked to traffic. Opal's front door stood open and the dock below Opal's house was swarming with men.

She looked around for Judd and finally saw him talking to Mike. Behind them, other officers were taking two men and Opal, in handcuffs, out to the waiting police wagon.

"My God, they must have had Caleb," she said out loud. How could she have been so wrong? And how had Judd known?

She ran forward, her eyes searching for someone bringing out the baby, but instead saw two officers come out carrying huge plastic bags. As the horrible possibility that the baby might be dead sank into her thoughts, she started to run.

Judd caught her arm. "I thought I told you to stay in the car. Dammit, Adrienne..."

But instead of reacting to his anger, she clutched his arm. She felt a little woozy and sick to her stomach. "You were right, Judd. Maybe I shouldn't have been working with you on this case. Maybe I don't even know what I'm doing. I should have known something was wrong. I should have known it immediately." Adrienne felt as if she were braced on the edge of hysteria. Angry with her own ineptness, she suddenly wondered if there had been other times in the past when she'd missed some vital piece of information.

As unrelated as it was to the moment, she had to admit she'd certainly been clueless when it came to her relationship with Judd.

Judd took her by the arms and shook her lightly. "What the hell is the matter with you?"

She looked at him fully for the first time and saw both annoyance and concern in his eyes. "They killed him, didn't they?"

"Killed who? What are you talking about?"

"Don't try to soften it, Judd. I'm supposed to be the expert on missing children and I didn't even sense . . . oh, my God . . ." She covered her face, and if Judd hadn't been holding her arms, she knew her knees would have buckled.

Judd pulled her against him, supporting her and letting her burrow against him.

In a matter-of-fact voice, he said to Mike, "If you don't need me any longer, I'm gonna split."

"We're all set. Great police work, Judd."

Still supporting Adrienne, he drew her away and beneath an old tree with low-hanging limbs, he said, "Angel, look at me."

"I can't. I should have known. I should have—"

He kissed her to stop her words, sliding his hand into her hair and holding her steady. Not a passionate kiss, it was more to stop her from dissolving into tears.

Then, in a soft whisper against her ear, he said, "None of what you saw had anything to do with the missing baby. When I went into the kitchen, I looked around for any signs of Caleb, just as you were doing. What I found were dozens of plastic pieces with coke residue. Then I saw Boris Skodie on the dock. We've been trying to get him for over two years for drug-cutting and intent to deliver. Apparently, Boris, Opal's husband, and his friends were using Opal's house to cut the coke for the street and to ship it via boat to receiving points along the coastline."

Adrienne stepped back and blinked in disbelief. "Then these arrests have nothing to do with Caleb."

He nodded.

"You suspected Boris would be there and you used me—"

"No!" He took a deep breath and cupped her chin. "You and I came here for exactly the reasons I laid out. To question Opal about the kidnapping. Finding Boris was one of those lucky breaks. I had to get you away from there because I didn't have any idea what was involved."

Adrienne sagged against him, feeling foolish that she had jumped to such a horrendous conclusion regarding Caleb. Hysteria, rushing to *any* conclusions and, most of all, railing at Judd without more proof but her own flawed assumptions, made her feel very embarrassed.

Carefully she said, "You wanted me to stay in the car so I wouldn't be hurt."

"Yeah."

"I could have messed things up, huh?"

"I was more concerned about you not getting hurt. I had no idea what I'd be dealing with."

As they walked slowly back to where Judd had parked the car, Adrienne understood for the first time the danger of a civilian's being involved in serious police work. Judd's not wanting to work with her went far beyond her gender, it involved her safety. Her lack of a calm and experienced approach had now, she had no doubt, only reinforced every stereotype about women he had.

She straightened and pressed her lips into a grim line. She didn't intend to make such a foolish mistake again.

Chapter 8

"We finally got the information from DMV on the license plate."

Judd had just returned to his desk at the station and Mike was filling him in.

"Her name is Lois Greeley. And she even resembles the sketch," Mike commented. "She lives in Louiston in a housing complex. Age forty-five, and from the info we got from the local police, she's never had so much as a parking ticket." Mike handed the pages to Judd and said, "Litchfield wants to see you to go over the next move. You know the chief, he doesn't want any time wasted."

It had been an hour since the arrests at Opal's house. Boris and his buddies were being charged and processed. Opal had been questioned as to what she knew and how involved she was in the actual cutting, packaging and delivery of the coke to the street. Adrienne had urged her to accept the lawyer the state would provide. Opal, realizing she was in serious trouble, had finally agreed.

Adrienne had then gone up to her own office to check through Child-Aid files in the hopes of finding Lois Greeley's name.

Now, with Mike at his side, Judd scowled as he flipped through the pages on the way to the chief's office. "You said you already searched the list of former employees as well as the list of former maternity patients at Seapoint Hospital?"

"Yeah, and no one named Lois Greeley was on either of the lists. And before you ask, yes, I went over the names twice."

"Maybe she used another name."

"We're checking that out."

Judd nodded.

"And even if there is no alias, that doesn't mean Greeley isn't the one we're looking for."

Judd stopped outside the chief's office. "Okay, let's say she is. But why Seapoint Hospital? What in hell is her connection to it?"

"Maybe there isn't one," Mike said. "Maybe it was a random choice. You know we've seen more and more no-apparent-motive crimes. She might just have arbitrarily picked a hospital and then carried out her plan."

"No," Judd said emphatically as they opened the door to the chief's office. "She had that blue rattle. Since we know from the call to the supplier this morning that it *wasn't* sold separately, then it had to come from one of those newborn packets. Afternoon, Chief."

"Dillon, Shelby, come on in and sit down." Frank Litchfield, the police chief, put out his cigarette and sat back in the wooden barrel-backed chair.

The office was cluttered with past commendations, but not so obviously displayed that a visitor would think he was bragging. They were scattered here and there as if Frank wasn't sure where to put them or if he really should have been honored with them to begin with.

He'd been a cop who had worked the streets, and at different points, he'd headed up homicide and narcotics. He was known to his men as a cop's cop. He backed his officers, had little sympathy for repeat offenders and continually complained about budget cuts that he said put his men at risk.

A middle-size man, he had a froglike face, bumpy skin and enough gruffness in his voice to have gained him an impressive reputation with most of Seapoint.

Judd had tremendous respect for him, but he also knew that a summons to the chief's office usually meant a stepped-up effort on a case. Now he sprawled in one of the chairs and braced his left foot over his right knee.

Litchfield said, "You look beat, Dillon."

"Just frustrated. A lot of possibilities that are going nowhere."

"That shouldn't surprise you. Look how long we've been trying to get Boris. More than two years. This kidnapping case is barely thirty-six hours old."

"Maybe I'm frustrated, because there's a baby involved—"

"And you're working with a woman and not another cop."

Judd shrugged. If it were only as simple as just working with Adrienne, but it was more than that and the "more" was what had him tied up in knots. It was being with her. It was opening up about the guy who hadn't stopped when he saw Diana and Travis were hurt, and it was the horror he'd seen on Adrienne's face when she'd thought the Whitewell baby had been found dead.

Sure he wanted the case solved so that the baby would be safe and back with his parents, but Judd also wanted the case over so he could go back to his solitary life, where Adrienne wasn't involved in it. He'd gotten used to making the rules, setting his own agenda and if there was any personal involvement with a woman in his life, it was on his terms. Nothing heavy, nothing serious and for damn sure nothing complicated.

He'd assumed that was what he'd had that night with Adrienne. In fact, he had purposely directed the evening so that he could control it. He'd made the moves, they'd gone to her apartment so that he could leave instead of trying to get her out of his place later. But most of all, Judd had definitely and deliberately ignored the temptation that dogged him for weeks afterward—call her to explain and apologize.

Perhaps that was why he'd been so silent. There was no explanation that wouldn't have made their night more complicated, no apology that would have justified his actions. Not just because sneaking out of her bed and leaving at dawn had confirmed his bastard status, but because he'd also been unable to forget her.

That was the rub. The last thing Judd wanted was to remember a woman longer than five minutes. Adrienne, of course, had never been in his "forgettable" category, by virtue of the fact that she'd been close friends with Diana.

But Judd had no one to blame but himself for sleeping with Adrienne. Desire and some deep need for her that he refused to acknowledge or accept had overtaken him. Yet he didn't need anyone, certainly he didn't need the emotional tangle of a woman in his life. His attempts to get past that night of lush kisses and sultry intimacies that he now found himself thinking about too damn much, however, had never been totally successful. Worse, being assigned to work with her meant spending time together and that could all too easily turn complicated. Hell, never mind that it could, it already had.

"Judd?"

He glanced up, his frown still very evident. "Sorry, I was just—"

"Trying to come up with a valid or, better yet, an official reason for me to take Adrienne Trudell off the case."

"Yeah, I guess I was," Judd said, wondering if that might indeed still be possible. That would sure clear up his problem...or would it? For sure it wouldn't be the best move for either the Whitewells or the police department.

"Not gonna happen," the chief said.

Judd nodded, reminding himself to stop thinking it would. *You're gonna have to deal with this, Dillon, so make the best of it,* he thought to himself.

Litchfield added, "You do realize that if it hadn't been for her knowing Opal French, you wouldn't have gotten Boris Skodie."

"I'm aware of that."

"We have female officers and you've worked with them in the past and never objected."

"Adrienne's not a cop. Today, when I realized what Boris was up to, my immediate reaction was to get her out of there."

"Which, according to the report you filed, was what you did."

"But it could have blown the opportunity to get Boris. Now, if she'd been a cop—"

"You probably never would have gotten into the house. We don't know yet how involved Opal French is, but you can be damn sure that she would have known—from Adrienne's mother, no doubt, since you said the two women were friends—that Adrienne was a cop. Not a possibility in hell, then, that Opal would have chanced your coming into the house."

"Okay," Judd admitted. "You're right on that, but it doesn't change the fact that in those few minutes, I wasn't thinking like a cop working with another cop, but like a cop trying to protect a private citizen."

"And still did your job." Litchfield studied him a few moments. "Maybe that non-cop thinking was good for you," he said slowly, as if fearing he was stepping onto personal territory. Then carefully, he continued, "Since you lost Diana, you've been so work-oriented that you've lost perspective a bit. That's not good for either you or the department."

"This coming from the cop who used to spend twenty hours of every day on the job?" Judd scoffed. "Come on, Frank. The department thrived when you were working straight-out and you know it."

"But my wife divorced me and my kids are still reminding me of all the baseball games I missed. Hey, look, it's none of my business and I have no complaints about your work. I'm just telling you that contact with the civilian world does have its advantages."

"I'll take a vacation when this is over."

"You've been saying that for the past year. In fact, I ran into your father the other day and even he asked me why we didn't hire more cops so his son didn't have to work all the time."

Judd managed a grin. "Dad just doesn't like to get dragged to all those family outings without me there to suffer with him. Mom doesn't listen to his excuses about having to work." Then he eyed the chief suspiciously. "Is my supposed stress factor the reason you called me in here? I was under the impression you wanted to discuss the Whitewell case."

Litchfield sighed. "You're a stubborn bastard, Dillon."

Judd turned to Mike, who had been listening to this with conspicuous silence. "And I don't want a lecture from you, either, Shelby."

Mike held up both hands. "Hey, I'm a quiet little mouse here, just doing my job. Far be it from me to offer advice if you won't take it from the chief."

A temporary silence thickened in the office, but finally the chief cleared his throat. "Let's get back to work here." Litchfield picked up his phone and punched out a number. "Evelyn, tell Adrienne I want to see her in my office." He frowned. "What do you mean she went home to change clothes?" Scowling fiercely, he barked, "Call her and tell her this isn't a fashion show. I want her in my office in fifteen minutes." He dropped the receiver onto its cradle. "God, just what I needed. A woman more worried about her clothes than the case."

"Chief, it's not that," Judd said, taking up her defense and not sure why. This was probably a good out for him, and the chief just might have some second thoughts about having put her on the case. But Judd couldn't do it. He knew why Adrienne had gone home to change and he knew it because he knew her. Dammit, it was just one more reason why being with her was too complicated.

"No? Then what in hell is it?"

"Adrienne was wearing shorts. Beach-type clothes for the visit to Opal. My guess is that she doesn't want to walk around the department dressed like that. She has a thing about being professional."

Litchfield thought for a moment, then conceded. "Okay, I admit I wouldn't have liked her parading around here in shorts." He glanced at Mike. "Take a run downstairs and keep an eye out for her. And instead of coming back here, see how Opal's questioning is going."

"Yes, sir."

Once Mike was gone, Litchfield turned to Judd. "Let me run this by you so you know what we're going to do."

"Why do I get the feeling I'm not gonna like it."

"Because you won't."

"Terrific."

"I just got off the phone with the Louiston police. They did some checking with the neighbors for us on the Greeley woman. She came home late last night, probably after Keith saw her. Apparently, one of the neighbors, a Hester Marple, knows Lois well. She saw Lois get out of her car and carry a wrapped bundle into her apartment. Then she came back out and carried in a bunch of bags and a small suitcase. The neighbor said she knew Lois had had her baby because she wasn't pregnant anymore and the bundle must have been the infant."

Judd sat up straight. "She wasn't pregnant anymore?"

"That's what she said."

"Or Keith was wrong and this is just a string of damn coincidences. Here we are trying to nail down this woman and the real culprit could be halfway across the country."

"Or Lois is the woman and she never was pregnant."

Judd gave Litchfield a long look. "She faked a pregnancy to divert suspicion for when she brought a baby home?"

"That's one of the things you and Adrienne are going to find out." The chief glanced up. "Come on in, Adrienne."

Judd, who still wore his faded jeans, glanced around to the door. She'd changed to a soft pink suit with a white blouse open at the throat. No necktie, he noted, and wondered if she'd left it off because of what he'd said. Probably not, he decided grimly. After the few conversations they'd had, Judd didn't get the impression that Adrienne was going to dress with him in mind.

She sat down in the chair beside Judd.

"How are you doing?" he asked softly.

"Still a little shaken, but I'm okay."

"Listen, I should have told you why I wanted you out of the way."

"You were probably afraid I'd ask too many questions."

"Maybe. Time was a major factor."

"I guess I was just so focused on the baby's being there . . . I overreacted. I shouldn't have instantly assumed the worst about Caleb."

They both glanced at a scowling Litchfield. "Could you two save the mutual apologies for another time?"

Judd straightened. Litchfield's eyes were hard and all business. Obviously, the case was central in the chief's thoughts and any diversion became an intrusion.

Hell, Judd wondered, what was wrong with his own focus, anyway? Getting all soft and mushy had never been his style. Thinking back on what the chief had said about working too much, Judd grimaced. Maybe he should reconsider taking a vacation. Working with Adrienne had all the earmarks of a high stress level.

Litchfield filled her in on what they had on Lois Greeley and then asked her, "What, if anything, did Child-Aid have on her?"

"No listing, but Evelyn is doing a national check with other agencies that deal with missing children."

"All right. Evelyn will keep me informed and I'll make sure you two get that information and any other we find."

Judd sat forward, immediately alert. "You'll make sure we get it? That sounds—"

"Exactly like it sounds. I'm sending you two up to Louiston for a couple of days."

"Oh, hell." He felt Adrienne stiffen beside him, but he didn't look at her. No doubt she didn't like this arrangement any better than he did.

"It's the best lead we've got. Keith Cokeburn ID'd the sketch, and we both know, given his own problem, he wouldn't have come to you if there had been any way he could have avoided it."

"And what if this Greeley woman is clean?"

"Then we've lost a couple of days. The alternative of her being the kidnapper and us either sitting on the lead or allowing her to get away would be worse. Besides, the entire department is on this, so we'll be checking out any new info that comes in."

"A two-day stakeout in Louiston." Judd shuddered.

"I think Louiston is a quaint little town," Adrienne offered.

"If you're comatose."

"It has a quiet, stress-free environment, Judd. You make it sound like it hasn't come into the twentieth century."

"And likely to miss the twenty-first, too."

"Okay, you two. You obviously have a difference of opinion. You can hash it out while you're there. Judd, I don't want you going in there as a cop, and Adrienne, you're not to reveal you're an expert on missing kids."

"Let me guess," Judd said sarcastically. "We're on our honeymoon. Our plans to go to the Cayman Islands changed, so we took our second choice. A mecca of tourist delights in beautiful Louiston."

The chief looked at Adrienne, his eyes amused. "Would you want to honeymoon with this guy? Even a fake one?"

"Not a chance," she said forcefully.

"Guess we'll have to go with plan two, Judd," the chief said.

"I can hardly wait."

"We want to make this as simple as we can. You two will be old friends of Lois's who have just returned from a vacation on Cape Cod. You've decided to stop and visit with her before you return to the West Coast. That should cover you as far as the neighbors. As to the Greeley woman... I don't want any false arrests, and if this woman has the Whitewell baby, you're going to have to be damn careful."

"Make sure it's the Whitewell baby and not really hers before we make any moves on her," Judd said.

"Yeah. You'll have to stay a couple of nights, so you'll need to bring changes of clothes. There a motel across the street from the complex where Lois lives, so you'll have a place to—"

"Wait a minute," Judd interrupted. "When you said a couple of days, I thought you meant that as the max time for a stakeout. Why are we staying in some motel? If we know where she is and she has the kid, why don't we move in on her rather than hang around asking questions? That's going to look as suspicious as hell."

"Judd's right," Adrienne added. "And it might make her run again."

Litchfield tapped a pencil on the desk, his face grim. "And that's the problem. She's already run again. She left Louiston this afternoon with the baby."

Judd closed his eyes and cursed. If the computers at the motor vehicle registry hadn't been down, they would have had that plate number confirmed hours ago. They could have moved in and gotten Lois before she split. Of course, there was still the possibility she wasn't the woman who'd taken the baby, but Judd wouldn't have placed any major money on that.

If he were truthful, at least with himself, he knew it wasn't going to Louiston or doing a stakeout that was bothering him. Most of a cop's life was hurry-up and wait. Dig out the evidence, piece it together and make sure it's ironclad. And in the process, the long lulls between gathering the evidence and putting the pieces together for an airtight case can take endless patience and multiple months of frustration. This was two days, minuscule by police time, and yet he dreaded it.

Taking a deep breath, he reminded himself that choice wasn't a high priority for a cop. You went and did the job and did it the best way you could. What he needed to make himself understand was that Adrienne had the same goal.

That's all that was involved here. Two very different people with two very different jobs. And one goal. Getting Caleb Whitewell home safely.

The tension between them, the personal reactions such as holding her when she'd thought Caleb was dead and even that kiss at his house... All of those could be put into context, they could be explained in a dozen different ways. None of them meant anything and none would lead to anything unless he let them. And dammit, he had no intention of letting them.

He glanced over at Adrienne and wondered if she was also riddled with thoughts about how they would deal with two days of closer than close contact.

But instead of looking worried, she only looked puzzled, as if she was trying to figure out why they were going to Louiston if Lois wasn't there.

"There's no other way this could be done. That's what you're telling me." Judd was already resigned to the inevitable and wishing like hell Lois would walk in here right now and give herself up.

"But why are we going if Lois isn't there?" Adrienne asked.

"This neighbor claims that Lois went away for a few days, but is coming back. Since we don't know who she went to see or where, waiting for her to return is the best move.

"I don't want to hang up my best detective for the fun of it. I'd like nothing better than to send a couple of undercover street cops, but Louiston is too small a town for that, it wouldn't work. For this case, a man and woman, a couple, are the ideal choice."

"Why can't we just get a man and a woman who are both cops?"

Adrienne leaned forward. "I'm on this, Judd, and I'm going to stay. Finding missing kids, no matter what the circumstances, is my job, and if you think you can maneuver me out because I don't wear a badge or carry a gun, you're wrong."

Judd straightened, a little surprised at the edge in her voice as well as the determination behind her words. "I'm not trying to maneuver you out—"

"Furthermore, Chief Litchfield asked Evelyn to put me on this case, and if anyone is going to get off it, it will be you."

"Now, wait just a damn minute."

"No, you wait a minute. You've made it clear what you think of working with me, but your opinion doesn't matter a fig to me. What matters is finding Caleb Whitewell and getting him back safely."

"And you think that doesn't matter to me?"

"I think you're afraid I might know what I'm doing and then you might—and I emphasize 'might'—have to change your opinion of me." She glared at him. "And heaven help us if the great detective Judd Dillon has to alter some ingrained judgment that was wrong from the beginning."

"Most of the time, I'm not wrong," he snapped, irritated that he was having an argument with her that had no possible outcome he was going to like.

"All the time, you've been wrong about me," she said so strongly, it immediately took on more connotation than their earlier conversations about working together.

Judd started to say something and then closed his mouth. She glowered at him, her cheeks flushed with anger.

He glared back at her, his mouth grim and his thoughts hopping around as erratically as a bag of jumping beans.

Litchfield stood. "I want you two on your way to Louiston by tonight. Let the Louiston police know when you arrive. They've promised any assistance you might need, but they won't interfere."

Neither Judd nor Adrienne moved.

"Okay," the chief said. "That's it."

Adrienne rose. To Judd she said, "I'm going home to pack some things. You can pick me up in forty-five minutes. And don't be late. If we get to Louiston before dark, we'll have some time to check things out."

"Thank you very much for the instructions, Ms. Trudell," he said darkly. "In your next life, you should consider being a cop."

"Only if it affords me the opportunity of working with a professional like you, Detective Dillon," she said with the kind of sweetness that dripped with sarcasm. "I'll see you in forty-five minutes."

She marched out of the office with her back straight, and not once did she look back.

Litchfield shook his head. "Whew. That is not a lady I would like to cross."

"Just be thankful you don't have to work with her."

"Judd..." He hesitated. "Is something else going on between you two? Something personal? Is that why you kept saying a female cop would be better?"

"Adrienne and Diana were friends, so I do know her outside her work for Child-Aid."

"My God, that's right. Look, maybe I can get Shelby on this with her."

"No."

"But if working with her is going to continue to be so distracting and scrappy, the time to make the change is now."

It was the perfect out. No more tension. No more impromptu kisses. No more risks of revealing stuff about himself. So why wasn't he jumping at the opportunity?

A helluva good question.

"I want to do this, Frank. Maybe it goes back to my not being available when Diana and Travis needed me. I should have been with them when they were going to visit Diana's parents. Instead, I stayed here to finish up some stray details on a case and planned to meet them the next day. But there wasn't a next day for them." Judd paused a moment as once again the memory of getting the news of the accident washed over him. "I know there aren't a lot of similarities between this case and the accident, but I'm not about to let a case go just because I'm not too thrilled about working with Adrienne. And you're right. The low-profile approach allows for more flexibility and a lot less chance that the Greeley woman or her neighbors will be on to us."

"Adrienne was right about one thing."

"Yeah? What's that?"

"You are a professional, Detective Dillon."

Judd grinned. "But I don't think she meant it as a compliment." He glanced at his watch. "I better get a move on. Knowing her, she probably will leave without me."

Chapter 9

Assertiveness definitely works. Especially when it came to dealing with Judd Dillon.

Adrienne came to both conclusions with a small smile as they left the interstate and headed down a two-lane highway toward Louiston.

Two hours had passed since she'd let Judd know at the police station that she had no intention of being some passive helpmate in finding little Caleb. She'd known for years that she was basically a strong woman, she'd had to be, since too often her mother hadn't been around to make the decisions and choices a parent usually made for their child.

In some ways, her mother's lack of attention had made Adrienne more capable, she'd had to develop a mature independence earlier in life. But she knew there was a wide difference between being strong and being demanding, between being assertive and being bitchy.

Yet Adrienne also relied on internal instincts. Often in her job, a low-key approach got the best results. She didn't need to prove she was skillful. That was the sort of thing those she helped and those she worked with would have to evaluate.

Still, she exuded a certain level of confidence, given her credentials and willingness to exact help from every available source when a child was missing. Success in finding children and getting them home safe was by no means a one-person crusade. Many people were involved and Adrienne viewed herself as the one who simply took all the elements and worked through the tedious details to the eventual locating of the missing child.

For the most part, Child-Aid was structured so that Adrienne ran the fieldwork and Evelyn, although technically her boss, was more a buffer and coordinator. The two women had each found her own niche and functioned beautifully as a team.

Now, however, working with Judd had brought her head-to-head with a man who viewed being in charge as not only his job, but his role. For the most part, she was willing to bend; she wasn't a cop, and Judd, as she'd already witnessed, was particularly adept at asking the right questions to get the information he needed. Working with him, she knew, would be insightful and educational but he did more than inspire admiration for his professionalism. He was also adept at throwing her emotions into chaos. Not only had she willingly participated in that kiss at his house when they'd gone to look for Travis's rattle, but she'd practically fallen into Judd's arms at Opal's. The latter encounter may have been excusable, but Adrienne had determined that her behavior had been improper and unbefitting, despite the circumstances. Not her terror that something awful had happened to the baby, but that she'd reacted in such an emotional way, thereby allowing Judd to see her weak and vulnerable. Obviously, his talk in the police chief's office of replacing her had been strengthened by her actions at Opal's.

The last time she'd been in such a vulnerable state, she'd been so convinced she loved him that she'd allowed him to come home with her and they'd spent the night in her bed. The humiliation of having exposed her feelings had been mortifyingly proven the next morning when she'd heard him sneaking out.

Although making love with him in her apartment a year ago and falling apart in his arms at Opal's were not even closely related, there was a principle involved. Pride. And given the direction the conversation in Chief Litchfield's office had been going, Adrienne knew she had to assert herself and make clear that her tears at Opal's had been the result of unusual circumstances.

She had no intention of acting passively acceptant of whatever he wanted and whatever he did. She realized that saying it and doing it were two different things, but standing up for her role in helping to find Caleb had proved—at least to her—that she could be forceful when necessary.

Sighing, she scooted lower in the seat and watched the rich colors of the August sunset sink into the horizon. She'd worn an apricot sundress with a laced-up bodice and a flared skirt. She'd chosen the outfit based on who she and Judd were supposed to be in Louiston—friends of Lois's who were finishing their New England vacation by stopping in to say hello to an old friend. She sat quietly as the miles sped by, her eyes getting drowsy.

Moments later, Judd asked, "You still awake?"

"Of course I'm awake," she said, blinking furiously and straightening in the seat.

"You haven't said five words since we left Seapoint."

"You haven't said anything, either."

Without looking at her, he said, "I'm nursing my wounded ego."

She gave him a sideways glance, but his expression showed neither amusement nor seriousness. It was such an odd thing for Judd to say, she wasn't sure if he was being honest or looking for her to apologize, so she opted for the middle ground. "I can't imagine that you would allow anyone, especially a woman, to wound your ego."

"Most that I know—men and women—don't chew me up in front of the chief."

There was no rancor in his voice and that puzzled her. Other men she'd known would have launched into a long lecture about exactly who was in charge and who should know their place.

Adrienne studied the passing landscape. Maybe she'd embarrassed him; that had never been her intent. She started to say just that and realized she might very well be falling into some trap.

Judd Dillon embarrassed?

By a woman?

Disbelief at that possibility had her dismissing the idea. He was far too sure of himself, too good at his job, too precise and professional to allow something as insignificant as a clash of roles to cause him any chagrin.

Turning in her seat and looking at him, she said, "All I was doing in the chief's office was letting you know where I stood. If I hadn't said anything, you would have found some way to get me replaced."

"Replaced because working with a civilian is tricky. You don't know the ropes and consciously or subconsciously, cops tend to be more protective of a civilian than of another cop. It's an entrenched mind-set." His profile couldn't be described as anything but grimly resolved. "And with you involved, there's a double complication because I also know you on a personal level. I don't want our being stuck together to become problematic."

Adrienne chose to ignore the implications of "problematic." "Pardon me, Detective Dillon, but we're not 'stuck together,' we're *working together.*"

She waited for him to come back with one of his Ms. Trudell comments, but he said nothing. A few cars passed and in the distance the lights of Louiston bled through the trees. Judd seemed to grip the wheel harder and center his concentration on the road.

Feeling more sure of herself, she added, "You know, these couple of days together could be a very enlightening experience for both of us."

He drove silently and then with a curse, he pulled off the road into an oval-shaped rest stop area. Stopping the car, switching off the engine and swinging around to face her, he snapped, "I don't need to be enlightened and you don't, either. We've been down that path once before and the residue of the experience has already affected our working together."

Adrienne glared back at him. "The residue? What a wonderfully complimentary word."

"Seeing it that way keeps things in perspective."

"For who? You're the one all hung up about that night, not me."

"The hell with that night. The hang-up is all about right now and how neither one of us can't get beyond it."

She folded her arms and scowled. "I don't know what you're talking about."

"Yeah, you do. That's why you're all stiff and tense and sitting there as if someone put you into a straitjacket."

Appalled that he'd so thoroughly described the way she felt, when she wasn't even sure herself, she narrowed her eyes and gave him a strident look. "If you're insinuating that I'm still carrying feelings for you because we slept together one time, you're, well, you're just plain wrong."

"Am I? I don't think so."

Adrienne was glad for the shadows inside the car. She knew her face was flushed and her pulse pounded with both anxiety and alarm. In as even a voice as she could muster, she said, "I am not in love with you, Judd Dillon, nor would I ever be so foolish as to even entertain the notion."

"Who said anything about love?" he asked so offhandedly that she knew the word, never mind the emotion, was no longer valid for him. In a dull, flat voice, he added, "My interest or need for that particular emotion died with Diana."

She sucked in her breath, feeling a wrenching twist in her heart. Suddenly, the irritation and the need to pick at him were gone. The emotionally dead couldn't be brought back to life with mere satisfying lovemaking. That was what he'd really said. That was what he'd learned that night with her, and now he wanted her to understand clearly and concisely that passing time with her, kissing her and even the obvious desire he still had for her didn't make a difference. She hadn't affected him.

Working with her was just that. And wasn't that exactly what she'd wanted them to be—co-workers, two professionals concerned only with the single-minded goal of finding a missing baby?

"We should get going," she said, desperate to get off the subject they were on.

She'd spent an entire year convincing herself she felt nothing for Judd and now in barely a blink of time, she felt barraged with uncertainties and emotions that threatened to leap forth and humiliate her.

"Damn," he muttered and shoved his hand through his hair.

"Judd…" Her voice trailed off, for she didn't know what to say. It wasn't that she wanted to comfort him or open any emotional wounds, but she also didn't want him to think she was going to be some gooey reminder of the past.

She reached over and touched his arm. To her astonishment, he jumped as if she'd snuck up on him. But when she started to pull back, he gripped her wrist.

Staring at her, he said, "You stir up too much of the past for me, Adrienne."

"I didn't want to," she said sympathetically. "I've already said too much to you already."

He watched her for a long time and she felt dizzy from the smoky intensity of his green eyes. He tugged her toward him, his words urgent. "Come here."

She stiffened. "That will only make everything more complicated."

"Probably." He drew her closer and she went, despite a dozen warnings that buzzed through her mind.

"After all we just said," she began uneasily.

"I still want to kiss you. That's my big problem with you, angel. Kissing you and hoping it will be enough."

His mouth came down on hers so quickly and so thoroughly, Adrienne went boneless. He released the seat to give him more room. Without preliminaries, he lifted his mouth long enough to pull her across his lap so that she sat straddled and facing him. The potent green of his eyes was both icy and hot and Adrienne wished she had the presence of mind to think about how close those two responses were to the way he'd looked at her that night a year ago.

You're going to get hurt.

You're going to be left bereft and lost.

Push away. Get away.

Tell him no. Tell yourself no.

Yet she didn't move. Her heart slammed and she could feel his as he wound his hands into her hair, dispensing with the gold clip that had held it in place, and once again, without words, pulled her mouth down on his.

This time, the kiss deepened and Adrienne found herself drowning in a churning pool of sensation. Tastes and textures and the tantalizing expertise of the one man whose mouth could make her forget all the reasons that she should be objecting instead of sinking deeper.

Her breasts tingled and the juxtaposition of their bodies allowed her thighs to grip his hips as she nestled into him. The flare of her dress bunched up in her lap, exposing her tanned thighs.

Judd groaned. "You're too good at this..."

"Maybe it will relieve the tension."

"Only when hell becomes a deep freeze."

The car windows were open and the evening sounds of crickets surrounded them. In the distance, the noise of civilization echoed but couldn't intrude.

Sinking deeper still and not sure she could stop the plunge, or that she even wanted to, she pushed her hands into his saddle brown hair and let herself move with the kiss. She shouldn't; she knew she should be pushing him away, objecting, reminding him who they were and why they were together. Yet, for just this single wickedly stormy moment, she wanted to forget the restraints and ramifications of later.

Judd, too, knew he was dangerously close to losing control of himself. Kissing Adrienne wasn't like kissing any other woman. That particular piece of insight had made itself known that night at the bar when the intent of the kiss had been light and teasing. Her taste had swamped him and he'd known then she was an experience he wanted, and wanted badly.

Kisses with Adrienne were heated and sultry, exhausting and satiating. Seductive kisses were for more blatant women. Always with Adrienne, the intimacy leapt ahead so quickly, Judd would be in up to his neck and wishing like hell he knew what had happened.

This time he knew. He'd taken the leap in a deliberate attempt to show her—not tell her—what their being together could become. Not would. Could. Hell, maybe he was counting on her to keep the restraints in place. And just maybe, those restraints were exactly what made her so desirable.

He ran his hands along the sides of her breasts, the cross-lacing on the bodice of her dress both intriguing and irritating. He pulled the cord loose and released the catch of her bra. Her breasts, warm and full spilled into his hands. His palms brushed her nipples, their tightness scorching him.

She arched her back just enough that any hope Judd might have entertained that she would halt where they were going collapsed.

With a supreme effort of will, he made himself slow down, ignoring the tantalizing possibility of taking this any further. Kisses in the car that later led to going to bed was exactly what had happened to them that night. This time, the trouble was that he didn't think they'd even get so far as a bed if he didn't stop them.

He eased her back a little, kissing her softly. For just a second, she protested and Judd cursed the inner voice that warned him that he could hold no one but himself responsible if she accused him of starting this.

"You're a dangerous lady," he whispered, brushing his fingers down her throat and across her breasts.

She shrank back, fumbling with her clothes.

Once she had the bra hooked, Judd tightened the laces on her dress. "Adrienne..."

"I don't want to talk about it."

"I started this and—"

"And you stopped it. What does that make me but some wide-eyed, silly female who falls into your arms as if I'm starved for a man's touch." She settled herself back in her own seat and refused to look at him.

He reached over and cupped her chin. She stubbornly wouldn't meet his eyes when he turned her face toward his.

In a gruff voice, he said, "You're not silly, you didn't fall into my arms and what in hell is wrong with your wanting a man's touch?"

The question puzzled her because it made sense. There wasn't anything wrong with wanting a man to want her, to touch her, to love her. Her problem was that she wanted those things from Judd, who might return them on a physical level, but beyond that...

Finally, she said, "Maybe I just don't know how to handle you."

Judd didn't say anything, but released her and once again started the engine.

"Let's just leave it at that," he muttered after a few moments, suddenly too damn aware her reticence wasn't even close to his problem of handling her, wanting her and refusing to consider anything beyond that. His difficulty was how to make an honest admission that something could exist between them besides sex.

No, dammit. No. He'd been down that road of reckoning called love-and-forever-after. Not again. Never, never again.

The tiny town of Louiston hadn't changed, Adrienne thought as Judd drove past a once-profitable potato farm that had been sold to a developer. A sign had been plunked at the edge of the property that read Coming Soon—Affordable Homes. Overdeveloped and then gripped by an exodus when the last of the old shirt and sweater mills shut down, Louiston had never quite recovered.

It was located too many miles off the interstate system to get any notice except by someone who had reason to drive there.

The town proper consisted of a main street that was called Main Street and a town square where a century-weary and paint-peeled statue of Paul Revere held center stage. There had never been any evidence of the midnight rider being in Louiston, but rumor had it that the town's founder, Amos Revere, claimed kinship. When Amos decided Louiston needed a hero, a statue of Paul was crafted and erected so that it would be seen by everyone who passed through town.

Adrienne studied the statue as Judd drove by and turned left, going toward the housing complex where Lois had an apartment. Wanting to put those last intimate moments they'd shared before they'd driven into town out of her thoughts and out of the conversation, she asked Judd, "Did you ever believe that story about Paul Revere riding through Louiston?"

Judd had said little in the past few minutes, and while his silence raised a thousand questions she shouldn't even be thinking about, she was grateful the issue of their kiss and its ramifications had been dropped.

Now he briefly glanced at her. "What? I was looking for the street names."

"My mother used to tell me that story, and when we came up here to visit my aunt, I used to wonder how Paul Revere knew it was Louiston, when the town wasn't even settled until after the revolutionary war."

"I have no idea. Louiston's history isn't high on my priority list."

"You made that clear back at the station—"

"And if the looks of the place are anything to go on, you can be sure I haven't had any second thoughts," he commented, making Louiston sound like an infected wart.

"How can you possibly have something against a whole town?"

"Because a lot of the criminal element in the state has operated out of Louiston. And every time the town is mentioned at the station, it's in the context of something illegal. And making it even less endearing to me, it was up here that I spent a few days tracking down the drunk who killed Diana and Travis."

"Oh."

"So, please spare me the bouquets about Louiston. It's a dump and the fact that the Greeley woman lives here says all there is to say about her."

"You know," she said, not willing to be so all-condemning, "I could take offense since I once had relatives in Louiston."

"Once had? Then they obviously came to their senses and moved."

"Actually, they died."

"So much for a long life in Louiston."

Adrienne sighed, thinking that Judd was overreacting, but understanding that the town wouldn't hold good memories for him simply because he'd spent some of the darkest days of his life here. Adrienne had known that the driver hadn't been arrested until over a week after the funeral; she'd also heard that Judd had pushed the rules so he could be part of the arrest team, despite his having been ordered to stay out of the case.

To be honest, she hadn't been surprised at his actions, but she'd been concerned that he might step over the line and forget he was a cop, forget that killing the guy who had killed Judd's family wouldn't bring them back.

Of course, she'd never said anything to Judd, but she'd held out hope daily while the driver was being hunted that Judd wouldn't destroy his own life by committing a crime himself. In the end, she recalled, he had let the law handle the drunk driver.

Sometimes, like now, she considered how entwined Judd was in her thoughts. When he didn't know it. When she would have preferred to be thinking about anyone else. When she faced the constant battle between a deep feeling for him that she feared, and the certain knowledge that he cared nothing for her beyond a single night of sex.

"There's her apartment house." Judd indicated a two-story building, its white paint peeling, its front walk a strip of cracked concrete.

There were more apartments all laid out in a row, showing that whoever had constructed them was more interested in getting houses built than in any kind of aesthetic arrangement.

"She must live on the second floor," Adrienne said, peering up at the windows. "It's all dark."

Judd stopped the car and got out. Adrienne did likewise. Together, they walked up the cracked concrete path and onto a skinny sheltered porch, if it could be called a porch. It was more a stoop with a roof. Four locked mailboxes hung to their left and Judd looked for names. Greeley was one of the names, although it was faded.

He said, "Looks as if she's not a new tenant."

Adrienne looked at the rest of the names. They all appeared faded, as if they, too, had been there a while.

Judd opened the front door that revealed a common hallway. They were greeted by the smell of sausage and the sound of a barking dog. He tucked Adrienne behind him.

"It sounds like a small dog," she said in a low voice and wondered why she was whispering.

"Yeah. The kind that eats your ankle instead of your leg."

Before they could start up the stairs, one of the first-floor doors opened a crack and a slice of face showed. "Who you lookin' for?" the woman said.

Judd took Adrienne's hand. "Lois Greeley."

"What for?"

Adrienne managed a smile that she hoped looked friendly and not strained. "We're old friends of hers from years ago. We told her we were going to be vacationing in New England for a few weeks and promised to stop by and see her."

"You don't look like any of her other friends."

Adrienne and Judd exchanged glances and both wondered just what Lois's friends did look like.

"Well, people do change, you know," Adrienne said, not having the remotest idea what she meant, but hoping it sounded plausible to the woman.

From what they could see of her expression, it was stone-like and suspicious. "She ain't here, so you two better be on your way." She started to close the door, when Judd quickly stopped her.

"You know when she'll be back?"

"No, and I don't care."

"Look, Ms.?" Judd queried, smiling.

The woman's chin jutted out. "I don't have to tell you my name. Now, go on, get out of here."

"Judd," Adrienne said, looping her arm through his, but smiling warmly at the woman, "I just bet this is Hester Marple. Lois mentioned her in some of her letters."

Judd didn't miss a beat. "Of course. I should have guessed immediately."

The door opened a crack wider, the woman's curiosity obviously outweighing her suspicion. They could see she was holding a small dog. "Lois talked about me?"

"Yes, yes, she did," Adrienne said.

Hester peered at Judd and then at Adrienne. In a defensive way, she asked, "What'd she say?"

Judd muttered to Adrienne. "Good luck."

Adrienne clutched his hand tighter. He was going to let her do this and she prayed she wouldn't mess it up. In a low and she hoped confident voice, she said, "I don't think I should say in front of Judd. Lois knew I would keep whatever she told me in confidence and I have. I haven't breathed a word to a soul."

Judd muttered something she couldn't make out.

Hester's eyes narrowed and the dog stretched to sniff Judd. The animal yipped a few more times and Judd took a step back.

"I think he likes you," Adrienne whispered.

"Or wants to chew on me."

Hester got a tighter grip on the dog. "I told Lois them were my secrets. She promised she wouldn't tell."

Adrienne nodded. "Lois is very good with secrets, isn't she?"

Hester snorted. "Not if she blabbed to you." Then, as if suddenly realizing something, she said, "Say, if you know so much about secrets, how come you didn't know she had a kid."

Without missing a beat, Judd said, "That's one of the reasons we stopped by."

Adrienne homed in on a new angle. "Lois did mention she wanted to keep the baby a secret, but she never did say why. Do you know, Hester?"

"Well, of course I know!" she snapped.

Adrienne felt her heart lurch. Judd must have sensed a change in her for he put his arm around her and drew her close.

Hester said, "Ain't gonna say cuz Lois wants it to be a secret. Said she'd be back in a few days. You can ask her then."

"But the baby is okay?" Adrienne asked, trying to sound only curious and not overly concerned.

"Yeah, sure. Cute little fellow, if you like kids. Me? I like my Prissy here. Kids grow up to be nothin' but trouble." She shuddered. "Nothin' but a pack of trouble." With that, she slammed the door.

Back outside, Judd shook his head. "Hester Marple and her attack dog, Prissy. God. It's like something out of a bad movie."

"But we know Lois has Caleb," Adrienne said, the excitement evident in her voice.

"No, we know she has a kid."

Back in the car, Judd turned to her. "Okay, how did you know her name?"

"It was on one of the mailboxes. Since the chief mentioned Hester Marple was a neighbor of Lois's, it seemed to fit."

Judd scowled. "So you took a shot in the dark that she was Hester."

She shrugged. "It's called taking charge and throwing the other person off guard by taking the initiative. I learned the strategy in an assertiveness class I was taking and it's been very useful in my work. Strangers don't expect you to know anything about them, and since most people have some secrets, it's simply a matter of looking and sounding as if you know more about them than you really do."

"What if she hadn't been Hester?"

"I would have thought of something."

"Is that some new method of finding missing kids? Some sort of wing-it type crapshoot where you hope you get lucky."

"Sometimes," she replied breezily, "you have to use unusual approaches to get the information you need."

"Maybe bringing you along was a good idea."

"Why, thank you, Detective Dillon."

"You're quite welcome, Ms. Trudell. And while you're coming up with all these great ideas, do you want adjoining rooms at the Sleepy Hollow Motel? Or do you want to further the enlightenment about our relationship and get a single?"

He was teasing her, she knew. What distressed her was how tempting it was to say yes, let's get a single. "After what happened a little while ago, we'd probably be better off in separate motels," she said grimly.

Judd drove to the next block and into the parking area of a long row of indistinctive motel rooms.

"Adjoining rooms, right?"

"Of course. I think we can handle that."

He gave her a long look. "Then all we'll have to worry about is one of us keeping a door locked."

Chapter 10

After registering, Judd unlocked the door to Adrienne's room and flipped on the lights. The air conditioner hummed and the room was blessedly cool.

The room was serviceable, with the standard bed, dresser, TV and a multicolored carpet that looked fairly new.

"Not too bad," Judd noted as he moved to the window and pulled the tan curtains aside. "Good."

"What's good?"

"I can see the apartment complex from here. I asked the desk clerk specifically for rooms with windows facing this direction. That way, I can keep an eye on Lois's place when we're not actually there."

"Good idea." Adrienne put her bag on the bed and then walked to the window and stood beside him. It was nearly nine o'clock and the cloudy night blanked out the moon and stars. "How can you see anything? It's almost dark."

"I come from a long line of vampires," Judd dead-panned.

Adrienne feigned astonishment. "Really. I can't imagine why I didn't think of that."

"Probably my charm. We're trying to upgrade our image from fearsome to fuzzy-warm."

"And you haven't quite completed the process."

"Fearsome is fun." He wiggled his eyebrows.

Adrienne chuckled. "Somehow, I doubt your mother would appreciate your ancestral conclusions."

"It's a secret. Hunt and I made a pact when we were kids that no one would ever know."

Adrienne's gaze, amused and glad for the lighter moment, found assurance in his offhand comments about incidents from his boyhood. "You're telling me."

"I thought you were good at keeping secrets. That's what you told Hester."

Adrienne nodded solemnly. "And the only ones who know about you and your brother descending from vampires are the two of you."

"And now you."

"And I'm sworn to secrecy."

"Hope I can trust you on this."

"Oh, absolutely. Cross my heart." She made an X just to the left of the lacing in her dress.

Lacing, Judd recalled with too much clarity, that less than an hour ago he'd deftly untied, while at the same time telling himself he was headed for major trouble.

Frankly, his reaction to Adrienne puzzled him. Controlling his sexual needs had never been something he'd thought a lot about. When he was married, he'd been a faithful husband; to be otherwise, in Judd's opinion, was neither an option nor a desire. And after Diana's death, he'd gone from months of celibacy to a few weeks of sexual saturation. Those experiences had left him empty and annoyed with himself.

Then there'd been the night with Adrienne.

One night and it stood there like a door between who he was before he'd slept with her and who'd he'd become afterward.

That revelation in itself was enough to terrify him. No experience, sexual or otherwise, should be that definitive, that vivid. Not repeating it had become such an obsession for him that he had made absolutely sure he stayed the hell away from her.

Well, he had managed not to have sex with her—just barely, if those moments in the car were any barometer. But staying away from her was now impossible.

Judd glanced in the direction of Lois's apartment. The second floor remained dark, but did get some reflective light from the street lamps. He wanted this case closed and filed—to have the baby home and Lois locked up where she belonged. But also to give him good reason not to see Adrienne anymore.

Judd stepped around her without touching her and moved to the door. "Lock this one behind me and unlock the connecting one."

Adrienne pursed her lips. "I don't know. Am I going to be safe with a vampire's descendant in the next room? You might swoop through in the dead of night and bite."

He raised an eyebrow, his gaze sliding to her throat.

Adrienne immediately covered the area with her hand.

Giving her a direct look, he took note of the amused blue of her eyes. "I left my cape and fangs back in Seapoint."

Adrienne let out a long breath as if she'd been holding it. "Whew, I was worried there for a minute."

He chuckled. "Lock the door."

"Yes, sir."

Judd was still grinning when he entered his own room. Nothing like a little banter to ease the strain. However, he was even more impressed with how easily she fell into the silly conversation. It was as if she were in total sync with him, a possibility that would be useful in solving this case, but could also be troubling. Perhaps because he'd never known a woman who could adapt to a situation or a conversation without at least one or two missed signals.

Her quick thinking with Hester had also impressed him and he immediately saw that as a valid tool for the role of "old friends of Lois's" they would be playing.

Yet, her adaptability was troubling because he didn't want to find things he liked about her personally. He'd already let down his guard too often and afterward had tried to convince himself there were extenuating circumstances. Kissing her was becoming an adventurous—and dangerous—habit.

First at his house where his memories of Diana should have been inherently strong, and yet he had not given a thought to his late wife when Adrienne had lain sprawled under him on the guest bed.

A few lighter kisses—and then what had happened a mile or so from Louiston. God, she'd felt good straddling him, her thighs clenched against his hips. Her stomach soft against his, the cumbersome clothes that only fueled his memories of what lay beneath. Her breasts, silky and flushed in his hands. Her mouth and tongue, the sweet heat of deep mystery.

Judd swore and shoved his hand through his hair. Forget the excuses. He'd stopped the car to do exactly what he'd done. Kidding himself into the idea that it had "just happened" was ridiculous. But why he'd wanted to kiss her and touch her and make her aware of what was happening between them wasn't as easily explained.

Or maybe he didn't want to know. Maybe he didn't want to face himself and the feelings that spooked him. And maybe he was worrying needlessly.

God knows she'd been more than clear about her feelings for him, and they weren't exactly love and promises. So what was going on was no doubt explainable, they had the hots for each other. Good old garden-variety sex.

Judd opened his duffel bag and pulled out his shaving kit. Opening it, he realized he'd been so rushed, he hadn't checked to make sure he had enough of the basic necessities. Long ago, he'd established the habit of keeping a supply of toiletries in the kit to speed up his packing process. That way, he didn't have to worry about forgetting the essentials.

Now glancing through the items, he found everything he needed and something he'd forgotten about. Besides the toothpaste and toothbrush and razor, there was an unopened box of condoms.

He'd bought them two months ago when, after a long, stressful case he'd concluded, he'd called a woman he knew in Boston and made plans to meet her. Judd had known just what he wanted. Lots of sex and lots of sleep.

He had easily accomplished one of his objectives, as the unopened condom box attested.

Carla had not been pleased. "Since all you wanted to do was sleep, why did you call me?"

Judd had apologized, but had immediately realized a deeper motive. He really hadn't been interested in having sex. Not with Carla or with anyone. Carla was exotic and inventive and any man would be a fool to go to bed with her just to sleep, but he had done just that.

Admittedly, Judd had indulged in some sexual high jinks in his younger years, but whether it was because he was older, wiser or more cautious, he'd become so selective that, as the experience with Carla proved, sex wasn't as much fun as it used to be.

The phone on the bedside table rang, interrupting his thoughts.

Judd answered. "Yeah."

"Judd Dillon?"

"Yeah. Who is this?"

"Have some papers with info you need. I'll meet you in ten minutes at the convenience store on the next block. Park beside the Dumpster."

"Who are you?" he demanded, trying to figure out who could possibly know he was here.

But the caller hung up, leaving Judd staring at the phone. Scowling, he debated his options. The idea that some trap had been laid seemed ludicrous. Sure he was keeping his real reason for being in Louiston secret, but not because he believed the Greeley woman was involved in some multilayered conspiracy. Still, whoever the caller was, he knew Judd's name and where he was staying.

He crossed to the adjoining doors, knocked lightly and when Adrienne called out an acknowledgment, he opened it.

She was still dressed, but he noticed she'd unpacked and a sleep shirt lay across the turned-back bed. She stood near the dresser and the mirror reflected her back. In her hand, she held a bottle of lotion.

"Everything okay?" she asked. "You look worried."

Quickly, he told her about the phone call.

"I'll go with you."

"No. I'll be fine. Not a lot is going to happen in a public parking area."

"But you don't know."

"Come on, let's not get carried away with the cloak-and-dagger stuff."

"If I were a real cop, you'd take me... No, correction, you'd want me with you as backup."

He wasn't about to debate that with her again. "Probably. But you're not, so you stay here."

"And if I refuse?"

"Not a good idea to refuse when a cop tells you to do something," he said, his tone filled with dire warning. "Then I might have to take extreme measures."

She wet her lips, and still holding his gaze, she whispered, "What measures?"

Once again, as with the vampire banter, he observed how easily she slipped into the conversation. The difference this time was that the mood was sexy and taut. Judd absorbed the depth of her eyes, the smoldering tenseness that slid between them and wrapped around them like an undulating veil.

"What we cops do with beautiful women..." He let his voice trail off.

Her cheeks were flushed and the bottle of lotion hung loosely in her hand, precariously close to falling. "I'm not beautiful," she said simply.

Judd blinked at the realization that she was stating what she truly believed. And in that instant, he recalled telling her the night they'd made love that she was beautiful and she'd confessed that no one had ever said that to her.

"You're more than beautiful, angel. You're ravishing and provocative and dazzling." He paused a few seconds. "Still want to know what we cops do with beautiful women?"

She nodded, but only marginally, as if she thought she might be stepping into some sticky web she couldn't escape.

"I'll have to tie you up with the lacings of your dress, find one of your neckties to gag you, lay you on the bed and lock the door so there's no possibility you could follow me and get hurt. Then when I came back . . ."

For a few pulsing moments, the silence thickened between them.

Then in a firm voice, she said, "When you come back, I wouldn't be here."

"Oh?"

"We women are more resourceful than you think. I'd figure out a way to get loose."

"Knowing you, I don't doubt it."

He crossed over to where she stood.

He took the bottle from her hand, unscrewed the top and sniffed. "Nice."

He turned the bottle and wet his fingertip. Then he touched her throat just where the tiny pulse hammered. Slowly, he moved his finger in a circular direction and she caught her breath.

"You're trying to distract me, aren't you? First with the teasing talk and now this," she murmured, the catch in her voice audible.

With a casual shake of his head, he once again wet his finger with the lotion. This time, he put the bottle down on the dresser. Watching her eyes, he said, "Now, if I wanted to really distract you, I'd unlace your dress and unhook your bra." His hand worked even as he spoke.

Adrienne swallowed and stood so still, she might have been hypnotized. With the lacings loose and the bra open, her cleavage showed, yet her breasts remained covered. Judd didn't disturb the loose fabric, but concentrated his finger on the warm length of skin between her breasts. When he drew down the opening, she shivered.

"Cold?"

"N-no."

"Hot?"

"You're s-seducing me."

His finger had moved along the inside of one breast, and at her gasp of words he stopped. "On second thought, I should know better than to look for trouble I don't need," he muttered.

He started to pull his hand away and she curled her fingers around his wrist. "Judd, what's going on?"

He uncurled her fingers and moved back toward the adjoining doors. "I gotta go."

"You mean trouble between us, don't you?"

"There is no *us*, dammit." Immediately, his voice softened. "Look, this was my fault. I came in here. I touched you."

"And I didn't object," she said instantly.

"Well, dammit, you should have. Tell me to stay the hell away from you. Tell me not to touch you. Tell me not to want—" He cursed then and stalked back into his own room.

Putting on his shoulder holster and checking his weapon, he said, "I'm going to see what those papers are all about." He glanced in her direction. "On the way back, I'll pick up a pizza and some beer."

"All right." Adrienne moved closer to the adjoining doors. The lacings moved slightly and she gathered them up and pulled them together, effectively covering herself. "Maybe Lois is with the caller."

"And she just wants to turn herself in so that the baby can be returned to the Whitewells." Cynicism cut through each word.

"It's possible."

"As likely as my vampire ancestors." He moved toward the outside door.

"Judd, wait."

She hurried forward, grabbing his arm before he got the door open. He swung toward her, his eyes dark and angry.

"A few more minutes, angel, and you're gonna be under me on one of those beds."

"Or you'll be under me," she retorted so fast, her words stunned him.

"And on that intriguing possibility, I'm leaving."

He stepped outside and closed the door before she could answer him. In the car, he started the engine, switched on the headlights and turned toward the convenience store they'd passed on the way to the motel.

In all honesty, the majority of his fury was easily explainable. At himself for allowing the liberties he'd taken, at Adrienne for being so damn appealing and even at Lois Greeley for creating the circumstances that had not only put an innocent child at risk and a family through a nightmare, but that had also managed to screw up a year's worth of work in staying away from Adrienne.

She not only distracted him, but it infuriated him that she affected him at all. A man who could be celibate for months, then equally bored with sex to the point where he'd slept through an inventive night with Carla... God, he shouldn't be so tied in knots over one Adrienne Trudell.

In a flash of realization, he knew why. It was one of the reasons Adrienne and Diana had been such close friends. Adrienne, herself, had briefly touched on it a few days ago when she'd stated in no uncertain terms that she was nothing like Diana.

Adrienne was right—one of the best proofs was her going to the diner, then doing such a convincing act at Opal's and, of course, her standing up to him in front of Litchfield. Diana would have backed away from all three with a firm shake of her head.

Adrienne didn't have the fragile, almost spun-glass quality that his wife had possessed in abundance. Adrienne was more straightforward with her feelings, her reactions, her emotions and even her words. She fascinated him because he was never quite sure how she'd react.

Diana would have been appalled by the vampire conversation. Judd recalled his mother's fury when a playmate's mother had called her and asked if she knew what her sons were telling their friends. Secretly, Judd and Hunt had thought it funny that grown-ups would take two kids so seriously.

Odd, he thought now, that he would recall the childish game here with Adrienne. Maybe it was a throwback to his own innocence, when such an obviously ridiculous conversation could be enjoyed simply on face value. Maybe that was the appeal of Adrienne. A core of innocence, a willingness to just go along for the ride and see where it took you.

He grinned in the dark car. No way in hell would Diana have ever come back with a "Or you'll be under me" comment. However, he wouldn't put that beneath the heading of innocence. Nor did he think she'd been teasing or flirting. No, Adrienne had said it to show him she could deal with whatever he threw at her. But could *he?*

Not only did her comeback intrigue him, but imagining it made him a little dizzy as he pictured himself sprawled across the bed with a naked Adrienne riding his...

Hell. He shuddered and shifted in the seat. He slammed on the brakes as he realized he was halfway past the entrance to the convenience store.

He swung into the lot, ablaze with lights. Some teenagers with a single radio blaring were eating from a huge communal bag of chips and swilling down soda out of cans.

Judd saw the Dumpster and parked, then glanced around at the other cars. A man with grizzled hair and a thick neck and dressed in slacks and a checkered shirt that just covered a sausage layer around his waist ambled toward Judd. He carried a folder in his hands. Judd opened his door and climbed out.

"Judd Dillon?"

"You're the one who called."

"Yeah." He clutched the folder as if it were top secret. "These came by fax for you. Litchfield said to get them right to you."

Judd took the folder and glanced through the pages. It was information on Lois Greeley. "Thanks, this will be helpful."

"If there's anything we can do. I mean, I know you're handling this, but the Louiston department is ready to assist if you give the word."

Judd nodded. "And you're—"

"Sergeant Sean Payton."

"Good to meet you," Judd said as the two men shook hands.

Payton nodded. "I'm off duty right now. I told the lieutenant I would get these to you on my way home."

Puzzled by the secrecy approach, he asked, "Why didn't you just bring these to the motel? Or at least tell me on the phone who you were."

"I thought this was an undercover surveillance."

"Yeah, it is, but bugged phones and someone's following you or even being curious isn't likely. This isn't that kind of operation."

"You can never be too sure, you know."

Judd was about to say that either police work in Louiston was slow or Payton was into conspiracy theories, but didn't do either. "Okay, I'll give you that." Judd opened his car door. "Anyway, thanks for the papers." He slid behind the wheel. "Oh, by the way, where's a place to get good pizza?"

"Maria's. It's two blocks down and on the left."

A half hour later, he returned to the motel with the papers, a huge pizza with six toppings and a six-pack of cold beer.

Once inside his room, he immediately noticed that the adjoining doors were both open. That and the empty silence.

"Adrienne?" He walked into her room expecting to find she'd fallen asleep. Instead, the bathroom door was wide open and her sleep shirt lay in a heap on the floor as if she might have quickly dropped it. The bed remained undisturbed.

A sense of foreboding coiled in his belly and he wasn't sure if he was worried or angry. Payton's words lingered in his mind. *You can never be too sure,* he'd said. Was there more to Lois's taking the kid than Judd realized?

He glanced at the folder of papers. Payton may have read through them when they came in. Maybe he knew something Judd didn't know.

Judd shook off the idea that the case was larger than they'd thought. No way. Litchfield would have contacted him directly with that kind of information. It would require new strategy and definitely more cops.

But dismissing the possibility of a larger case, where in hell was Adrienne?

Surely she hadn't tried to follow him, but since there was no other possible explanation— No, not possible. He would have seen her. Unless.

Judd swore. Unless she'd been hurt or someone had picked her up or... Or what? God, he didn't want to even think about it.

He stalked back into his own room about to call the police, when he saw the note propped against the phone.

Snatching it, he read out loud. "I know you'll be worried because I'm not a cop, but I do know what I'm doing. You don't need to call the police." Judd scowled. How in hell did she know he intended to? He read on. "Save me some pizza and a beer. Just maybe, we'll be able to celebrate."

"Celebrate what?" Immediately, his gaze fell to the box of condoms he'd tossed onto the dresser. Had she seen them and assumed he'd come prepared, just in case?

No, she'd probably be furious that he even assumed she might cooperate. No way would her having seen the condom box be any cause for celebration.

He opened a can of beer and drank while he paced between the two rooms. He walked outside periodically and looked for any sign of her. There was none.

Back in the room, he was about to pop the top on his second can of beer and call the Louiston police despite what her note said, when he glanced toward the apartment complex. Setting the can down, he stared without blinking for at least thirty seconds.

"Damn."

Then he vaulted out of the motel room, running and fighting a growing fear he'd never had before. A terror that tore at his gut and drove his steps faster toward Lois Greeley's apartment.

Chapter 11

Adrienne halted a few feet from Lois's apartment door.

Her heart pounded so hard and loud, she did some deep breathing to slow it down. She wished Judd were with her, but she hadn't wanted to chance waiting for him to return and miss what may be a significant opportunity to find Caleb.

Her concern that his meeting with the anonymous caller might be a trap dissipated when she thought about it more rationally. In the first place, he was an experienced cop, and knowing his dislike of Louiston, Adrienne guessed he was more than prepared for any surprises.

And in the second place, her own fear that something might happen to him didn't make sense, they had practically no personal relationship, a feeble friendship and what could she have done if she had gone, anyway. Her performance at Opal's had made her look less than professional. She cringed now, just thinking about her hysteria there and that Judd had had to take her into his arms to settle her down.

But moments ago, when she'd glanced out her motel window and seen the light in Lois's apartment, she'd known there was no time to lose. She'd seen it as an opportunity to prove she could be the professional she claimed to be.

The problem was, she realized worriedly, now that she was almost in front of Lois's door, she didn't know what she should do. In more ways than one, she fully understood why having a plan worked. Like it had at Opal's, and when they'd first arrived in Louiston and spoken to Hester. Even originally at the hospital, Judd had spoken with her at some length before they'd gone into Tanya's room, and certainly his questions had been thought through. Adrienne recalled complimenting him later and how testy he got. Well, if she messed this up, testy wouldn't even begin to describe his reaction.

But there had to be times when a cop didn't know what situation he'd find himself in. In those circumstances, he would rely on instinct.

Instantly, she realized exactly why Judd had wanted a female officer. She would know what to do right now, while Adrienne was standing here in the hall desperately thinking...

Wait a minute, she thought suddenly, catching her breath. She wasn't some neophyte, she wasn't just a civilian in need of protection. She worked for Child-Aid and was, in fact, an expert at finding lost children. That's why she was here and why Chief Litchfield had asked specifically for her. So was she relying on her own knowledge and instincts of how Lois would act? No. She was in some sort of panic in the hallway.

"It's all your fault, Detective Dillon," she muttered under her breath. Being with him had not only managed to mess up her astuteness when it came to her job, but it had sent her emotions into overdrive and chaos.

She crept closer to the door, which she realized wasn't quite closed. From inside, she could hear footsteps. Adrienne listened and concentrated. Either this was Lois or it was someone else, an obvious conclusion, but one that brought her up short and made her definitely scared.

If the latter case was true and someone other than Lois was in the apartment, using the plan she and Judd had worked out—that they were friends who wanted to visit with Lois—would be perfect. However, if it was Lois . . .

Her heart desperately wanted to find Lois and little Caleb and the thought of botching this up sent new fears through her.

She eased the door open wider. The light came from the kitchen area and threw long streaks across a faded carpet. The smell of old newspapers and dust made her cover her mouth to prevent herself from sneezing. A living room was to the right and clogged with furnishings—dark and heavy with lace coverings on the arms. A Tiffany lamp, probably fake, tottered on a spindly piecrust table. A couple of plants in need of water sat on a windowsill.

Adrienne took a few more steps. The bedroom looked as if a hasty departure had been made. Clothes thrown aside on a carelessly made bed. Costume jewelry spilled on the dressing table. Against the far wall stood a brand-new crib. A mobile hung above it and a blue blanket with teddy bears and puppies was folded neatly over the railing.

Adrienne found the sight both encouraging and troubling. The new crib and the accessories indicated Lois wasn't a total monster, but at the same time it indicated a plan, not a spur-of-the-moment action. And that troubled Adrienne. For if the woman had gone to so much trouble to fake a pregnancy and buy baby equipment, kidnapping Caleb must have been in the plan also. Or at least the kidnapping of a baby boy.

A sensation of being watched gripped Adrienne. With her heart pounding, she swung toward the hall light.

There stood a hard-looking woman with dull yellow hair that was tied back, beetled eyebrows and wearing a dress that barely contained her ample bustline.

In the shadows, Adrienne couldn't tell if the face matched the sketch, but the woman's size was much more generous than what Tanya had described.

"Just who in hell are you, girlie?"

Assertiveness, Adrienne reminded herself. Peering at the woman, she said haughtily. "I might ask you the same question."

"You might, might you?" A huge plumber's wrench was in one hand. "Miss Uppity sounds like to me. You one of them whores the cops been tryin' to run out of here?" She drew closer. "You don't look the type, but these days a body can never tell."

As she walked a few more steps into the room, she swung the mammoth wrench. Adrienne tried not to show any panic. If the woman hit her with it, the blow would kill her. Her eyes darted around as she tried to find a way out of the room, out of the apartment.

She eased to her right. "Look, I thought you were Lois—"

But the woman waved away the words. "Never mind that a body has to come up here in the middle of the night cuz old man Foley in 1B is gripin' 'bout some leaky pipe drippin' and stainin' his matchbook collection, but I got to put up with some whore lookin' for her john."

Adrienne narrowed her eyes. "I'm not a whore. I'm a friend of Lois Greeley's and—"

"Yeah? You don't look like her type of friend."

Adrienne scowled, recalling that Hester had made a similar comment. "People change," she snapped.

"And I got work to do." The woman shrugged and turned back toward the kitchen. "Lois ain't here."

"I know that now," Adrienne said briskly, now that she was pretty sure the woman didn't intend to slug her with the wrench. "I saw the light and I thought she might have come back."

"Well, she didn't, so beat it, huh?"

Now that her fear had subsided, the idea of just leaving without finding out anything was too disappointing to contemplate. Maybe the woman knew something about the baby. She ambled back to the kitchen and Adrienne followed.

Here, too, everything seemed outdated and faded. Old appliances, mismatched dishes, a wall clock shaped like a rooster and a Formica-topped table with four chairs. In the center of the table was a bouquet of tiny flowers in a vase shaped like a baby's cradle. Lying beside the vase was a blue rattle like the one she and Judd had found at the hospital, like the one that had belonged to Travis.

Adrienne's mind raced and she wished she'd looked around more closely in the bedroom. If Lois was the thief who had taken the newborn packets from the maternity floor storage room, then the other items were certainly around also.

Not a chance in a million she would just leave now. Maybe if she posed a few pertinent questions, she might get lucky. Although the woman was hardly the friendly, forthcoming type, still, Adrienne wanted to see if she could learn even a scrap of information about Lois.

"You know," she said as if she were just carelessly tossing out information, "Lois and I haven't seen each other for years."

The woman sat facing the underbelly of the kitchen sink. An array of cans and rags had been pushed aside to give access to the pipes. Adrienne immediately noticed they weren't the new white PVC pipes that were under her sink at home. These pipes were old and looked rusted. Trying to force the wrench, the woman grunted loudly.

Her voice strained, she asked, "You still here?"

Adrienne ignored the rudeness and said, "And I understand that she has a new baby."

"So what else is new? Everyone's got babies. Twelve-year-olds are havin' kids," she said in disgust. "When I was twelve, I didn't even like boys. Liked horses..." Her voice trailed off and Adrienne sensed the woman's love for horses had been very important to her when she was growing up. But she wasn't here to find out about her.

"Has Lois had other babies?"

"Hey, I thought you were her friend. Don't you know?"

"As I said, I haven't seen Lois in years."

"Seems mighty strange to me that you wouldn't know if she had kids." She shrugged as if thinking about why Adrienne wouldn't know took too much thought. "Don't know if she had no other kids. All I want from her is the rent on time every month. There's some paper and a pencil over there. Write her a note and leave it by the phone with your number. She don't got many friends. Keeps to herself, so she'll probably be callin' you right quick."

Adrienne glanced at the cluttered counter and at the bulletin board beside the phone. She gave the corkboard a cursory glance but then realized exactly what was on it and looked more closely. Phone numbers, a calendar, a menu from a take-out place and an old curled photo of three women. She felt as if she'd stumbled upon a gold mine. The woman working on the water leak still had her back to Adrienne.

"The note is a good idea," she said as she glanced through the phone numbers, not having the faintest idea which ones were important and which were not. Most were jotted down haphazardly, with either just a first name and in some cases only an initial. There was a "Call Lucy" on the calendar date of the day Caleb was taken. Adrienne quickly jotted down the number that had the initial *L* after it. She also made a mental note to ask Hester.

Then her attention was drawn back to the curled photo. Adrienne eased the tack out of the picture, took the photo down and turned it over, but no names appeared on the back. It was old and deteriorating, no doubt from constant exposure to light. The shot had been taken with an instant camera. Three women were at a table at some kind of celebration, but it was the wall with a grouping of oval-shaped framed paintings that hung directly behind the women that looked vaguely familiar. Enough so that Adrienne knew she'd seen it before, but she couldn't recall when or where.

She turned the photo more to the light and concentrated. She mentally scrolled through the places she'd been recently, but none brought back anything that looked like the painting display.

She scowled and stared at the women in the picture. The one in the middle looked somewhat like the sketch of Lois, but the others she didn't recognize.

"...have to pay the damn water bill on this place, I sure wouldn't be up here doin' this."

Maybe Judd would recognize it, but to take it out of the apartment would have him furious and accusing her of stealing. She stared at it, trying to memorize the details.

"Hey!"

Adrienne glanced toward where the woman was working. "What did you say?"

"I asked you what you're doin' over there?"

"Just trying to think of all I should tell Lois." Her mind raced. What possible connection could there be between a grouping of paintings that she knew she'd seen before and Lois Greeley? The hospital? My God, there were hundreds of rooms in the hospital and—

"You ain't takin' stuff off her bulletin board, are ya?"

"I was just admiring an old picture of Lois." Quickly, she tacked the picture back up on the board.

"Looks to me like you're bein' some nosy bitch." The woman got to her feet. "I don't know who you are, but I betcha you ain't no friend to— And who are you?"

Adrienne swung around to find Judd glowering in her direction. Her immediate reaction was to call him over to look at the picture, but his obvious fury forestalled that idea. Despite the distance, his eyes burned into her. His mouth was grim, and for a brief moment Adrienne feared him more than she had feared the woman with the wrench.

In a low, seething voice, he asked Adrienne, "What in God's name do you think you're doing?"

The woman, who stood as if Godzilla himself wouldn't intimidate her, held the wrench in one hand and propped the other hand on her hip as she studied them curiously. To Judd, she said, "And who are you? One of Lois's buddies, too? Or you the john Miss Uppity here is lookin' for?"

Adrienne sprang forward. "Judd, darling, I thought I'd left you asleep."

He glared at her momentarily, but then responded as if they'd done a dress rehearsal of this scene just moments before. "Sleep? With you around, baby, I never get any sleep."

The swagger in his voice, the double meaning in his words, sent her pulse racing and an unexpected flush to her cheeks. She ducked her head, embarrassed by her own reaction.

"So you two know each other," the woman said.

"Not as well as I thought," Judd said evenly. He sauntered over, glanced in the direction of the bulletin board—if he saw the picture, he didn't act as if he noticed anything familiar about it—and then slung an arm around Adrienne's neck as if she were his personal possession. "We'll be on our way, Mrs. Grobes. And I certainly do appreciate your kindness and patience."

"Kindness and patience!" Adrienne began, but Judd squeezed her hard enough to let her know he didn't want her to say anything.

In a tone that set Adrienne's teeth on edge, he said, "My woman here has been so eager to see Lois, and when she saw the light in her apartment, she got a little overanxious."

"Yeah, yeah, yeah," the woman said, obviously tired and wanting to end the whole conversation. She turned back to the sink.

"I am *not* your woman," Adrienne whispered cuttingly.

"Thank God," he muttered back.

"Then stop manhandling me like I'm some rebellious child."

"How about if I put cuffs on you like you're a grown-up trespasser?"

"Oh, for heaven's sake." Adrienne glowered at him, but the look he returned raised a cold sweat throughout her body. Never had she seen him so angry.

As he hustled her out of the apartment, she started to say, "Judd, when I tell you—"

But he pushed her back against the wall just outside Lois's apartment and kissed her. Not in a zillion years could she have called it anything but a "shut-up" kiss. It took Adrienne's breath away with its intensity and she hung supported only by his body and the force of his mouth. He touched her everywhere and yet touched her nowhere. It was the oddest, most disconnected sensation she'd ever had.

Ever since she'd known Judd, she was aware of his reputation as an always-in-control cop. Tempers and anger didn't belong on the street and cops should always show restraint, whether trying to deal with the law-abiders or even the law-breakers. Yet, in those few moments in the apartment, Judd had been furious, and although she doubted the woman would have noticed the anger having such deep roots, Adrienne had and had reacted immediately.

This kiss was like some built-up pressure release for him. She had no doubt that when they got back to the motel, he would savagely lecture her on all the reasons that she shouldn't have done what she'd done.

Perhaps valid from his standpoint, but she didn't intend to wait on him like some terrified underling. He'd thrown her off balance by charging in there with all that "my woman" talk. Maybe this was the perfect time to make her own case for rushing off to Lois's.

He lifted his mouth, his breathing heavy. To Adrienne's astonishment, she found herself more than excited, very close to aroused. She slid her arms around him, found his body hot and humming with tension. She touched her own mouth to his chin in a wandering brushlike stroke.

Immediately, he froze. Pulling back from her, he cupped her chin and held it so she couldn't look away.

"What in hell is going on, Adrienne?"

"Nothing. I wanted to kiss you back, and, uh, well . . ."

"Well what?"

"I wanted you to know my going into Lois's wasn't wasted and I'm not angry with you for the way you acted in there."

"The way I acted?" He blinked and glanced up at the ceiling, closing his eyes and shaking his head.

"As if I were your property," she snapped.

"Perhaps I should have shown her my gun and badge and you could have pulled out your credentials."

"Don't be sarcastic."

Stepping back from her, he dropped his voice to a low snarl. "Then don't try to charm me into making some idiotic apology."

"I'm not! But you're not being fair or giving me a chance to explain—"

"Later." He took her arm and held it firmly while they made their way down the dark staircase.

Getting out of the building without encountering Hester wasn't going to happen. With Prissy yapping behind her, Hester peered through a crack in her open door.

Scowling at Adrienne, she said to Judd, "See you found her."

"Yeah. Thanks, Hester."

She gave Adrienne a superior sniff. "If you'd stopped and asked me, I would've told you it was old lady Grobes up there."

Adrienne gave her a tight smile.

Outside, Judd held her arm firmly, despite her efforts to get free.

When she continued to struggle, he reached down and lifted her in his arms and then unceremoniously heaved her over his shoulder.

For a long fifteen seconds, she simply hung there, so appalled and astonished that Judd would do such a thing and do it in public, that she said nothing. "Damn you to hell, Judd Dillon!"

But he said nothing, walking on as if she weighed no more than a bag of feathers. A carful of teenagers drove by and slowed down. Leaning out the windows, they hooted and whistled.

"Hey, man, you sure know how to treat them."

"Make her purr, man."

"Here, kitty, kitty."

Judd walked faster and Adrienne pushed her hands against his back with all the strength she had, but still he wouldn't release her.

Turning into the motel parking lot, Judd waved and said good evening to the desk clerk who stared from his office doorway. Once Judd was past him, Adrienne saw the man's head spring forward at the sight of her flung over Judd's shoulder. She considered calling out for him to call the police and then grimly realized that Judd was the police.

Trying to look dignified when she probably resembled a road-kill was impossible. The man just kept staring, adjusted his glasses and then, as if still not convinced, he took them off, cleaned them and put them back on again.

Adrienne closed her eyes in mortification.

"Everything okay, Mr. Dillon?" he asked what Adrienne thought had to be the understatement of the year.

"Just fine. See you tomorrow."

"Sure thing." The desk clerk watched, obviously determined not to get involved, until Judd had the motel door open and they were once again inside. He walked through the adjoining doors and dropped her onto her bed. She lay in a heap like a rag doll. Her arms ached from pounding on him, trying to get free. Her head swirled dizzily and she closed her eyes, dragging in gulps of air.

Judd snapped, "I'm gonna take a shower and I suggest you do the same. It will give us both time to cool off. Then you're going to explain exactly what in hell you were doing."

Her eyes flew open. Not even an apology for embarrassing her in front of the desk clerk, not a word about those crude kids and as far as cooling off... Never did she intend to cool off from this.

In a brittle voice as dignified as she could manage lying sprawled on the bed while he towered over her, she said, "You are a barbaric, sexist, horrible, sadistic monster and if it wasn't for Caleb, I would walk back to Seapoint ~~right~~ now."

"And if I didn't need you for the sake of this longtime friendship with Lois, I'd send you back with a police escort."

"I hate you."

"Good. And while you're nursing all that energy, try and come up with a plausible explanation for who in hell gave you the right or permission to go into Lois's apartment."

"You make it sound as if I broke in."

"Did you knock and did Grobes invite you in?"

"Well, no."

"So you walked in."

"The door wasn't closed tight. I just gave it a little nudge and it swung open."

He leaned down, his voice edged with anger. "And you know what Hester was going to do if she hadn't recognized you?"

Adrienne glanced away.

"Look at me!" When she did, he said, "She would have called the cops. Seems there's been a lot of prostitution in the neighborhood and the residents are very suspicious of lone women prowling about."

"I was not prowling." She bit out the words, her anger taking on a deep seething quality.

He touched the lacing on her dress. "I'd hardly call this a looking-for-clues outfit."

She slapped his hand away. "Well, perhaps you'd like to choose my clothes for me and instruct me on how to be your most obedient servant."

He straightened and walked toward his own room. "I'm going to take a shower. Afterward, we can eat cold pizza and drink warm beer and we'll take a look at some papers I got tonight on Lois."

She sat up and blinked at those last words. "Papers on Lois?"

"Yeah. Just a lot of boring routine kind of stuff that's gotten legally."

She stuck out her tongue at his back as he walked away, peeling off his clothes as he went.

Twenty minutes later, she emerged from her own bathroom, dressed in her thigh-length sleep shirt. Her hair was still damp and she felt only marginally less angry than before she'd showered.

She halted when she saw Judd sprawled on her bed wearing only a pair of ragged faded white jeans. The contrast against his dark hair and tanned skin made Adrienne stare more than she should want to, given the way he'd treated her. His hair looked as if he'd combed it with his fingers, the front fell forward, giving him an approachable appeal that made her fingers itch to push it back. He was barefoot, his ankles crossed as he lay against two bunched-up pillows.

Beside him, the pizza box was open and two pieces were missing. She noticed that one beer can was crumpled, too. A folder of papers lay across the empty side of the bed.

He glanced up, his eyes absorbing her rather than sliding over her in a casual manner. "Pizza's great. That's a sign of good pizza, you know. When you like it cold as well as hot."

Adrienne just stared at him, unsure what to say or do. His tone had changed dramatically and he appeared entirely too relaxed and friendly. She damned the rush of sensation that churned through her.

She was still furious at him for his earlier treatment and she wasn't about to let herself be wooed back by cold pizza, warm beer and an obvious attempt to get into her good graces.

"Come here."

"Why?"

"So I can apologize."

Immediately, she was suspicious. "You said earlier you wouldn't."

"I changed my mind."

"Why? Because you think you can control me better by being nice."

"No, I treated you exactly the way you accused me of. And the fact that I was scared as hell you might have gotten hurt or into a dangerous situation you couldn't get out of, isn't a good excuse."

Judd scared? It seemed nearly impossible to believe and in fact too simple to just accept his apology. "You didn't act scared, you acted furious."

"Yeah, I know."

"Why did you?"

"Are you going to come over here?"

"I don't know."

He offered his hand and she took a tentative step forward, but then stopped. "Why can't you apologize from there?"

He sighed. "Because I want to kiss you, hold you..."

"Oh."

"Nothing you don't want, angel."

She took another step, her mind racing with questions. Kissing and holding weren't very professional, but then again the last couple of hours hadn't been, either. She also knew her heart too well when it came to Judd; kissing and holding, especially in this charged atmosphere, would go way beyond kisses and touches.

And then there were her own reactions to him, a sense of false hope that she might mean something to him. She didn't, and tonight, of all nights, she didn't want to be reminded that anything personal between them meant nothing to him. For certain, she didn't want to be left wondering how to act the next morning.

She cleared her throat. "Does that mean you think I want you to kiss me or are you saying you'll stop when I say so?"

Judd slowly swung his legs to the floor and stood. His jeans rode low and snugged his body so sexily, Adrienne felt her mouth go dry. From her dresser, he pulled one of her neckties. She watched him drape it around his neck as he moved closer to her.

"Judd..." She licked her lips to ease the dryness. When he touched her throat and then curled his hand around the back of her neck, a distinct shiver went through her.

"I want you, Adrienne.... I want you more than I want my next breath."

Frantically, she tried to get her emotions in perspective. "Maybe it's not a good idea," she said weakly, her eyes sliding closed when he kissed the side of her neck. His hands coasted up high on her thighs, beneath the sleep shirt, taking the garment with them.

"It's the best idea I've had in a year." He lifted his mouth long enough to pull the garment up over her head and toss it aside.

Before she could object, he circled the tie around her neck, and holding the ends, he tugged her against him, taking her mouth in one continuous motion.

Adrienne touched his waist, her fingers brushing the snug denim, making him groan and deepen the kiss.

She couldn't get close enough. Then, as if some pent-up accumulation of response had been suddenly let loose, she felt those words that had stayed so carefully hidden bubble to the surface. How she wanted to say I love you, how she wanted to pour out her heart, how she wanted him to know that she felt as if she'd loved him forever. She'd carefully concealed them for so long, she couldn't even be sure if her feelings and the words connected to them were true or just a trumped-up fantasy.

What was so confusing for Adrienne was where to go with her emotions. She knew he didn't reciprocate them. Oh, that one night had been sensational and spectacularly fulfilling for her, but in the end it had turned out be a one-night love. And as much as she treasured the memory of it, she knew better than to look for anything more from Judd than what she got. Sex.

And now this... Maybe it was the same thing for him, but for her, now, it was as it had been a year ago....

Then his hands slid around her neck and she realized he was pulling back and fiddling with the tie.

She took an unsteady breath. "Just a minute ago, you said..."

He went through the process of knotting the tie and then smoothing the ends down between her breasts. He leaned back and grinned. "Now, this kind of professional look has lots of possibilities, Ms. Trudell."

She raised an eyebrow and deliberately touched the front of his jeans. "And you look too damn good in these, Detective Dillon."

"Guess we make a perfect match."

This time, he lifted her into his arms and carried her into his room and to his bed.

Chapter 12

Judd kissed her neck, her ear and then opened his mouth hungrily over hers. Her hands slid into his hair, holding him as if he might suddenly change his mind. Beside his bed, he lowered her to the floor where the back of her knees hit the mattress edge. He yanked the covers back, then laid her down. Her damp hair clung to her cheeks, her eyes were luminous.

"I thought we promised ourselves we wouldn't get involved," she said, but with little intent of resisting or even questioning.

"Guess we lied to each other." Judd's breathing wasn't just erratic. He felt as if some inner demon of reckoning was clawing at the marrow in his bones.

She ran her hand down his jeaned thigh and back up the inside seam. Softly, as if it were only a passing observation, she murmured, "At least this time, I know you won't run out on me in the morning."

He flinched, still far too aware of his behavior that night. By any standard, Adrienne should despise him. She brushed her fist across his flat stomach and then tucked her fingers behind the closure button on his jeans. Her knuckles burned into his belly, shooting the fire low.

Swearing, he muttered, "Keep that up, angel, and I won't be able to walk in the morning."

She grinned and Judd read the sweep of pleasure in her eyes.

"You'd love that, huh?" he asked.

"I have to admit, it's a powerful thought. The cool, heartless Detective Judd Dillon overcome by a woman."

"It's you in that tie." Again he smoothed the narrow edges of the silky material across her breasts. When she closed her eyes and sucked in her breath, a new spiral of heat tore through him.

He then gripped her wrist as her fingers wandered lower. Judd knew he wasn't just hard, he was in pain. Not a pleasant state of arousal—too deep and consuming and one he'd never come close to reaching with any woman but Adrienne.

Diana had been very good in bed, yet he'd always kept himself on an automatic restraint. Nothing substantial he could point to or even explain, but a part of him had always held back, had always been fearful he might shock her. Some sense that certain things were off-limits, not what a lady should do or would want to do. Not the kinky stuff like whips and chains, but explored enjoyment rather than embarrassed refusal. Once or twice, he'd tried with Diana, but she'd shrank from him as if she suspected he'd been practicing the art of erotic seduction in his spare time.

Glancing now at Adrienne, he felt a keen sense of profound need. Her allowing him to knot the tie, her mouth slightly swollen, while knowing he was deliberately turning professionalism between them as upside down as when he'd tossed her over his shoulder, her obvious turn-on to his wearing the snug jeans and the wideness of her eyes when he'd come off that bed, showed him her desire for him was candid and sincere.

It was an extraordinary revelation to him of what the potential between them was. Somehow, she'd become the ideal fantasy.

Wanton and yet not jaded.

Wanting and not afraid to say so.

Willing and yet still a little stunned by her own boldness.

A helluva combination, he concluded, drawing her against him and closing his eyes. It was as if something about her reached inside him, seized him and locked itself on like some long-missing piece.

In a low voice, he said, "Wanting you shouldn't make me feel so desperate." At her rather curious expression, he added, "As if no matter how much I have, it won't be enough."

She swallowed, stunned by the thick desire in his voice. He started to pull away, to shed his jeans, when she stopped him. "No, wait. I want to look at you..." She paused, then in a very low whisper so loaded with meaning, Judd clenched his teeth. "Oh, Judd, I want to touch you and kiss you..."

"No damn wonder I can't forget...no damn wonder," he muttered more to himself than to Adrienne.

She sat up, scooting to the side of the bed, sitting with her legs apart. Then she pulled him so that he stood between her thighs, his body lean and tight as it loomed over her. His hands slid into her hair and he tipped her head back. He bent his head, kissing her once, twice and the third time taking her mouth deeply. She flung her arms up and around his neck.

Judd considered all that he had done, was doing this very moment, and where he was going with every action that involved Adrienne. Wanting her and fighting against that want had been an issue, a drive, an endless internal debate since he'd walked out of her bedroom a year ago.

If only everything began and ended with sex. And while he'd concluded that Adrienne hadn't taken him to her apartment that night with any expectation beyond experiencing a few pleasurable hours, that had been his initial reasoning tonight.

Waiting for her to finish her shower, he'd thought about his fierce reaction when he realized she'd gone to Lois's apartment. Fear of a botched-up case? Fear Adrienne might get hurt? Hell, maybe both. Maybe even what he suspected was the real culprit. Too many tense hours with her, of wanting her, of just being too damn worn-out by the fight to steer clear of any personal and sexual involvement.

He'd been aware from the moment she came out of the bathroom and eyed him with suspicion that his shift in mood had been abrupt. No longer could he deny that he wanted her. But he also knew Adrienne was too smart to fall for some seduction scenario.

Besides, he despised moves like those. They were calculated and usually proved little beyond an ability to turn someone on. No, he wanted her for a far simpler reason. Pleasure, yes. To ease the pain pounding like a jackhammer in his gut, definitely. However, beyond those very obvious ones, his reasons were more selfish.

He wanted to forget how terrified he was that she'd gone to Lois's apartment alone.

He wanted to forget how that terror had turned to relief that in turn had become fury when he saw that she was all right.

He wanted to forget even the remote possibility that something could have happened to her. That she had been hurt or kidnapped or even shot had filled him with a chilling panic. He'd felt protective, yes, but far beyond a cop with a civilian, beyond a man with a woman and even beyond a friend with a friend.

This was more intrinsically linked to some deep core inside him, something that rose within him and wanted to bind her to him, wrap her in a cocoon of safety. Judd didn't understand it, nor had he figured out why he was tossing away all his hard-won, hands-off approach when it came to Adrienne. But there was no question something had definitely shifted inside him.

Carrying her out of the apartment complex like a sack of potatoes had been a nice touch, he thought grimly. He just hoped all the posturing and positioning had convinced Hester and anyone else peering out from behind closed curtains, that he had very definite ideas on "his woman" and what she was allowed to do and not allowed to do.

Her hands had gotten his jeans opened and the zipper down. He reached down behind her and pressed his palm against her back, urging her forward so that the heart of her rested against his jeaned thigh. She wrapped her arms around his waist and rubbed her mouth against his belly, brushing it lower into the Y of his jeans until he got dizzy with the possibilities.

He groaned. "You're lethal, angel. Easy..."

Even as she kissed him, she moved the vee of her own body closer against his thigh, swaying slightly, just a little unsure and managing to send about four rockets off in his head. Within a few seconds, her hips picked up a natural rhythm that needed little encouragement.

"Oh, man..." He held her against him, his back breaking out in a sweat. "Yeah, just like that..."

She mewed, her breathing catching and stopping for a few seconds. In a tiny gasp the words spilled, "I have to stop or..."

"Don't stop. Shh, I want you to. I want to feel it...see it..." He moved her body into a quicker, more intense pace against his thigh so that she trembled and he felt her first ripple of pleasure.

"Oh..." Her fingers dug into his flesh and he knew she'd leave marks. He lifted her higher so that the very heart of her was pressed into him in a rubbing motion. "Judd..." She tried to pull back, but he wouldn't allow her to give up the sliding rhythm. "This is wicked—"

"No such thing, angel." He tugged her tight and felt her body react automatically. "You're almost there..."

She stiffened again, then her back arched and her eyes squeezed closed. Standing above her allowed him to watch her spiral up and then go totally still, leaving only the flush in her face and the tantalizing smile of satisfaction. As the shudders lessened, she sagged against him, her chin burrowed into his chest.

He massaged his fingers on the back of her neck, feeling a drench of pleasure within himself at her release. He held her against him for a few minutes, his fingers his only motion. His own body was so wired, he needed a few seconds to get a hold on himself.

The next thing he felt was her mouth, the warmth of a very wet kiss and a nip at his skin.

In a muffled voice, she whispered, "You want me," in such a pleasured voice, he grinned.

"Nah, I never get turned on by a woman doing what you just did."

"That happened the last time, remember."

"Yeah. In the car. Before we even left the restaurant."

"It was all your fault, you know. All that suggestive talk about what you wanted."

"Sex talk."

"Just the same, afterward, I was very embarrassed."

"You were great then and even better a few minutes ago."

She kissed him, once, twice and then tipped her head back to stare up at him. Judd traced the moisture on her mouth with his finger.

Kissing the pad, she whispered, "We made love four times that night."

"You've got a good memory."

"Yes."

"So let's make a few new ones tonight."

She studied him, her blue eyes deep and misty. Slowly, her gaze never leaving his face, she lowered his zipper the rest of the way. Then as she pushed at his jeans, he took both her wrists and pulled them away and settled them so that her hands were at her sides.

He stepped back, got rid of the jeans and retrieved the box of condoms.

She looked at the box, a tiny grin playing at the corner of her mouth. "Don't tell me they were giving away free condoms with the pizza? Or was it with the beer?"

"If I told you I brought them with me, would it matter?"

She blinked, the question unexpected and, knowing how fiercely Judd had not wanted any involvement, a definite contradiction. "If I say it matters, does that mean we have another fight and don't make love?"

He chuckled. "Don't credit me with that much willpower." In a thoughtful tone, he added, "Then again, if it doesn't matter to you why I have them, I might think you were hoping I would lure you into bed."

She studied him, realizing with some astonishment that she had indeed wanted him to lure her into bed. She'd wanted that for a long time, despite all the reasons that it was not a smart idea. "Hmm, neither of us look good either way."

"Good isn't what I want from you."

She pursed her lips as he settled down beside her and then lifted her so that she sat astride him.

She sucked in her breath as he slid deep inside of her. "Why do I have the feeling your having them has nothing to do with me."

"Jealous?"

"How could I be jealous? I have no strings on you," she said breezily. "We don't even like each other, remember?"

He peered at her, at the position of their bodies and the fact that he was sweetly buried inside of her. "Just uncontrolled, unbridled lust, huh?"

"Well, maybe a little more than that. I do sorta like you...sometimes." She gathered fistfuls of the hair on his chest and tugged gently. "But I don't like you when you're heaving me over your shoulder."

"I'll try to keep my barbarism under better control," he said sagely. He cupped her breasts and drew her down so that he could kiss each tip. She gasped at the tightening sensation and he blew softly across each nipple before taking each into his mouth and savoring the texture and the taste. He slipped his hands down her sides to her hips.

She tossed her head back and took a sharp breath.

Judd held her steady against him, his body swelled tight and threatening to burst inside of her, bringing her up and then down. Up and then down...

She shivered, her fingers digging into his belly. Never had she felt such intense pleasure, a bounty of sensations pouring as though from an endless supply of bliss.

Oh, God, if only she could let go of all her reservations about Judd, let go of her fear that if he knew what she felt for him was more than sexual, he would totally reject her. She wished she could take what was offered and not want more. Her mother had done that and Adrienne had always been so critical, so determined to hold on to some idealistic view of what men and women should feel with each other.

Sex without love, without commitment seemed so self-centered and so reckless, but in some ways it was certainly safer for the heart. Perhaps that had been her mother's choice; maybe she had only wanted to protect her own heart. Since Adrienne had striven to do the same thing by staying uninvolved with Judd or any man, she could hardly sit in judgment on her own mother for choosing a different method.

In a fierce resolve to enjoy and forget the pain that would inevitably follow once they were home, she tossed her head back and clutched him to her with a sweet tightness. Her body arched as once again she felt the swelling climb to satisfaction.

Judd hauled her down and rolled her to her back in such a smooth motion that she forgot to breathe. The walls of her body closed around his and he groaned from the slick heat of her. Adrienne gasped as channels of fulfillment opened inside of her. Judd buried his mouth in her neck as his body exploded in the mindless pleasure of replete gratification.

For many minutes, they lay still. Judd sprawled on top of her, Adrienne clutching at him, her arms feeling heavy, her body satiated. She kissed his shoulder and he muttered something she didn't hear. She smiled to herself, unable to stop the torrent of thoughts that raced through her.

Right this moment, she was totally happy. Content in a way she'd never been in any other facet of her life, whether it be work or fun or just a well-deserved lazy day off. In many ways, it was the same feeling she'd had after that night a year ago; a sense that being with Judd was where she needed to be, where her heart yearned to rest, and yet, she knew he didn't feel or want lofty thoughts and a tied-down relationship.

Sighing at the new pain that left her feeling suddenly leery and ashen, she confronted the cruelness of being with him. Why, oh why, had she been unable to forget a man who wanted nothing more than a night in bed? And how could fate throw them together so that once more she would be left with a shattered heart and an empty place inside of her?

To her horror, she felt a sheen of tears and damned such a showy reaction. Tears were for babies and immature females who viewed their own wants and needs about a relationship as the key to happiness ever after. Some key, she thought wistfully. All she'd found was how fraudulent happiness was—fleeting, encapsulated in a few moments of very good lovemaking and then, like the early-morning dew, it was gone and soon forgotten.

Grow up, she told herself tersely. Isn't that what her mother had always told her? Don't allow yourself to get hurt. Face life as it is, not what you wish it could be. Happiness and love are frauds dressed up to entice and lure and then leave a woman empty and cold. Such a cynical philosophy, Adrienne thought. Yet she knew her mother believed it and perhaps for her, it had been safe and comfortable. Adrienne couldn't envision herself taking the same approach as her mother, but she knew that there would never be another man in her life that she would love as she loved Judd Dillon.

She'd always wanted to believe in a perfect, unrestricted love between a man and a woman. Her problem was wanting it with a man who didn't want it with her. She knew he'd

adored Diana and never had he given Adrienne any reason
to believe he was seriously interested in her.

Oh, she knew he tolerated her, maybe even on occasion
desired her and just maybe their sexual attraction was
stronger than most, but then what? A long string of nights
spent in sexual exhaustion?

She pushed her questions aside and decided that spoiling
the hours she did have would make things doubly painful.
Judd muttered something and eased himself off of her.
Propping himself up beside her, he brushed a strand of hair
from her cheek.

"You okay?"

She was glad for the shadows. "Sure."

He cupped her cheek and turned her face so he could see
her. Studying her, he asked, "If I hurt you..."

She shook her head fiercely.

He slipped his hand down her body, between her thighs,
watching her for any reaction. Instead of a wince, she sighed
and curled around him. Judd felt a huge roll of content-
ment at her response. He lowered his head and kissed her.
"You really liked it, didn't you?"

"You're very good."

"You were sensational."

She squeezed her eyes closed and before he had a chance
to say anything, she flung her arms around his neck and
buried her face in his chest. *I love you,* her heart screamed.
*I love you so much and I don't know how to make you love
me back.*

Twenty minutes later, they were eating cold pizza and
going through the papers Judd had gotten from Litchfield.
He'd already told her about the chief faxing the file on Lois
to the Louiston police. Adrienne had pulled her sleep shirt

on, but hadn't removed the tie. Judd wore his jeans, zipped, but unbuttoned.

"Is that beer cold yet?" she asked.

He'd gotten a bucket of ice from a machine near the motel office and the cans were now buried in the melting liquid.

"Probably." He pulled one out, felt it and then popped the top, handing it to her. "I read through these papers while you were in the shower earlier, so let me give you the condensed version."

"I have some things to tell you, too." Her eyes were as eager as her voice.

"Let's do these first."

Adrienne nodded, sipped the beer and listened.

"From what's here—by the way, some of this info came from Child-Aid. Evelyn coordinated with Litchfield."

"Proving that we have a valid role in the police department."

"You never had an argument from me on that."

Adrienne's eyes widened. "When we first moved our offices in there, I heard you were furious."

"Not at Child-Aid's being there. At having to see you every day."

"And you think it was easy for me?"

"It wasn't a personal dislike, Adrienne. But getting sexually involved—"

"Yes, I know," she said, thinking of how involved they'd just been. Even as wonderful as it had been, despite the softness, the teasing, the smoldering looks, what they had together meant nothing to him. "You would have found it too difficult to maintain that heartless cold demeanor you're so famous for."

"It's safer for all involved."

"Sanitized words, Judd. You made it quite clear what your feelings about me were and I felt the same way about you."

He studied her a moment, watching the askew necktie, trying to keep at bay the desire to reach out and drag her across his lap. "This case has thrown that resolve all to hell."

"I'm sure we'll have no trouble avoiding each other in the future," she said stiffly, making herself look at him and not flinch from the new pain that tore through her. Keeping her guard up with Judd always seemed to be a necessary defense. The alternative was unending emotional pain.

She shifted, putting her unfinished pizza aside. Her appetite was gone. She should also get off the bed, get some clothes on and start acting like the professional she was supposed to be. They were here to find Lois Greeley and get Caleb back safely. Rolling around in some provocative and carnal activity would only make being together at the office far more tense and difficult.

She took a deep breath and tried her best to appear unmoved and unaffected by all that had happened personally between them.

"Let's get back to Lois," he said gruffly.

His body was tense, his eyes dark and she noticed the hardness of his jaw. Perhaps it was just as well that he was annoyed. It would make walking away much easier for her. "And Lois is why we're here."

"Yeah." Without looking at her, he spread the pages out and scanned them for a few seconds as if searching for relevant information. Finally, he pulled out a few of the pages. "Here we go. Lois is single, never married, late-thirties, does volunteer work and—" he glanced at Adrienne "—she's had a major problem involving a kid in the past."

"You mean she has a record?"

"She was arrested for taking a kid she was baby-sitting. Lois had the idea that she would be a better mother than the kid's own mother. It seems she'd had a lot of miscarriages and could never have kids. According to a court-ordered psychiatric test, she felt inadequate and useless. Having a child became an obsession."

"Was this before she took the child she was baby-sitting or afterward?"

"Sorry, I'm trying to fill you in on the background at the same time. No, the test was given after she kidnapped the kid. This is what happened with that. Apparently, the parents of this kid worked and were having a hard time with bills and juggling jobs and family time. Lois lived in a nearby apartment and volunteered to baby-sit. What they didn't know was that Lois had suffered her fourth miscarriage at about the same time their kid was born. Lois convinced herself that the mother didn't really deserve her baby because the woman worked. So Lois devised a plan to first gain the parents' trust, then take the kid and run away. She planned to be the mother, and in another town no one would be the wiser. The boy was about eight months old and Lois had been taking care of him for about three months before she actually abducted him."

"So how did they find her?"

"Real lucky. The father had forgotten something and came home within an hour of Lois leaving. Ordinarily, he would have thought she'd simply taken his son for a ride in the stroller, but the baby had just gotten over a cold and they'd told Lois specifically not to take him outdoors. Then a neighbor saw Lois with the infant and said she was struck by the fact that Lois was carrying a stuffed diaper bag. Fortunately, the father called the cops and they found Lois a few hours later."

"Thank God. I bet the parents were frantic."

Judd stretched out his legs and crossed his ankles. "Like the Whitewells."

"What about why she did it?" Adrienne asked. "I mean, Lois's thinking she could be a better mother might not be so odd on the face of it, but most women wouldn't go so far as to kidnap another woman's child. Besides, it sounds more like the mother and father were stressed-out and over-whelmed rather than bad parents."

"Probably the reason they jumped at Lois's offer to baby-sit."

"How long ago was this?"

"About four years ago. Nothing since. At least nothing she was arrested for. The judge put her on probation and ordered counseling. A year later, she moved East."

"East being here in Louiston."

Judd nodded, a frown creasing his face. "And that puzzles me. Why here? Why not Kentucky or Arizona or Maine? Why Rhode Island?"

"A job offer? Maybe she lived here once before and liked it? Maybe she wanted to make a fresh start where no one knew her? What about family? Maybe she has family here."

"Lots of questions, but an even bigger one is why Seapoint Hospital and why the Whitewell baby? It's too specific to be just a coincidence."

Adrienne caught her breath. "Judd, there was a photo on the bulletin board in Lois's kitchen. It was of Lois and two other women. They were seated at a table as if they were at some celebration. You know the kind, where a photographer gets a few people together for a group picture."

"What are you getting at?"

"This is all your fault, you know. If you hadn't acted like some Neanderthal and if we hadn't made love, I might have thought of this sooner. When I saw the picture, something struck me as familiar but I couldn't place it. When you were shuffling those papers, it came to me. When they did all the hospital renovations, the staff dining room was one of the rooms that was remodeled. It's been over a year and I'd forgotten what the old one looked like."

Judd gave her a direct look. "What are you talking about?"

"The photo of Lois and her two friends... The one I saw at her apartment. It was taken in the Seapoint Hospital staff dining room before the remodeling. The only people that eat in there are hospital staff and hospital volunteers."

Judd scowled and then closed his eyes as if something had fallen into place. Then he went through the papers again. "I know I saw something here," he muttered.

Adrienne drew closer. "Yes, you did say something about her doing volunteer work."

"Here it is. Adrienne, you are definitely an angel." He leaned over and kissed her hard. "Remind me to apologize for all the grief I gave you for going into Lois's apartment. She never worked at Seapoint as an employee. That's why her name never showed up on the lists Fairfax gave us. She was a volunteer. That's handled by the hospital auxiliary. That's where her name would have been."

Before she could respond, he was off the bed in one fell swoop and reaching for the telephone. He had the receiver in his hand and was punching out the numbers when he swore again and dropped it back on its cradle. "Damn, I forgot, she's not home."

Adrienne grabbed his arm. "Who's not home?"

But instead of answering her, he once again picked up the receiver and punched out an obviously memorized number.

"Who are you calling? Judd, it's one in the morning."

"My old man."

She blinked. "Your father? But why?"

"Because Mom is on one of her bridge club vacations in Vegas, I think, and I need to get her number."

"Wait a minute. Back up."

He slung an arm around Adrienne's neck and kissed her deeply. While the phone rang, he said, "Mom heads up the volunteer program for the auxiliary. She took it over a few years ago. She would know what happened with Lois."

"Oh." Everything was suddenly happening so fast, Adrienne felt as if she were playing catch-up.

"Dad? Yeah, it's me. I know what time it is, but I need a number where I can reach Mom." He waited a few seconds while Bart Dillon swore and grumbled about people who worked ungodly hours and expected the rest of the world to work by their timetable. "Okay, shoot." Judd scribbled down a number. "Thanks. I know the manager there, so this may be easier than I thought. Oh, and before I let you go back to sleep, have you heard from Hunt? Last time we talked, he didn't sound so good." He listened a few seconds, obviously disturbed. "Nothing, huh? Look, when I get done with this case... Yeah, I know, he doesn't want us worrying about him...."

Adrienne touched Judd's back and felt a wall of tightness. She really didn't know enough about the Dillons to be asking a lot of questions, but anyone watching the range of reaction in Judd whenever he talked about his older brother would notice his distress and concern.

Judd tightened his hold on her as if she might pull away. To his father, he said, "Someone called you about buying my house? You know it's not for sale. Tell them—" He cut off his words. "Look, I've already got too much to think about. I'll call you when I'm back in Seapoint. And Dad, sorry about waking you, but thanks for the number." He got the dial tone again and punched out the long-distance number.

After working his way through a number of the casino workers, he got the manager's office. After a few pleasantries were exchanged, Judd told him who he wanted and that it was an emergency. He left the number and the manager promised to locate Judd's mother, but said it might take a while. Judd thanked him and dropped the receiver onto the cradle.

Then he lifted Adrienne in his arms and swung her around in a wide circle. "Let's go to bed."

"What?" Incredulous at all these sudden mood shifts, she was beginning to wonder if Judd did this to throw her off guard or if it was his way of not having to think too hard about what he was doing.

"Mom's in Vegas doin' the slots. By the time Rocky finds her and she calls me back, at least an hour will have passed."

"So you want to have sex while we wait?"

"Better than cold pizza."

"Judd Dillon, I—"

But he covered her mouth with his and slid his hands under her sleep shirt, finding her warmth and a moisture that made him grin.

He lifted his mouth so that their lips were barely touching. "Tell me no," he whispered, while his hand stroked her inner thighs. "What I'm feeling is sure sayin' yes."

Refusing to just sink into the incredible pleasure his hand was creating, she said, "You're a bastard."

"And horny, like you."

She made a weak attempt to get free. "Forget the sex talk, Detective Dillon. This time—" He leaned down and whispered what he wanted to give her in very specific and very erotic words. Adrienne closed her eyes and her earlier objections collapsed.

He chuckled as he drew her against him.

"I fully intend to start hating you again when I get back to Seapoint."

"Hmm..." He nuzzled her neck. "Right now, you can want me, angel, the way I want you."

On the bed, he dispensed with his jeans and not until he was deep inside of her and her legs were wrapped around his hips and her pleasure mounting, did she remember that the condoms were in the other room.

Her good sense was falling under the rising tide of sensation between their bodies. She should stop him. She should push him away. But instead, she pulled him deeper and his groan of satisfaction when he climaxed filled her ears and her heart.

Chapter 13

"Costume jewelry on Lois's dresser? So what?"

"Don't you remember she wore that garish ring?"

"Oh, yeah," he said flatly. "Tanya mentioned it was the color of blood."

"I know her owning costume jewelry doesn't mean anything by itself, but it's one more reason to support our belief that Lois Greeley is the woman we want." Adrienne studied him, he was a bit rumpled, a little grumpy and despite the pleasure they'd shared just hours ago, she guessed he didn't like revealing any need for her. "I'm surprised you didn't remember Tanya's comment immediately. I recall you were rather stunned by it at the hospital."

"My memory lapse is probably because I don't do sex on most investigations."

"Gee, does this mean I might have distracted you, Detective Dillon?"

"Ms. Trudell, you've been a helluva lot more than a mere distraction."

She clasped her hand to her heart and pretended to swoon. "Oh, my, a real honest-to-goodness compliment. I may never be the same."

He scowled. "Try and enjoy yourself."

She made herself not laugh, but she couldn't suppress the grin. It wasn't that she wanted to make light of his obvious irritation with her and with himself—then again, she realized suddenly, maybe she did want to be frivolous.

Maybe blitheness was the best way to handle her feelings, the best way to keep them from spilling into tears and distress. Being upbeat and unconcerned was a shield against showing her true emotions. And it was certainly a lot safer for her heart.

Leaning forward and giving him her most sincere look, she said, "I'm sorry. I'll be good. I promise."

It was close to nine in the morning and they'd gone to breakfast at the small restaurant attached to the motel. The food wasn't bad, although Adrienne had to admit it didn't come close to Macko's Diner either in quality or generous servings.

They'd made love again after Judd talked to his mother and learned that yes, Lois had been a volunteer at Seapoint Hospital and that she'd been dismissed when Corrine Dillon had learned Lois had stolen items from the maternity inventory room—namely, the newborn packets.

She hadn't reported Lois because the woman was so distraught and ashamed that Corrine thought that getting caught and then dismissed had been enough of a punishment. Privately, his mother admitted, she'd also feared a theft would give the spotless volunteer program a stain they wouldn't be able to escape.

Judd, to Adrienne's surprise, hadn't been overly upset that his mother hadn't reported the theft. When Adrienne questioned his stoic reaction, he simply said his mother had always practiced the sometimes sticky approach of offering a second chance to someone who showed genuine remorse.

Now Judd pushed aside his partially eaten plate of bacon and scrambled eggs and refilled their coffee mugs from the pot that had been put on the table. He'd been annoyingly silent about what he'd planned as his next move in locating Lois. She had noted a particular preoccupation with Lois's apartment building across the way as if he was expecting something to happen imminently.

In fact, he'd even chosen their seats for breakfast so that he could watch the building for any movement. She couldn't help wondering if he had a hunch he wasn't ready to verbalize or if he was just making sure nothing in his observation of the building was overlooked.

In an almost too-casual tone, he said, "You know, if Mom had been in Seapoint when Lois kidnapped the Whitewell baby, you and I wouldn't be here."

Obvious in his comment was that they wouldn't have made love or faced any temptation with each other.

Adrienne said, "You mean, she would have seen the sketch and called you."

"Yeah."

Both were quiet for a few moments, as if considering how Corrine Dillon's vacation and consequently her absence from any of the local news might forever have altered many lives. Certainly those directly connected to the case—the Whitewells and their baby, Lois Greeley, if, God forbid, her plan succeeded.

But Adrienne also recognized the effect on her and Judd. They'd gone from each barely acknowledging that the other existed less than a week ago to a profound intimacy that made Adrienne flush at the memories of her own boldness.

Without realizing it, Adrienne shifted slightly in her seat.

Judd stared at her. "Sore?"

"A little." She met his gaze.

But he didn't apologize, and what struck Adrienne suddenly was that he didn't have to. She saw the pain in his eyes, but what she didn't know was whether he truly regretted that they'd made love or just that they'd done it too much. Maybe both, but she lacked either the courage or the desire to ask.

She wanted to treasure those moments and the fantasy that surrounded them for a little while longer. Reality would return soon enough. At least this time she was prepared for the emptiness and loneliness.

This time she would handle it better.

This time she was fully aware of Judd's next move and wouldn't be blinded by idealistic hopes of a relationship.

This time she was reconciled to no future with him.

He glanced out the window, narrowing his eyes, then glanced back at her, the silence soughing between them. "Okay, so what do we have so far? Lois was a volunteer at Seapoint Hospital as recently as a year ago. She closely resembles the police sketch of the woman who took Caleb. She can't have kids, so we know the pregnancy was a fake."

"That in itself makes her a strong suspect. Why would a woman fake a pregnancy unless she'd planned to do this?"

"Definitely premeditated," Judd commented. "We know she likes costume jewelry and that she's a thief. I saw the crib in the bedroom when I came looking for you and there was a blue rattle on the kitchen table, just like the one in the newborn packets."

Adrienne grinned, more than pleased with what they'd both learned. "We really have a lot of pieces, don't we?"

"Still, the key is missing. Why did she take this particular baby at this particular time. So far, as we've learned, and from the questioning of the Whitewells, there isn't a direct connection."

"Lois is obviously not stable. Maybe her reason doesn't fit into an obvious pattern."

Judd's eyes darkened. "Go on."

"Well, doing specialized work with Child-Aid has shown me that quite often the motives for someone's taking children without permission aren't always plausible or reasonable to the objective observer. I worked on a case where a father kidnapped his daughter and left his son behind. We puzzled over that because the mother said that he'd never shown partiality."

"Until the abduction."

"Yes, later we learned that he took his daughter because he wanted a say in the boys she dated when she grew up. Apparently, the father had a sister who had gotten into all kinds of trouble when she was a kid. He said it was because his sister had had no father to prevent her from dating losers."

"That seems a little simplistic. In fact, you're a good example of just the opposite."

"Me?"

"You grew up without a father—"

"But, in my case, my mother..." Her voice trailed off and she stared at the table. Clearing her throat, she added, "I was going to say that she set a bad example, but now I think she handled her life as best she could."

Judd was silent. He turned his mug around and around as if contemplating how much to say. "I've always thought you were too tough on your mother."

"I have been tough and I can't say that I approve of how she's handled her relationships, but, she is the only mother I have. Hearing you on the phone with your mom, it sort of made me envious."

He nodded. "Yeah, sometimes you have to consider the pluses. For example, did she leave a string of kids behind by all these men?"

"No. I'm her only child."

"And did she flaunt her sexual habits in front of you?" She shook her head.

"And hasn't she always been supportive of you whenever you made a decision?"

Adrienne nodded slowly, feeling increasingly sheepish. "You make it sound as if I've always been wrong to be critical of her."

"Maybe you should just be less critical. Parents make mistakes and having their kids hold it over their heads as if proclaiming themselves judge and jury only severs the relationship. Most parents aren't perfect, but if they love their kids, despite all the flaws, they should be spared all the moralizing and second-guessing."

He paused a moment and Adrienne swallowed hard. She didn't disagree with what he said and in fact, she more than conceded he was right. As if his words had given her some new insight, she made a vow to call her mother when she got home and get some things settled. And she wanted to offer an apology for being such a critic and judge. Her attitude certainly hadn't helped their relationship, it had made it more stressful.

But what else was going on with Judd? she wondered. He was rarely this talkative and the obvious deeply felt passion in his voice made her wonder who was talking, the cop who'd seen too much disaster or the father who had lost his own son and no longer had the highs and lows of child-raising.

Watching him and not missing that he was no longer relaxed, she said, "You're not just talking about me, are you?"

Sighing, he shook his head. "Don't ask me why I'm telling you this, because I don't know why."

"How about because we're friends?"

"Yeah, maybe. I sure in hell hope that's all it is."

Adrienne frowned at the odd comment, but wisely said nothing.

After drawing a long breath as if it took a lot of courage to do so, Judd said, "I have another brother besides Hunt. His name is Crew Sabin."

Adrienne recalled his saying something about a younger brother a few days ago and she'd been puzzled and curious. "I didn't know."

"No one does. A woman my father had an affair with about thirty years ago had his kid. Dad never told anyone, but he sent money to the woman and made sure the kid was taken care of. The woman died a few years ago and the old man's bastard son paid Dad a visit."

Adrienne stared in astonishment. Bart Dillon owned Dillon Construction, a very successful business that employed a lot of Seapoint residents. Judd's father had been a model for anyone who started out with little money but a lot of ambition and the drive to succeed. Despite his wealth, Bart had never lost his gruffness or acquired a totally nonmacho approach to women. Adrienne found it plausible that he'd been involved with another woman, while at the same time she knew he was a devoted husband to Corrine and good father to his boys. She wasn't sure just how his having an affair and being a family man blended, but with Bart Dillon they did.

To Judd, she asked, "Was it blackmail?"

"Hell, that would have been easy. No, just the opposite. Instead of wanting money, he wants no part of it. Crew flung a huge sum at Dad. About a quarter of what Dad had been sending to support Crew and his mother. Then Crew swore he'd pay back the rest if it killed him. Dad tried to reason with him, but Crew wanted nothing to do with him. I walked into Dad's office at about the time Crew was leaving. I really felt sorry for Dad, but Crew was a sight to see. Hard and angry and bitter. From what Dad told me later about Crew's mother, I think she would have been devastated at Crew's actions.''

Adrienne reached across the table and folded her fingers around Judd's wrist. "I'm surprised you told me all this."

He stared down at her hand as if he, too, was surprised by his candor. "Yeah, me, too."

"Does your mother know?"

"I don't know. She's never given any indication she does, but then, she'd be more inclined to find a way to give Dad the benefit of the doubt."

"The second chance, as she gave Lois?"

"Yeah."

"How do you and Hunt feel about Crew?"

"Hunt has never met him, but I like the kid. He's hotheaded and sometimes seemingly without conscience when it comes to taking on anything that will earn him big money. He's obsessed with paying back every dime to Dad."

"I assume from the way you told me all this that you and Hunt aren't resentful of your dad for his having been involved with another woman."

Judd shrugged. "It was a long time ago. The really odd thing is that I think Dad would like to acknowledge Crew, but Crew is so bitter and resentful that the likelihood of that happening is remote."

Adrienne sat back and gave him a quizzical look. "Is your intent to compare Crew's anger at your father with my feelings toward my mother?"

"No, but I guess I see similarities. Parental ties are strong and evoke strong emotions. I know how I felt when I lost my family. And I saw that terror in both Tanya and Ronnie over their missing son."

Judd's sudden candor was too curious to ignore. He rarely talked about himself and was usually so focused on his work that this side trip about another brother was more than just a chance conversation.

She had also noticed his too-often glances in the direction of Lois's apartment. Something was definitely going on.

Then in a nonchalant voice, she commented, "You know, I feel as if I'm in some role reversal with you. You're the one who is so careful about never revealing yourself. The cop with no heart. Now, here you are using your own awkward family situation to make a point about me becoming more tolerant of my own mother."

"At least you owe her the benefit of the doubt. No one says you have to approve of or even like her life-style and her choices, but getting beyond that to accepting her for who she is rather than what she's done would bind rather than sever your relationship. And in a curious way, your mother and all her boyfriends had a positive effect on you. Diana told me that when you two were in college, you were so careful about who you went out with that a lot of the guys felt as if they had to meet some impossible standard."

She nodded, recalling how her friends had teased her. "I was just very careful. Even after graduation and after I started with Child-Aid, I couldn't just shun the cautiousness. By that time, it was probably entrenched."

"Which makes me very curious," he admitted. "Curious as to why you weren't cautious that night in the restaurant with me."

"I guess because I knew and trusted you."

"Sounds a little flimsy."

"It was a year ago," she said firmly as if knowledge and trust could be bracketed in time slots. "Besides, it was probably the result of a lot of sexual chemistry, the close dancing, the drinks we had. All those things can destroy inhibitions."

"Hmm. And what about a few hours ago?"

She stiffened. "I haven't asked you a lot of questions about why you wanted me. I certainly don't intend to explain my, uh, feel—my actions with you."

Judd watched her intensely and she held his gaze for long straining moments. The clatter in the restaurant faded away. The morning traffic crawled by as the street leading out of town filled with cars headed to the South County beaches.

"I think we've gotten away from the real issue."

"Or was that your intent? Keep us here talking about anything, even personal stuff, while you wait to make your next move?" She glared at him, not at all sure she wasn't being used. "You're generally not so open about yourself, Judd, so please don't insult my intelligence by saying you've suddenly turned over a new leaf."

He closed his eyes for a moment. "All right, I admit I was stalling for time."

"And keeping me in the dark as to why? Damn you!" She slid from the booth and stood. Disappointment overwhelmed her. She'd thought their relationship had progressed and it hadn't. "Nothing has changed as far as our working together, has it? You still view me as out of my element and nothing I do will change that opinion."

In a clipped voice, he snapped, "There's plenty of time later to chew me out."

"There isn't enough time in a millennium to chew you out, Detective Dillon."

"Yeah," he muttered. "Probably not." But if she was looking for any warmth in his voice, or softness in his face, she didn't find it. "Lois and our next move. Can we get back to that?"

"After you answer one question. Why do you keep staring at Lois's apartment?"

He shoved a hand through his hair. "Hester went out earlier while you were getting dressed. I wanted to make sure I saw her come back. The restaurant gives the most unobtrusive view of the building, besides the motel room. For reasons we both know, the restaurant is safer for us."

Adrienne couldn't argue with that. "Why didn't you just tell me that?"

"Because it's important that we appear casual. And after last night, we've raised enough questions. We're going to have to move today. If it's not already too late."

Adrienne sat back down and gave him a stricken look. "Then you think because I went to Lois's apartment, I could have botched up this whole thing?"

"I think the suspicion level about us shot up at least fifty degrees. This neighborhood views any outsider as an intruder—"

"Oh, God."

"Don't fall apart on me now." Judd reached for her hand, but she pulled away.

"You blame me, don't you? If Lois has gone into hiding and we don't find Caleb, your hesitation at having to work with someone who isn't a cop will be proven correct." She made herself face that, but on the other hand, she wasn't doing this to prove anything about herself. She was here to find Caleb and if her pride or her self-image was wounded in the process, she would survive that.

To launch into some discussion of her qualifications, coupled with anger at Judd because he didn't immediately embrace them, wasn't very professional.

"Adrienne, I'm not blaming you. In fact, your visit to Lois's place got us some vital information. But you're also antsy and I was afraid if I told you we were going to just sit here and do nothing until Hester returned, you'd get so eager and jumpy—"

"That I'd blow it."

Judd didn't argue with her assessment. "The motel owner seems very curious about our relationship and since he's also right over there, I thought a rather dull and mundane breakfast would better suit our needs." He leaned back and studied her. "As to Lois and our next move... You said something that stuck in my mind."

"What?"

"That Lois faked the pregnancy because she had planned this. And since a pregnancy doesn't last just a few months, she would have had to plan for some time."

"You think there's significance to the fact that she stole a baby born in the Seapoint Hospital in August?"

"It would certainly provide some clues to a plausible motive." Judd took a last sip of his coffee. "Oh, and while you were in the shower this morning, I tried that number you wrote down from Lois's calendar."

"And?"

"No answer and no answering machine."

"Oh. So what's next?"

He glanced out the window for what must have been the twentieth time. "She just came home. So we go and shake Hester down."

"She wasn't all that interested in talking yesterday."

"She's our best hope, and I have a feeling she knows where Lois is."

"But why wouldn't she tell us? She doesn't know we're who we really are."

"She's suspicious of you," he said blandly.

"Me?"

"You finished eating?"

"Yes. She's suspicious of me because of last night? She said something to you, didn't she?"

Judd slid out of the booth and dumped some bills plus a generous tip on the table. He guided Adrienne out the door, his hand on the small of her back.

The hot August morning enveloped them. Adrienne had worn a white eyelet dress with cap sleeves and a scoop neckline. A red belt cinched her waist. It was too warm for nylons and heels so she'd opted for white sandals. Judd wore jeans and a dark lightweight sweatshirt with the sleeves pushed up. When she'd questioned him earlier about the shirt, he'd told her it was easier to hide a weapon with a loose-fitting shirt.

She squinted into the sun. "You didn't answer my question."

He peered off toward Lois's apartment. "The answer is yes, I'd love to take you back to the motel and let you kiss all the scratches you left on my back."

She crossed her arms. "Shall I tell you about the marks you left on me?"

"Where?"

She gave him a mercurial look, but truthfully she treasured each love bite, as well as the slight soreness from their intimacy. However, not about to give him any satisfaction, she stated emphatically, "You know damn well where they are."

He grinned and took her arm as they crossed the street and headed toward Hester's.

As they drew closer to the run-down building, Adrienne asked, "So what did she say to you?"

"She thinks you're a cop."

Astonished, Adrienne stopped and stared at him. "You're kidding. Did she say that outright?"

"Hardly, but your going into Lois's last night had her in quite a state when I got there. She was on the phone when I arrived. A call, I might add, that she hastily concluded when she saw me there. She was so rattled, she forgot to hold on to that floor-mop mutt of hers. The animal practically attacked me."

Adrienne grinned as they continued to walk toward the building. "Prissy probably thought you were an intruder."

"Yeah, sure. The mutt hates men."

"I'll go in first, Detective Dillon, and make sure the dog doesn't hurt you," Adrienne said in her most serious and sober voice.

"Very funny." But he stopped her before she opened the door. "We're going to have to admit to something beyond the ploy of old friends looking for Lois. I have a hunch about that number you found on Lois's calendar. If you can keep Hester busy..."

"Doing what?"

"I don't know. Make something up. You're into plants and she's got enough in there to supply a funeral."

"Is this like the deal at Opal's?"

"Yeah, but a helluva lot more is riding on it."

Moments later, a polyester-robed Hester cracked open her door. She blinked when she saw Judd and Adrienne. "Yeah? What do you want now?"

"Hester," Adrienne said in her most contrite voice, "we have to talk to you."

"I ain't got nothin' to say." At her feet, Prissy yipped and strained to get through Hester's legs. The woman tried to close the door and Adrienne burst into tears.

Judd said, "Come on, sweetheart, maybe Hester can't help us."

"But she's Lois's friend, so she has to know where she is." She turned her stricken gaze to Hester. "Please, you have to help us."

Hester looked from one to the other. "Who are you, anyway? And don't give me none of that bull 'bout bein' old friends lookin' to renew some moldy friendship."

"Can we come in?"

"Why?"

With one arm firmly around Adrienne, Judd said in a low voice, "Hester, Lois doesn't want anyone to know who she really is and for the past year we've honored that wish, but now she's gone too far."

Hester's eyes widened. Adrienne decided it had to be the woman's curiosity and the intriguing depth in Judd's tone of voice, for she eased the door open. She swooped Prissy up and tucked the dog into the folds of her robe.

"Okay, you got a few minutes, but leave the door open. If I gotta yell for old lady Grobes, I wanna be heard."

Adrienne went in first. The room was large and filled with plants, just as Judd had said. Live ones and barely alive ones. There were large leafy ones in pot-bound planters. African violets that sagged, a Boston fern with as many brown spokes as green ones and sitting on the table beside the telephone was a drooping foxtail, its long pink fuzzy tubelike flowers spindly at best. Its leaves hung limp, a sure sign it needed water.

The foxtail wasn't common and for that reason Adrienne decided she might use it to distract Hester while Judd did whatever he wanted to do. Which, she reminded herself, he hadn't given her much clue about. Just as he hadn't at the hospital, or with Keith at Macko's, and at Opal's and on and on. Sighing, she concluded he might be right. Her hysterics at Opal's and her fury last night had certainly shown she had an overreactive nature. Well, she intended to prove now she could do her job and let him do his.

Judd followed her in, urging Adrienne forward while he eased his way closer to the telephone.

Hester frowned, her entire face folding like an old accordion. "So? What's this that Lois went too far doin'."

Adrienne walked closer to Hester and whispered, "She steals things. It's really very sad and unfortunately a compulsion, but we've been her victims. And I see you have, too."

"Huh?"

Adrienne threw a sympathetic look at the wilting foxtail. "Why, I know you have. I saw a foxtail in her apartment and everyone knows that a real plant expert buys them in pairs. And from the looks of this apartment and the variety of greenery in it, I would say you're a lover of plants."

Hester seemed to relax. "Well, yeah, I do like 'em. Makes it seem pretty in here, like I was livin' in the country instead of in this cramped apartment."

Adrienne cast a glance in Judd's direction. He was behind Hester and gave Adrienne a wink of approval at the direction she was taking the conversation with the woman. Adrienne suddenly felt good, too pleased, in fact, by his obvious admiration. Just remember, she told herself, the most important thing about later is seeing Caleb back with the Whitewells. You and Judd aren't going anywhere but your separate ways.

Hester peered at Adrienne who had picked up the dying foxtail and was walking toward the kitchen. "Hey, what are you doin'?"

"Giving this poor depressed thing a drink."

"Depressed?"

"Because its mate is gone." She swung on Hester. "Surely, you've noticed how upset this poor plant is." Beyond Hester, Judd worked quickly near the telephone, going through what appeared to be an address book.

Hester nodded sadly. "Uh, well, sure, but I had no idea that Lois—she steals things, you say?"

"Yes. Have you noticed any of your things missing?"

Hester scowled. "Now that you mention it, I had a gold brooch. Belonged to my Aunt Ida Mae. Maybe Lois took it?"

"It's very possible," Adrienne said gravely.

"Is that why you were up in her apartment? Lookin' for evidence?"

"Exactly. I should have stopped and warned you, Hester. I do apologize, but I was afraid Prissy would bark and well, you know, alert Mrs. Grobes."

"She's not in on this, is she? I mean you haven't said anything to her. She's a blabbermouth."

"No, we've only told you, Hester. We know you can keep a secret. Just as you've done with Lois. Keeping all her secrets."

"You a cop?"

"Absolutely not. Like I said earlier, I'm one of Lois's victims, too. Just like you. I want back what she took from me."

"Yeah? And what'd she take?"

"My little boy, Hester. Lois took my little boy."

"Oh, my God." Hester leaned against the cluttered counter, allowing Prissy to slip from her hands. Her face was as pale as white bread.

Adrienne helped the woman into a chair. Hester's eyes rolled back, and before Adrienne could get a cold compress of wet paper towels, Hester had fainted.

Judd came into the kitchen. "What in hell happened?"

Quickly, Adrienne explained what she'd said.

Judd shook his head derisively. "I have to admit, Ms. Trudell, working with you is an experience I won't forget."

Adrienne ignored his comment and lightly slapped Hester's cheeks. "Hester, can you hear me?" A few seconds later, the woman's eyes fluttered open. Judd helped keep her steady in the chair while Adrienne got her some water.

"What happened?" she asked, blinking and rubbing her eyes.

"You fainted."

"Balderdash! I never faint."

"Where's Lois, Hester?" Judd asked. "I found a telephone number for her sister, but no address. You called her and told her we were looking for her, didn't you?"

"Yeah, I called her. Lois said she don't have any long-lost friends."

"Where is she?"

"Why should I tell you?"

"Because if you don't, I'll see that you're charged with being an accessory to kidnapping after the fact."

"You are the cops."

"Just me. Now, you're going to be a good citizen and for once in your life do the right thing."

"I didn't know nothin' 'bout her takin' no kid. I thought she was hatchin' her own."

"Sure," Judd said impatiently. "Give me an address."

Hester looked from Judd to Adrienne and even at Prissy who sat a good distance from Judd and seemed to be studying the entire scene.

"Am I gonna get any reward for talkin'?" Hester asked, a definite gleam in her eyes.

"Try doing something once in your life, Hester, because it's the right thing to do."

"Ain't no profit in that."

"But in your case, I might just put in a good word for you and keep you from doing about five years in prison."

"Prison! Hell, I ain't goin' to no prison," she yelped and lifted her chin belligerently. "She's out at her sister's, pretendin' she's mama of the week. Old Situate Road, about fifteen miles west of Louiston. Lucy lives with her boyfriend. You can't miss the place. Her mailbox looks like a cow."

Judd took Adrienne's arm and within five minutes they were in the car and headed out of Louiston. Judd pushed the speed to sixty and then to seventy.

Adrienne simply held on. "You're afraid she'll warn Lois."

"I know she will. The Hesters of the world never want to cooperate with the cops."

"But with the threat of prison . . ."

He shook his head. "She knows it's only a threat. The worst she'll get is probation."

"But if she warns Lois, then Lois will run—"

"If she hasn't already."

Chapter 14

"What do you mean you don't know? She's your sister, isn't she? Where in hell has she gone?" Judd snapped out the question with the precision of a well-trained drill sergeant.

The drive from Hester's to Lois's sister's house on Old Situate Road had been a series of hairpin turns at high speed on a strip of broken asphalt that was too narrow a road for such recklessness.

Judd had said little, giving the winding and bumping road all of his concentration. Adrienne had sat stiff, seat belt secure, her neck aching from the tension and her eyes glued to the passing houses for the telltale cow-shaped rural mailbox.

Then suddenly they had both seen it.

Judd had deftly turned into the weed-choked driveway. Adrienne had been filled with hope and anticipation that they were just seconds away from finding little Caleb.

That prospect had vanished when the woman in the doorway said no one was there but herself. Judd's obvious frustration and fury had exploded into a direct accusation. Her terrified gasp had given away more than Adrienne guessed the woman intended.

Leave it to Judd to skip all the preliminaries and leap right in with the question he wanted answered. The sledgehammer approach bothered Adrienne, but on the other hand, he had given the woman no chance to think, only to react, something Adrienne had no doubt that Judd intended.

Now the woman shrank back, her eyes wide, her body seeming to shatter at the prospect of having to deal with Judd. Her red hair had been wound into a ponytail that topped off a plump, but square frame. She wore shorts and a generous halter top that only emphasized the rolls of flesh. Freckles added interest to an otherwise plain face.

Judd loomed over the woman and Adrienne stepped in front of him. But before she could say a word, he gripped her arm and held her, a definite signal to not interfere.

"You're Lucy, aren't you?" Judd asked in such a way that neither a yes or no answer was going to keep her out of trouble.

The woman glanced at Adrienne as if seeing her for the first time. "I don't know nothin'."

"And I'm Santa Claus taking a vacation. Don't try to jam me, lady."

"Judd, take it easy," Adrienne said, while at the same time she guessed that Judd had taken just about all the runaround he intended to take on this case. Playing the waiting game as they'd done with Lois had grown tiresome quickly and, given the jeopardy possibility to Caleb, Judd had simply run out of patience.

He deliberately dropped his voice to a low pitch. "You're Lucy, and Lois Greeley is your sister, isn't she?"

The woman's head bobbed up and down, her eyes directed away from Judd.

"How long ago did she leave?"

When Lucy only swallowed and tried to back away, Judd reached out and caught the door so she couldn't close it.

"You don't wanna talk, then you won't mind if I have a look around." It wasn't a question, for he was already setting her aside as if she were no more of a hindrance than a cheap lock.

When she realized he had passed her and walked into the house, she yelped, "Hey!"

"Lucy, it would be best if you just do as he said."

"Good advice. If Lois is here and you've been lying to me, you're going to jail."

"Jail!" Lucy screeched. Then her mouth trembled. "I didn't do nothin'. I don't even know what's goin' on." Judd stalked into what Adrienne assumed was a bedroom. "Hey, wait a minute," Lucy shouted.

"He's only going to look around." Adrienne glanced at the neat but definitely lived-in living room.

"He ain't got no search warrant."

"But he has probable cause to believe that Lois is here or has been here. Your sister is alleged to have kidnapped a baby boy from Seapoint Hospital a few days ago. We were told she came here to see you."

"Who told you that?"

"In her own way, Lois did, but Hester Marple confirmed it."

Adrienne amazed herself at how calm and controlled she was. Especially given the good possibility that Lois had been here. Her hysteria at Opal's had definitely been the result of her having been overwrought. Not that anyone could be unemotional about an abducted infant, but giving in to tears and desperation helped no one, including the baby. Keeping one's head was the best approach.

Judd, she decided, listening to him stalk through the rooms and then hearing the back door slam, was not keeping his head. She'd known at Hester's that he was worried and more than irritated that Lois just might get away.

"You cops?"

"He is, yes," Adrienne said. "Actually, Judd is a detective and I work with Child-Aid. It's a—"

"I know about Child-Aid," Lucy said. Her eyes widened with awe and respect, as if she'd just been presented to royalty. "Neighbor up the road found her runaway daughter through Child-Aid. Some specialist in missing kids..." She scowled. "Don't remember her name."

"Her name is Adrienne Trudell," Judd said matter-of-factly as he came back into the room. His eyes found Adrienne and he shook his head. She knew he hadn't found either Lois or the baby.

Judd loomed up behind Lucy, who swallowed and tried to find somewhere to go.

"Was Adrienne Trudell the name of the Child-Aid specialist?" Judd asked. His hands rode low on his hips, his eyes as cold and hard as Adrienne had ever seen them.

Lucy pressed her shaky fingers to her mouth, looking not at all sure if even that nonanswer might get her into trouble. Finally, she said, "Yeah, sounds like it."

"Well, this is your lucky day. You're looking at the very capable Ms. Trudell."

Lucy swung back to Adrienne. "Are you really? Oh, my neighbor was just beside herself when you found her little girl, Debbie-Jean."

Adrienne said, "Child-Aid was glad we could help. Now, Lucy, since you know about the work we do, you must know that when we come into a case, it's serious. Just like when the police are called. Your sister is in a lot of trouble. The parents of that infant are beside themselves with worry."

"Evidence in the bedroom indicates an infant was here, Lucy. Now, enough of the stall. Where did she go?"

"Lois don't mean no harm. She, well, she's always been gooney about babies. Personally, I never did know why. It's not like they stay little and sweet. Grow into little monsters."

Judd cursed. "For God's sake, lady, are you listening to what in hell I'm asking you?"

Adrienne quickly stepped in between Lucy and Judd, who was bearing down on her. In a firm voice, Adrienne said, "Lucy, you must tell us. Judd doesn't quit and neither do I. We're not going to go away. Now, I don't think you want your house here crawling with cops drilling you with questions."

"Oh, God..."

"Please tell us what you know."

Lucy eyed Judd, and Adrienne could fully understand her fear. He looked awesome. Fiercely determined, wired tight and dangerously secure in the knowledge that he held most of the cards. Although Adrienne doubted he'd break any rules that cops were required to follow, he was definitely pushing the envelope of intimidation.

"Lucy?"

"She, uh, told me she wanted to go to, uh, Boston. Yeah, that's it."

Judd and Adrienne exchanged looks.

"Lucy," Adrienne warned, "I know that's what she told you to say, but you don't want to lie to us, do you?"

Biting her lip and hugging her arms to her body as if she felt suddenly chilled, she sagged with relief when a battered pickup pulled into the yard.

A beefy man flung himself from the cab and came toward them. He wore a bill cap, pulled low so that it crushed his shaggy blond hair. He had arms the size of tree trunks and wore a T-shirt advertising a popular beer; it hung over old black jeans. Work boots kicked up the dry August dust as he strode forward.

Lucy broke away from Adrienne and ran to him. He caught her to him, his arm sliding around her protectively. He walked Lucy back to where Judd and Adrienne were standing. He nodded to Judd. "You a cop?"

Ignoring the question, Judd asked his own. "You know anything about the kidnapped baby?"

He sighed. "Yeah."

"Tony, no, you can't—"

"Baby, you're not helpin' her steal a kid. I warned you that it was only a matter of time before the cops showed up. You ain't takin' no fall for Lois."

"She's my sister and we've always stuck together."

"She's also got a few lights burned out in the attic," he said, tapping the side of his head. "Back when she took that kid in Wisconsin, the judge should have locked her up instead of just tellin' her to see a shrink."

"That was a long time ago. Lois swore to me the baby was hers. I saw her when she was pregnant."

Ignoring her, he said to Judd. "Look, we don't want no trouble. Lois is plannin' a bus trip down South. Fact is, I just took her to get her ticket." He consulted his watch. "Her bus leaves in about twenty minutes, so if you get a move on, you might still catch her."

Adrienne started toward the car. Judd gripped her arm and stopped her. "Stay here."

She scowled, but Judd had already moved toward Tony and was taking the man's arm to move him away from the house. At first, Tony balked, but Judd's cold look quickly changed his mind.

When they were a sufficient distance away, Adrienne watched while the two men talked. After a few minutes, she noticed Tony's shoulders slump dejectedly. Judd walked back to the car, signaled Adrienne and in a few minutes they were back on the bumpy highway.

"What did you say to him?" she asked. "Judd, you didn't threaten him, did you?"

"What do you think?"

"You did, didn't you?" For reasons she didn't want to think about, she wasn't as outraged as she felt she should have been.

He shrugged. "Just told him I knew he was banging Lois and I'd be more than willing to pass on the news to Lucy. If he wanted to keep his happy home happy, then he'd better give up Lois or face some rather unpleasant moments with Lucy when she got him alone."

Adrienne stared, her mouth agape. "How did you know?"

"That he's getting it on with Lois? I didn't. But Tony's saying he'd driven her to the terminal when we know Lois has her own car was enough to make me want to question Tony a little more closely."

"She could have sold the car."

"Or even junked it."

Confused, Adrienne asked, "Then how—"

"Instincts, a hunch." He shrugged. "I don't know. Something just didn't ring true."

"So you decided to bluff. Adding an accusation of a cozy relationship between Lois and Tony."

"Don't look so stunned. It was a shot in the dark. Just like him trying to send us on some wild-goose chase to a bus terminal. If Lois knew we were on our way, she'd hardly be hanging out in one place for an extended time. She'd be on the move."

Adrienne was confused. "So if she's not at the bus station, where are we going?"

"To a local park."

"He told you she was at a park?"

Judd slammed on the brakes and made a sharp left turn. "Good ole Tony. Funny thing about guilt and fear. They tend to make confession a high art."

"So if she's at a park, she's obviously not running from us. Then she doesn't know we've located her."

"A major break, angel. Tony said Hester talked to Lucy after Lois went to the park. Then Tony went to warn Lois that we were on to her."

"But—"

"He chickened out. Tony's tale of Lucy's not taking a fall for Lois was only a smoke screen. This guy knows the score. Once I gave him a few salient facts about his own situation, should Lois disappear again, he got the picture. Complicity and aiding and abetting can be real trouble. Tony might be horny, but he isn't stupid."

Adrienne swallowed, trying to absorb the incredible turn of events. What astonished her was how quickly Judd had latched on to the ruse. She thought Tony had sounded credible and genuinely worried that Lucy might get into trouble for harboring Lois. Instead, when his own hide was at stake, he couldn't wait to confess.

If one could call three benches, a few spindly trees and more dirt than grass a park, then this one barely qualified. A parking area had a number of cars, a couple of vans and some compact station wagons. To Adrienne's amazement, the absence of the usual amenities hadn't detracted from the laughter and camaraderie of the mothers and their young children. A swing set was getting a lot of use and a sandbox was occupied by three little girls with plastic buckets and shovels.

Judd slowed down. "Check out the license plates." He gave Adrienne the plate number, but none of those in the area matched.

"Maybe she did sell or junk the car," Adrienne commented, the disappointment audible in her voice.

"Or she parked somewhere else." Judd took the sketch from his pocket, studied it a few moments and then methodically searched the crowd of women. "What do you think? Spot anyone who resembles the sketch."

"I saw that picture of Lois on her bulletin board, remember? Leo did a good job on the sketch." Adrienne searched the crowd. Her gaze passed over a woman with a carriage and then came back to her. She was walking near the park edge in a methodical gait, paying little attention to the other mothers.

"Judd, look over there."

"The one who's turned and is coming this way?"

"Yes." She opened her car door and started to get out.

Judd stopped her. "What do you think you're doing?"

"My job."

"Wait a minute. You can't just walk up to her and say, 'By the way, are you the kidnapper I'm looking for?'"

"How about if I walk up to her and say 'Hi, would you mind if I admire your baby?'"

"Adrienne..."

She narrowed her eyes and glared at him. "You really don't have any confidence in me, do you? Giving in to my being assigned to work with you was just because you couldn't easily get rid of me without getting a lot of hassle."

"I'm not questioning your ability."

"Yes, you are. I just witnessed your hardball approach in dealing with Lucy. Unless you didn't notice, you didn't learn a damn thing from her. All you did was scare her to death."

"In case you missed it, we're here because I did get something out of Tony."

"Threats and intimidation and, worst of all, an accusation that may not even be true. But if you'd followed through and told Lucy, he would have never been able to prove otherwise."

"What are you talking about?"

"You said yourself that accusing Tony of sleeping with Lois had been a shot in the dark. If he hadn't caved in and told you what you wanted to know and you'd told Lucy—it would have destroyed their relationship."

"You're breaking my heart," Judd muttered.

"You really don't understand how a relationship works, do you?" In that moment, Adrienne suddenly realized why Judd had avoided her, why he would never want her. Not because he didn't want a relationship, but because he would have to trust her, trust himself, and that terrified him. Losing his family hadn't just made him cynical, it had made him hollow and unable to believe in anything except what he could control.

He gripped her chin, his voice low. "I don't give a damn about Tony and Lucy's relationship. They got themselves into this by choice. I do, however, give a whole lot of damn about Caleb being returned to his parents. Besides, unless I've missed something, I thought that was what you wanted."

"It is!"

"Thank God, we finally agree on something." Then in a move that stunned her, he reached across her and opened her door. "Lead the way."

Not wanting to take the time to ask him why he'd suddenly changed his mind, she swung her legs out.

"Angel?"

She turned her head and he caught her mouth in a sudden kiss that made her melt.

"Be careful. I'll be just a few yards behind you."

She nodded and got out of the car. Suddenly, she felt as if she'd won the battle and lost the war. She made herself focus on the present and finding Caleb; there were weeks, months and years ahead to figure out how she could have been so foolish as to allow Judd back into her life.

Adrienne approached Lois slowly. She certainly didn't want to alert her or startle her. The sun beat down and Adrienne felt the pearls of sweat slide between her breasts and break out across the back of her neck.

She sensed Judd behind her, moving so as not to look as if he was following her.

Taking a deep breath, she slipped her hands into her pockets and made herself sound friendly. "Hi. Beautiful day for a walk, isn't it?"

Lois glanced up, her eyes anything but friendly. The carriage was old, the plastic bonnet faded and the wheels looking none too steady. Lois held the handle firmly. No noise came from inside. Instead of answering Adrienne, she turned her back.

"I'd love to see your baby."

"Go away."

"Oh, I won't wake him."

"How'd you know it was a him?"

Adrienne damned herself for the slip. "A friend just had a baby boy, so I guess infant boys are on my mind."

The woman grunted. "Go away. I don't show no one my baby. Lot of sick people out there. I don't take no chances."

"Do you come here often? I've been looking for a nice place to bring my niece and—"

"Why are you askin' me questions? I don't know you. Lots of others to talk to. Why you comin' over here and askin' me?"

Adrienne had to think fast. "Actually, I was hoping I could tell me a little bit about the area. I'm new around here. Just moved to Louiston." She watched carefully for any sign of anything unusual. All the while she talked, she cautiously moved closer. Carefully opening her purse, Adrienne reached inside and felt around for the plastic object. Finding it, she said, "Here, I have something for your son."

The comment seemed to throw Lois and her eyes darted around.

Adrienne took the object from her purse and the woman immediately stiffened.

"Where'd you get that?"

"I brought it for your son."

"He don't need no blue rattle."

"But all babies love rattles." Adrienne held it up and then rattled it. The woman leaped back as if it were alive. "Lois," Adrienne said softly, "I want you to let me have the carriage."

"No! Get away from me. You can't have him."

"He's not yours, Lois," Adrienne said softly while all the time moving closer. "I know you want him to be and I know you wouldn't hurt him, but he needs to be with his real parents. You're not his mother, Lois. Do you understand me?"

The woman began to sway back and forth, her voice keening and rife with pain. Adrienne reached for the carriage handle.

Suddenly, she shrieked, "He's mine! I been waitin' and waitin' to get him and you ain't takin' him from me."

"Lois, he's not yours. You know he isn't. You took another woman's baby. That's against the law." All the while she talked, Adrienne felt the cold sweat of terror and desperately tried to keep it from her voice. More than anything, she didn't want to startle the woman into running with the carriage and possibly hurting Caleb. She really had no idea what Lois's mental state was, but she knew that an in-your-face approach rarely worked in cases dealing with missing children. The idea was to get the suspect off guard so that the approach became more of a mental dismantling rather than a swat team attack.

Lois, however, tugged the carriage closer to her and away from Adrienne. She knew then that Lois wasn't going to just hand over the baby. Instead, she gave Adrienne a piercing look that was truly frightening. And for the first time since she'd approached Lois, Adrienne wondered if Judd's intimidating approach might have worked better.

Snarling at Adrienne, she said, "I been wantin' a baby for so long and I finally figured out how to do it. You can't take him. You can't." She started to run, shoving the carriage ahead of her. It rocked back and forth and Adrienne heard the squall of the baby.

"Lois!"

She also heard Judd swear behind her. She started to run after Lois, and within moments Judd had passed her. Lois was no match for either his endurance or his speed. He grabbed the woman, while at the same time reaching around and snagging the carriage before it tipped over.

Adrienne hurried up and took the carriage handle. Lois, however, didn't give up. She kicked and screamed until most of the women in the park were gathering around and watching in stunned disbelief.

Lois shouted, "He's tryin' to kill me and she's gonna steal my baby. Help me! Get them away from me. My baby, oh, my poor baby..."

Judd swore and gripped her harder. She managed to kick him before Adrienne swung around and slapped her face.

For about five seconds, Judd gaped at her, and Lois, so taken aback by the sudden move, lost her momentum. Adrienne sucked in her own breath and turned to the women who seemed about to herd together to pull Judd away from Lois.

In a firm voice, she said, "He's a cop, and if any of you want to be charged with assaulting an officer, then go ahead and touch him."

They all halted. "What's going on?" someone asked.

"I'm from Child-Aid. The baby is Caleb Whitewell. He was abducted from the Seapoint Hospital a few days ago."

"Oh, yeah, I heard about that. You mean, this is the woman who took him?"

"She's going to be charged, yes." Adrienne glanced up to see two police officers walking toward them.

Judd had managed to get Lois's hands tied behind her back. He said nothing to Adrienne, but when the two officers came up to him, he said, "You guys did it just right."

"Yeah, we figured you were trying to fake her out so the kid wouldn't get hurt."

"Adrienne faked her out."

One of the officers gave her an impressed smile. "That slap did the trick, Ms. Trudell. A little unorthodox, but given the circumstances..."

Lois glowered at Adrienne. "I'm gonna charge the bitch with assault."

"Shut up, Lois. By the time all the charges are tallied against you, you're gonna be damn glad the slap stopped you from makin' things worse," the officer said.

Adrienne lifted the baby from the carriage and held him against her body. The thumping of his heart and the screaming coming from his healthy lungs had never felt so good.

Judd came over beside her. "He okay?"

"I think so. He should be checked over at the hospital, but one thing to Lois's credit. She didn't hurt him."

"Cute little kid," Judd murmured. "By the way, where did you get the rattle? It was a brilliant move."

"Remember the one I got from the hospital? I still had it in my purse. I decided to use it to see if my having it would throw her off enough so that she'd make a mistake."

"Well, it worked." He put his arm around her and gave her a brief hug before letting her go. "All in all, a pretty incredible performance, Ms. Trudell."

"Ah, one of those compliments again, Detective Dillon. You're surely going to turn my head."

He grinned and dropped a casual kiss on her mouth. "Come on. Let's go home."

Adrienne felt both a burst of enthusiastic satisfaction and a sense of letdown. Happy that Caleb was safe and would soon be back with his parents, but more than a little miserable that her time with Judd was at an end.

How easy it would be to mention something like a celebration dinner. Or some time together to relax and bask in their good work on the case. Nothing unusual about that, but she knew it wouldn't happen.

He didn't want it and she knew that any extended time with him now would surely reveal her heart. She felt as if she were facing unending dark loneliness.

And it was no one's fault but her own.

She'd managed to break all her self-imposed promises.

She'd fallen in love with Judd Dillon all over again.

Chapter 15

Back in Seapoint, four days later, Judd's desk work at the police station should have been back to its usual routine. But it wasn't.

Nothing in his life had returned to ordinary. Nothing.

Swearing at the situation he found himself in, pummeled by emotionally laden reactions to every thought about Adrienne, he damned the fact that his life was no longer singly his. The hell of it was that he knew why and he didn't like it. He didn't like it one little bit.

He finished up his expense sheets and tied up the loose ends of his report on the Whitewell case.

Caleb had been given a thorough check at the hospital and had been found to be in excellent health. Tony and Lucy, apparently seriously concerned about their own culpability, had notified the police, which accounted for the timely arrival of the officers at the park. And as Judd had suspected, Lois had parked her car so that the plate couldn't be easily spotted. Since the arrest, Lois had been charged with kidnapping and was being held at the women's detention center. At her arraignment, the judge had denied bail and ordered psychiatric evaluation. It would be months before she came to trial, but Judd was certain the evidence was strong enough and the witnesses plentiful enough that Lois would go to prison.

Judd wished his private life were as cut-and-dried. Over and over, he tried to tell himself that working with Adrienne had been a new experience; he'd adjusted and could honestly admit that she'd given him a new perspective on working with a woman. Now, if that attitude were only from a work standpoint, then he could pat himself on the back and that would be that.

But it was more than an enlightened viewpoint. It was Adrienne and him and what had happened between them. She'd changed him and he wasn't sure if he welcomed that.

It would be so simple to just fall back on Diana as an excuse. Despite occasional problems, he'd loved and cherished his wife, but in many ways, Diana had been an easy woman to love. She'd rarely hassled him about anything, had never argued or challenged him the way Adrienne had, but more important was that Judd had found something with Adrienne. Something he'd thought he would never want again. A woman's love.

Mike Shelby stopped by his desk. "I thought you were gonna leave early today. Litchfield said he ordered you to take a week off and he didn't want to see your face around here after four o'clock today."

"I wanted to get this paperwork finished up."

"Not like you, Judd. You usually get that stuff out of the way within twenty-four hours of finishing a case."

"Yeah, well, I've got a lot on my mind," he murmured.

As if Mike knew exactly what was on Judd's mind, he said casually, "I saw Adrienne a few minutes ago. She didn't look too happy."

Judd glanced up. "What was wrong with her?"

Mike shrugged. "Beats me. But she did say she asked to be transferred out of here to another branch of Child-Aid. The chief tried to talk her out of it, but she was insistent. Something about professionalism."

Judd's lips set in a grim line. "Has she left? I mean, for the day?"

"Yeah. Maybe you ought to talk to her, Judd. You two seemed to hit it off. Litchfield wasn't pleased about losing her." Mike waved to another officer who was passing by. Judd scowled, staring at his desk. Mike continued, "Oh, by the way, you know how we've been trying to get a reason out of Lois Greeley for why she took the baby at the particular time she did?"

"Yeah."

"You won't believe it. It was right under your nose." Mike told him what he'd learned and Judd closed his eyes in disgust that he hadn't zeroed in on it. He knew why. One Ms. Adrienne Trudell—and making love to her—had dominated his thoughts. Instead of using the kind of logic and reasoning that any first-year rookie would use to figure out the whys of Lois's actions, he'd been busy thinking of Adrienne. What was more disturbing was that he hadn't even bothered to follow up on Lois himself, to learn if she *had* revealed her motive for having taken the baby when she did.

"Does Adrienne know?" Judd asked.

"Don't think so."

He shoved his chair back. This gave him a valid excuse to see her and maybe, just maybe—what? A sharp pain hit him somewhere uncomfortably close to his heart. Who was he kidding?

He could tell her about Lois on the phone. Given his new insight about his feelings for Adrienne, if he really wanted not to act on them, he could do the professional thing. Call her and keep it short and to the point. But even as that possibility leaped into his consciousness, he dismissed it. No, he wanted to see her.

More than he wanted just about anything, he concluded emphatically. He realized that every stalling tactic he'd used in the past to avoid any relationship with her simply didn't work anymore.

He wanted Adrienne, and as much as he may have wanted to dismiss it, he knew he wanted more than sex.

Getting to his feet, he said to Mike, "Oh, by the way, I'm putting the house on the market." Another decision he'd made since returning to Seapoint. Not particularly long and involved, but in his gut he knew it was the right decision. The time had come to let the past rest in peace. "My dad had a call while I was in Louiston. Someone is interested, but I know you said that if I ever decided to sell, you and Susan would be interested. I'll give you first refusal."

"What changed your mind?"

"Time to really move on, I guess. Time to finally settle the past and get on with my life."

"A reckoning of sorts, huh?"

"Yeah." He shrugged into his jacket. "Let me know by the end of the week, okay?"

"I can probably say yes right now. Susan has always had a soft spot for that house. In fact, we drove by there last Sunday and she commented on how much she'd love to have it."

"Well, talk it over, anyway. One thing I learned about women after working with Adrienne is that they hate us men making assumptions about them."

A half hour later, he'd parked beside her compact at her apartment building, but instead of getting out of the car and casually going in to see her, he found himself waiting it out, shaky and unsure.

Perhaps because the last time he'd been in her apartment had been that night a year ago.

Perhaps because he'd learned a few things about his feelings for Adrienne that felt a helluva lot like serious stuff—stuff that included love and caring and wanting. All feelings he'd sworn he'd never allow himself to feel again.

The trouble with Adrienne was that from the moment he'd made love to her a year ago, he'd known he wasn't casual about her. That was exactly why he'd avoided her.

"So what in hell am I doing here?" he muttered out loud in the empty car. Why was he sitting here contemplating doing something that rattled him more than the most dangerous police work?

Damn.

He shoved open the door, slammed it closed, stalked up the walk and leaned on her doorbell in the security alcove. He rang it four times before she finally responded.

"Yes?"

"It's Judd."

A moment of silence. "Judd?"

"Yeah, remember me? The detective."

"What do you want?"

"To talk to you."

"About what?"

On the tip of his tongue was a raunchy comment, but he held it back. "Adrienne, please. This isn't something I want to discuss through an intercom."

She buzzed him in and moments later she opened her apartment door. If he'd expected shyness or nervousness, he would have been dead wrong. Her expression was aloof and her eyes watchful.

Judd took an unsteady breath.

She wore a light blue robe belted at the waist that stopped just above her knees. She was barefoot, but the most intriguing part was her hair. It was wound up turban-style in a huge Turkish towel, a few wet ends sticking to her neck. Obviously, she'd just gotten out of the shower.

"I'm surprised you let me in." God, he hadn't felt this gauche and jumpy since he was ten years old.

"Why? You've seen me in less than this."

"Brassy as hell, aren't you?"

She lifted her chin. "Yes."

Then she turned and crossed the room, which was arranged with the light airiness of wicker that contrasted with the strong colors of drapes and cushions. Plants bloomed everywhere, but most profusely in a small window greenhouse where the sun streamed in.

Judd stepped inside cautiously, the flood of memories from the last time he was here almost overwhelming. "I heard you asked to be transferred to another branch of Child-Aid."

"That's right. Would you like some iced tea?"

"No." He shoved his hands into his pockets. "Why?"

"I thought you might be thirsty." She took a sip from her glass and then went over and picked up the watering can.

"I'm talking about your leaving the station."

"I would think that would please you. One less woman who causes havoc in the ranks. Despite that rather raucous comment of yours to Fairfax at the beginning of the investigation, I don't think the entire department is that in awe of me."

"The comment about your reputation as a tough broad?"

"Yes."

"Maybe a slight exaggeration to let Fairfax know he wasn't talking to some empty-headed female, but the larger issue of your being respected was true."

She paused a few moments, as if it wasn't the answer she'd expected. "Thank you for that," she said, but the stiffness of her body language definitely indicated nothing had been settled between them.

Judd decided to cut right to the point. "You're leaving because of what happened between us, aren't you?"

She whirled, her eyes snapping. He realized immediately that her anger was deeply entrenched.

"Don't flatter yourself, Detective Dillon. I managed to survive sleeping with you a year ago, I imagine the adjustment this time won't be any more of a problem."

Judd flinched. "It's gonna be a helluva problem for me," he said, the words coming almost by themselves.

"You? You walked out of here before the sun came up the last time and never gave me a second thought. And maybe that's the way it is with one-night stands, but it doesn't mean I have to allow it to happen again." She took a deep breath. "In Louiston, well, I let my guard down, but I can't just sleep with you, Judd, because we—as you so profoundly put it—have good sex."

She then turned her back once again and proceeded to overwater every plant.

Judd knew he needed to get the words out, to tell her how he felt and yet they stuck in his throat with the tenacity of a damn confession. "Adrienne, there is something else I came to tell you. It's about the case."

She turned and faced him, her eyes suddenly concerned. "Nothing's wrong with Caleb, is there? I talked to Tanya on the phone before I left my office today and she didn't say anything."

"No, this is about Lois. She told us why she took Caleb at the time she did."

"Why?"

"Choosing Caleb was due to the mere fact that he happened to be there when she planned to grab a baby. It wasn't Caleb in particular, just Seapoint Hospital. She did know the hospital routine, as we conjectured, but more important, she knew that she'd get away with it that particular week."

Adrienne frowned.

"My mother always goes on vacation that particular week in August," he said. "And she's the only one who never forgets the faces or names of any of the volunteers. They usually come and go, and unless they've made some huge contribution, none of the staff ever remembers them. Lois would have attracted zero attention from anyone but my mother. And because Lois stole those newborn packets and Mom gave her a break by not turning her in, Lois would have been a real standout if Mom had seen her with Caleb."

"So Lois took advantage of the period when she knew your mother would be gone?"

"Yeah. Mom's bridge group chose that week years ago and Lois knew it. Apparently, she did call the hospital just to double-check, but since Mom was probably the only one who would have instantly recognized her, Lois used the time to make her move."

Adrienne shook her head in disbelief. "It's so simple. We should have figured it out once we learned your mother knew her and knew of the theft."

"*I* should have figured it out."

For long beats of silence, they stared at each other across the span of the room that separated them.

Adrienne swallowed. "Thank you for coming and telling me."

"Sure."

Again, a tense stillness swept between them.

Judd watched her, and then he spoke, his voice low. "You don't have to transfer because of me."

"Actually, the branch I'm going to needs some skilled hands, so it'll be for the best."

"No." He closed his eyes a moment then shoved a hand through his hair and swore. "Look, I'm not doing this very well because I don't know exactly what to say to you."

She looked everywhere but at him. Now that Lois and her motive had been disposed of, there seemed little left to say that wasn't personal.

"Would you excuse me a minute? I have to get my hair combed out before it dries in a snarled mess." Without waiting for him to answer, she edged out of the room.

Judd expelled what had to have been five minutes' worth of breath. God, why was it so damn difficult to just say what he wanted to say, what needed to be said? He knew why. Terror. He was terrified she would tell him to go straight to hell.

God, maybe he should just leave.

God, she hoped he'd leave. Or did she really hope he'd stay? Hope he'd sweep her up and—dammit, she knew better. Judd Dillon was never going to sweep her up.

Never. Never. Never.

Adrienne sat at her dressing table, dragging a comb through her hair, wincing at the pricks of pain and barely able to see her reflection through her tears. She'd done what she'd determined to do. She'd kept herself loose and casual; she hadn't shown any cracks or let her guard down. She'd been flawless in handling herself and hiding the storm of pain and deep agony her heart was struggling with. The result was that she had what she wanted.

She was alone and he would most likely leave just as he'd come. Her pride and her personal professional image would be whole once again. And once she'd transferred out of the police station, she would no longer have to worry about running into him.

She'd be free.

She'd be miserable.

The familiar squeak of the floorboard brought her head up and widened her eyes when she glanced into the mirror. Judd. The comb fell from her hands.

"Don't send me away, Adrienne."

She swallowed, a rush of desire and need spreading through her. "Judd..."

He moved into the room. "Since I saw you that first day of the kidnapping and knew I'd be working with you, I've tried to tell myself you mean nothing to me. I didn't want you to mean anything."

She watched him come closer, unable to speak because she didn't know what to say. Where was all this going? A few moments of lovemaking? What really worried her was her own intense reactions to him. She loved him and she wasn't sure she could hide that or deny him, no matter what he wanted.

He'd taken off his jacket and as he walked up behind her, she watched in the mirror as he pulled his shirt off, flinging it across her rose-point upholstered chair. The low-riding jeans he wore were snug and she fleetingly thought of their silly conversations about her neckties and his jeans. He did look good—too good—and she blanched at the blatant reverse sexism of her thoughts.

She brought her gaze up to safer places, only to encounter a strong chest that sent too many sensual images singing through her. He'd stopped right behind her chair.

"What do you want, Judd," she managed to ask.

"I want inside you, Adrienne."

The bold words shimmied through her. "Judd, having sex again—"

"Making love, angel."

"It's not love. You don't want it to be love."

"But it is, and whether I want it to be or not doesn't seem to have a whole lot of relevance to my heart or my thoughts." He gently pulled her up and away from the chair, keeping her back to his chest, sliding his hands down inside her robe. Her breasts were full and nestled in his hands so sweetly, he sucked in his breath.

Adrienne fought off the clamoring need for him. "What did you say?" So confounded by his touch, she was sure she must have misinterpreted his words. His mouth brushed kisses along her neck as his fingers did magical things to her nipples. "If you're trying to prove we have a sexual attraction..."

"No need to prove that," he murmured, the mastery of his hands and mouth befuddling any sensible thoughts she could conjure up. "It's already true. What it took me too damn long to figure out is that wanting you and loving you come from some source far more powerful than my ability to resist you."

She closed her eyes, basking in the deftness of his hands on her breasts, her belly and along her thighs. She leaned back as he worked the robe off, his mouth at her neck, her shoulders. When his fingers moved between her legs, she whimpered.

"Ah, Adrienne, yes..."

His hardness pressed against her and when she heard the hiss of the zipper, she knew she had to stop things. "Judd, we can't. I don't have anything to protect—"

"It's okay."

"No...I could get pregnant..."

"Shh, that's okay, too. We're going to get married."

She went totally still, fighting her way out of the smoky passion that clouded her head. Then, in a moment of total lucidity, she flung his hands off her.

He took a step back, momentarily off balance from the abrupt action.

Swinging around and trying to shake herself from the sensual haze he'd created, she said. "We're going to do *what?*"

"You want to just live together?"

"I want to know what in hell is going on."

He moved to the bed, where he perched on the corner, his hands gripping the mattress. As he lowered his head, Adrienne was struck with how right he looked here in her bedroom. Rumpled and gorgeous, and oh, so right. She recalled his reaction that day in the glass walkway at the hospital and how uneasy he'd been. The same uneasiness she'd often felt from him after they'd been intimate—

Her thoughts stopped with a rush of hope, fear and warmth. Judd felt things for her he was afraid to face. That had to be it. Making love to her had given him insight he hadn't wanted, just as sunlight revealed things not always clear otherwise.

He raised his head. "The only thing going on is that I love you and I don't know how to tell you."

Her heart took a gigantic leap and she realized she was standing half-naked in front of him and probably looking shell-shocked.

"You just told me," she murmured, expecting and waiting for him to grab back the words.

"Yeah, but words are easy, angel. Sex is easy. It's the forever after that's hard, the forever after that makes them real. After I lost Diana, I made up my mind that forever after was too risky. Being alone was safer and it definitely prevented getting hurt in the future."

"You made that pretty clear the night you came back here with me."

"Did I? God, I tried like hell to make it casual. Right up to walking out before dawn."

"It was all . . . deliberate?"

"You told me you loved me."

She clamped her hand over her mouth. "No! I never said that."

"Not in words, but you didn't need to. Your body, your heart, your total involvement told me more than words. I knew you, remember? I knew that Ms. Adrienne Trudell was no one-night-stand type and that because of your mother, you were very cautious of men, leery of showing any kind of vulnerability."

"And all those things are why you left?"

"Yeah. All those things were what I wanted and what I was afraid to take."

"Oh, Judd, I thought you just wanted sex."

"That's what I wanted you to think." He paused and then grinned. "Then again, making love with you is pretty spectacular."

She drew in a breath, and moved closer to him. "I didn't want to love you again. What happened in Louiston scared me because it made me remember just how much I wanted you, how much I loved you. I knew I couldn't work with you again and keep you from knowing."

He slipped his arm around her and kissed her deeply, drawing her down onto the bed. Sliding his hand under her hips, he pulled the robe out from under her and tossed it aside. He dispensed with his jeans and rolled on top of her in one swift motion, entering her with one long stroke.

"You're going to make me pregnant."

"Damn right. Then you'll have to marry me to save your professional image."

She laughed, an incredible joy spilling from her heart. "Really, Detective Dillon. You could get on your knees and ask in a proper way."

"Now, Ms. Trudell, I was thinking you could get on your knees and thank me—"

"Judd!" But she grinned and pulled him against her.

"Today we make a baby. Tomorrow we buy a ring. How about we get married the following day?"

She kissed him. "Right now, let's just concentrate on making the baby."

"Yeah," he murmured, his hips moving against her. "We could concentrate on that for a dozen weeks or so."

"I love you."

"Forever and forever."

"And ever."

* * * * *

Get Ready to be Swept Away by
Silhouette's Spring Collection

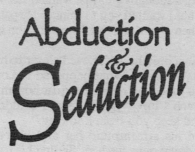

Abduction & Seduction

These passion-filled stories explore both the dangerous
desires of men and the seductive powers of women.
Written by three of our most celebrated authors, they are
sure to capture your hearts.

Diana Palmer
Brings us a spin-off of her Long, Tall Texans series

Joan Johnston
Crafts a beguiling Western romance

Rebecca Brandewyne
New York Times bestselling author
makes a smashing contemporary debut

Available in March at your favorite retail outlet.

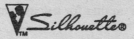

MILLION DOLLAR SWEEPSTAKES (III)

You won't want to miss...

by Merline Lovelace

Starting in May 1995, Merline Lovelace brings her
new miniseries, CODE NAME: DANGER, to Silhouette
Intimate Moments. And the first title, *Night of the Jaguar*
(IM #637), is also an INTIMATE MOMENTS EXTRA.

Alias: Jaguar. *Agency:* OMEGA. Secret Agent
Jake MacKenzie hadn't planned on rescuing
Sarah Chandler and three frightened children from
the jungles of Central America. Then a drug bust
gone awry made him an unwilling savior—
and all-too-willing lover.

Coming your way in August 1995 is
The Cowboy and the Cossack (IM #657).

Join the excitement of Merline Lovelace's
CODE NAME: DANGER, as the daring men and
women who comprise the Omega Agency find love
despite the most perilous odds, only in—

the exciting new series by
New York Times bestselling author

The MacKade Brothers—looking for trouble,
and always finding it. Now they're on a collision
course with love. And it all begins with

**THE RETURN OF RAFE MACKADE
(Intimate Moments #631, April 1995)**

The whole town was buzzing. Rafe MacKade
was back in Antietam, and that meant only one
thing—there was bound to be trouble....

Be on the lookout for the next book in the
series, **THE PRIDE OF JARED MACKADE—
Silhouette Special Edition's 1000th Book!**
It's an extraspecial event not to be missed,
coming your way in December 1995!

THE MACKADE BROTHERS—these sexy, trouble-
loving men will be heading out to you in alter-
nate books from Silhouette Intimate Moments
and Silhouette Special Edition.
Watch out for them!